Magic: A R

Nathan McGrath

Reality is merely an illusion, albeit a very persistent one.
Albert Einstein

Chapter One

The prison ambulance rumbled off the smooth tarmac road and headed into the forest along a cracked lane distorted by tree roots and weeds. Ripples of sunlight washed over the matt grey surface as it swerved left and right to avoid potholes and large rotting branches that had lain untouched for months.

Inside, a lean, balding guard with a lewd smile on his face watched a young woman's body twitch on the gurney, her head turning from side to side.

Lizzy's thoughts dragged up through a heavy, drugged stupor just enough to sense motion. She drew in a long breath that seemed to reach deep into her and awaken a long forgotten energy.

She wasn't in her bunk. They'd taken her from the prison laboratory. She'd seen friends, fellow inmates on gurneys; hair-thin sensor needles inserted deep into their brains, being put into prison ambulances like this one. She recalled stories of her friends being taken to some ancient ritual site where Lycus hoped to detect the channels to other-world signals that gave magicians spell-casting powers. Few of those that came back survived, most died soon after; with no memory except `the last days of their lives.

Recalling her friends got her wishing she'd never begun to wake up. Hopefully she'd just die too, quickly, not end up like so many of her friends; Jill, Rose, Carol, Mary, Sarah.

She tried to let go, fall back into that heavy sleep. But instead she found herself floating in the air above the ambulance.

She watched as the ambulance lumbered off the broken tarmac road and churned down a long-neglected track, sometimes disappearing under the trees. It crunched over saplings, broken twigs and branches, the rumbling growl silencing birdsong and the scuttle of creatures across the forest floor. Finally, the ambulance grunted down a gear and entered a large clearing, following a track alongside a sharp incline to park up by some rusty oil barrels. A pile of bones and burnt clothes half buried under the ashes of an old fire lay on the edge of a steep incline that dropped down to a dry stream bed.

With a final throaty rumble like an old beast clearing its throat, the engine cut out and the sounds of the forest returned. Birdsong rose through the treetops, Two small birds chased across the clearing, leaving ripples of ghostly echoes trailing behind them.

A large raven had been following the ambulance since it left the prison laboratory. Now it swooped down, its wide ebony wings outstretched and circled the clearing to settle on a high branch. It gave a little shudder and ruffled its feathers then jerked its head side to side. It gave a satisfied nod then took a couple of sideways steps to get a better view and fixed its gaze on the prison ambulance, tapping a claw impatiently.

Two burly guards dressed in sharp black uniforms covered in military supplies logos stepped down from the drivers' cabin and headed to the back of the vehicle. They walked with eager steps, trampling over charred fragments of bone and wood, undoing jacket buttons as they went.

The driver banged the side of a fist on the back door and his doughy face twisted into an ugly sneer. The other guard spat out a piece of gum and wiped the back of a hand across his stubbled face.

A lean man in a sharply ironed, pale grey outfit opened the rear door and muttered something which made all three men laugh as they disappeared into the vehicle, the metal door clunking shut behind them.

Something, someone, grabbed her legs and everything went dark again. Hands, all over her. Now she wanted to wake up, fight back. Soft energies flowed through her cells, rising from beyond the genes that shaped her; beyond the atoms, the quarks, the quantum realm. Subtle forces of a deeper nature and physic began to resonate. Her magic was coming back. She had to wake up, before...

The rear door smashed open and a cloud of smoke and flames bloomed out across the clearing. A squall of birds scattered in the sky. Lizzy, dressed in thin, faded pink pyjama bottoms and faded grey T-shirt that hung loosely over her body stumbled out and fell to the ground. Behind her, crimson and gold flames gushed across the walls and cabinets, swarming over the guards writhing and screaming on the floor.

The ambulance door slammed shut, muffling the blaze and screams of the three men inside, then the sides of the heavy metal vehicle crumpled and fell still.

Around Lizzy, the forest was a hazy, tangled blur of browns, greens and golds. She slowly got to her feet and instinctively inched her hand up her fingers twitching.

The raven, who had been watching intently, lifted into the sky and flew off with a "Kraaa," that sounded almost jubilant.

Lizzy rubbed her eyes and looked up, blinking in the bright light to see the bird disappear beyond the treeline. Around her the forest phased in and out of focus. Lizzy turned and stumbled away into the haze.

Behind her the ambulance let out a tortured metallic groan like a dying beast. It crunched and buckled inwards with slow, jerky motions. The door dislocated and snapped open from the top and hung outwards, held only by the bottom hinge. The stench of burnt flesh and plastic, cut with the sharp, acrid smell of chemicals and metal bled out across the clearing.

Lizzy ran, pushing branches and bushes aside until, breathless, she collapsed behind a tree.

The boom of the ambulance exploding sent out a blast wave that shook branches and dropped a shower of leaves and twigs over her.

The noise quickly faded away and she lowered her arms and opened her eyes. Things were a little more in focus and she brushed the debris from her head and shoulders. A yellow medical wristband caught her attention and she stared at it, wondering who'd clipped it on, and when.

Elizabeth Francis. 693082.

Lizzy ripped it off and threw it aside. She stood up unsteadily and headed away from the burning vehicle, gritting her teeth and forcing herself not to cry out whenever she stepped on something sharp. After several steps, she growled angrily and stopped, clenching her fists. The ground warmed and softened beneath her feet and the forest came into focus, the blur in her vision retreating to a barely visible line on the border of her eyesight.

She set off again and didn't stop until she came to a steep incline. She only hesitated for a moment then scrabbled down and splashed along the shallow stream, following the gulley's curve away from the fire.

Going deeper into the forest, the ground levelled off and she clambered out onto the shallow banks of a large, dry pond. Thin streaks of sunlight stretched down through branches to form a shimmering mosaic of gold and green around her and she sat down on the trunk of a fallen tree.

The forest seemed to go on forever; so much space, colour. After all those years of grey walls, long corridors, cold laboratories the sights, sounds and colours of the forest were overwhelming. The whistle and chirp of birds, the buzz of insects and a rustling breeze full of warm, soothing odours filled the air. Lizzy suddenly felt lost, exposed and scared. She leaned forward, rested her elbows on her knees, and closed her eyes.

Five, she was five when she last cast a spell, last had focus. Any magic now would do her more harm than good. She'd have to wait, for the focus and memories to return, for this fear to go away, then she'd be strong again; wouldn't she? Grief rose up and she began to cry, something she hadn't done for thirteen years, not since she saw her parents executed when she was just five years old.

Lizzy swallowed down the lump in her throat and stood up. The thin slippers she'd been wearing were already gone, lost in the stream. Her flimsy T-shirt and pyjamas, now torn in several places, were covered in spots of blood. She had to keep going, get as far away as possible.

She followed a narrow path down to a wide track. In one direction the track sloped up and deeper into the forest; in the other, it curved down to a tarmac road and lay-by where a trailer café was hooked to a transit van. A line of brand logos of foods, various car repair and maintenance product ran around the top of each vehicle.

Two motorbikes were parked up in front of a large billboard advertising Nu 8G clothes declaring 'Be More'. The two bikers sat at a small fold-up table, chatting animatedly as they ate. Beyond the billboard, van and trailer, a field of golden rapeseed stretched to a distant green hill.

A woman, her long blonde hair tied back, counted notes which she put into different pockets of her jeans. Beside her, a man wearing dungarees and a brown baseball cap, scraped down a hot plate. A teenage boy, wearing a similar cap fitted loosely over neat, straight black hair, emerged from behind the trailer and put a bright red bucket down by the steps.

One of the bikers threw his head back and laughed, "Vampires?" He laughed some more, "H," he said, shaking his head, "that's crazy even for you." His broad shoulders bobbed up and down as he chuckled. The man wiped a paper napkin across his mouth and dropping it onto the table, stood up, running his hand over his black-and-grey beard. "The accident brought magic, not bleedin' vampires. You should watch proper news." The bikers climbed onto their bikes and rode off. The smooth rumble of their bikes brought back memories of her rides with Dad.

The smell of fried bacon drew Lizzy's attention back to the food trailer. The teenager had spotted her and didn't look worried or scared. He pointed at her and said something to the couple in the trailer.

The woman glanced towards Lizzy's hiding place then said something to the man beside her. The man nodded and the woman took her apron off and wiped her hands on it as she stepped out of the trailer. She opened the back door of the transit van and looked up and down the road "Come on," she called with a quick wave.

Lizzy hesitated for a moment then ran down the track and across the road. The woman grabbed her hand and helped her into the back of the van. Lizzy found a seat between cardboard boxes of small bottles, snacks, plastic cups and paper plates and sat down. Surrounded by a constellation of brand logos scattered across everything, Lizzy closed her eyes and rubbed her brow with the ends of her fingers.

The woman slid the door so it was only half open, pulled out a thin canvas sheet and threw it over the boxes. Lizzy looked up and relaxed, "Thanks."

"My God," the woman said, looking Lizzy over, "you poor thing." She gently touched her flimsy, smoke-stained clothes and ran a hand over Lizzy's bald head, dotted with red and blue spots. How on Earth did you escape from the Secure Unit?"

"The ambulance, there was a fire."

"A fire?" the woman said, alarmed.

Lizzy dropped her gaze and the woman changed her tone, "Well, you're safe now." She rummaged around the back of the van and found an old plastic first aid box, "What's your name?"

"Lizzy."

"I'm Diane," she said, ripping open a sterile wipe and handing it to Lizzy. "Clean those scratches on your arms." She gave Lizzy's ash-covered feet, a curious look them wiped them clean.

Lizzy peeled a small plaster off her arm, looked around for

somewhere to put it, and Diane took it from her.

"Where did that come from?"

"They keep taking our blood," Lizzy said, "and..." her voice trailed off.

"What?" Diane said, glancing at Lizzy's scalp, "What else did they do to you?"

Lizzy looked away, "Stuff, they liked to hurt us."

"Monsters," Diane said. She worked quickly, cleaning the scratches and putting plasters over the bigger cuts.

Lizzy took a wipe and scrubbed at her face.

"Not so hard," Diane took the grubby, scrunched-up wipe and gave her another clean one. "There," Diane said, a few minutes later. "Feeling better?"

Lizzy nodded.

"Good," Diane smiled, "now, we'll have to get you away from here, fast." She looked Lizzy over again and shook her head. "This is unbelievable, you poor girl."

The van's side door slid open several inches and the young man looked in, "Dad said to leave some milk, rolls and eggs before we go. Is she a—?"

"Yes, open the back door, Bill, we'll unload from there."

"Yes, Mum."

The young man disappeared and Diane said, "You're lucky you found us, Lizzy. We'll get you to a safe place."

The back doors opened and Bill and his father stood outside.

"Is she okay?" the older man said, picking up a couple of boxes and handing them to his son.

"Yes," Diane said, "the ambulance she was in caught fire."

"Fire?" the man gave Lizzy a fearful look.

"An ambulance, not Salem. She needs our help, John." Diane climbed out of the van.

"I know, Di," John lifted the end of the canvas sheet and pulled out a box. He looked in the direction Lizzy had come from, then glanced at his watch.

"John!" Diane said, "Lycus will be everywhere soon."

"No they won't, ambulances go to the Research Centre in Bulford. That's an hour away and the guards won't find a working phone box around these parts."

"We should hurry anyway," Diane said, "Bill can come with

me and take her on the 'zuki to Ozzy's place. I'll come back here."

"Good thinking." John turned to his son, "You okay with that, Bill?"

"Sure, Dad."

Bill and his dad lifted out some small boxes and closed the rear doors, then Diane pulled at the side door and it shut with a metallic clunk. Bill climbed into the passenger seat and took a quick look at Lizzy before clipping on his safety belt.

Diane climbed into the driver's seat and looked over her shoulder, "You okay, Lizzy?"

"Yes."

The van bumped out of the lay-by and onto the road. A large raven sitting on the fence just behind the billboard took off in the opposite direction, towards the Prison Laboratory.

With her feet pressed against the floor, and both hands pushing down either side of her, Lizzy looked over the canvas covered boxes rattling around her then leaned back and closed her eyes.

The journey seemed to take ages. Lizzy shifted uncomfortably on the seat, her arms getting sore from keeping her balance and her elbows knocking against the boxes either side.

After two sharp turns the van stopped and fell silent. Bill and Diane got out then the side door slid open and Lizzy saw the rear entrance to a house.

"We're here," Diane said and helped Lizzy out onto a smooth, cold stone doorstep. Chickens clucked restlessly nearby somewhere and she heard goats bleating.

"You have a farm?"

"Just for our own eggs and milk. This way," Diane led her up some stairs and down a short hallway. A window at the end overlooked a clearing beyond which stood a small supermarket and café attached to a petrol station with two pumps.

"This way," Diane went into a room but Lizzy stopped in the doorway. Sunlight drifted in through an open window and lit up a soft autumnal room of faded browns and yellows.

Everything in the room, curtains, the armchair throw, bedding, even the rug, was made from a patchwork of faded fabrics and cloths. It had a feeling of home, it felt safe, something she hadn't sensed for a long time. Lizzy wanted to say something but only managed to murmur, "It's nice."

"It's a mess, but thank you," Diane put some keys on the chest of drawers then took a towel out and handed it to Lizzy. "Here, have a quick shower. The water cuts out after five minutes so be quick." She pointed to a door. "I'll get you some clothes, hope you don't mind wearing some of Bill's, you're around the same size."

"Okay."

"Good, when you're done, I'll make you a sandwich then Bill will take you to Ozzy's. Hurry now."

Being in a room full of soft fabrics and colours, after all those years locked up, felt strange, Lizzy felt lost and out of place.

The window over the chest of drawers looked out across a long, fenced garden. The end had been separated out into two sections with a chicken coop in the corner of one and a small shelter for the goats in the other. Several chickens wandered about pecking at the remains of goat feed. Two goats stood by an old metal bath. A boy and girl faun leaned against the fence chatting. He would sometimes scrape a hoof along the ground as he spoke. The girl said something and they both laughed. Lizzy glanced over to the bedroom door, she'd see things Diane and Bill would only glimpse in dreams.

In the shower, a bottle of 'Local West Country' shampoo and a bar of soap stood on the shelf. Lizzy removed her ripped pyjamas and T-shirt and stepped into the cubicle. She barely flinched under the blast of cold water and washed under it for a few seconds before it occurred to her to turn the temperature up.

She gasped as hot water rained over her for the first time in years. Lizzy squeezed some shampoo into her hand and let it drizzle out of her palm and through her fingers. Then, with a smile, she slapped what was left onto her head and scrubbed the bruises and crop of black hair covering her scalp. She then picked up the soap and raised it to her nose, taking in the fragrant smell. She washed quickly and began to hum a tune she used to sing as a child when having baths back at home. Then, realizing what she was singing, stopped and fell into a sullen silence, letting the water fall over her. She didn't move when the shower cut off. She just stared blankly at the white tiles for several seconds then stepped lightly onto the bath mat and wrapped herself in the large, soft towel, her mind a blank. Being locked up from the age of five and experimented on for 12-13 years did something to your mind, your memories.

Back in the bedroom, muffled music drifted up from somewhere down the hall beyond the door. The song ended and someone started talking about some brand new thing that would transform the way people saw you.

A pair of socks, small boxers, a pair of faded denim ' 2L - bLack fLag' branded jeans and a pale grey *Clash* T-shirt were laid out on the bed. A pair of *ZZ* trainers lay on the floor. She put the boxers on and picked up the T-shirt just as the door opened. Lizzy turned, thinking it was Diane, but Bill stood in the doorway, gaping at her, his face flushed.

Lizzy put her arms through the T-shirt. "Hello," she said and slipped the T-shirt over her head and pulled it down.

"Oh," Bill looked down at his feet then over to the window. "Sorry, I need the keys," he raised a hand towards the chest of drawers under the window, "for the garage."

"Okay," Lizzy picked up the jeans and put them on while Bill quickly crossed the room, snatched the keys and rushed out. Lizzy looked over her shoulder when the door clicked shut, then sat down to put the socks and trainers on. Fully dressed, she examined herself in the full-length mirror: the first time she'd seen herself in years. She was slightly taller than she imagined, and older.

A photo was stuck in the frame of the mirror: Diane and her husband with Billy, still recognisable as a small boy. Diane was smiling down at a baby in her arms. Lizzy touched the picture and wondered what happened to the little girl.

She smiled and saw her mother's eyes and father's smile in the mirror. This time the memories flooded back and with tears in her eyes, rushed into the bathroom and locked the door, just like she did as a child.

A minute later, Diane's voice came from the far side of the bedroom. "Lizzy?"

"Coming," Lizzy splashed water over her face then scrubbed it with the hand towel that hung over the radiator. The bedroom door was open and she headed down the short hall to the kitchen, stopping by Bill's room to look inside. Old, frayed pictures from music and film magazines covered the walls, and a stack of CDs was piled on the edge of a cluttered desk. Some clothes and comics lay scattered across a double bed. An acoustic guitar leaned against the wall by a chest of drawers.

In the kitchen, Diane stood with her back to a worktop, a mug of tea in her hand. "You look better," she smiled and pointed to a fried egg sandwich and glass of milk on the table. "Eat up. Bill will take you to Ozzy's place once you're done."

"Thanks," Lizzy sat down, "is it far from here?"

"About half an hour's drive, near Bristol," Diane sat beside her and put an old grey NY baseball cap on the table, "This should help, you look like an escaped convict."

"I am," Lizzy murmured and slipped the cap on. Beyond the window a silvery creature swooped across the sky and curved up into the clouds. She shot a glance at Diane and continued eating.

Diane sipped at her tea, "That's a nasty old bruise on your arm, what happened?"

"They gamble, make us fight. Sarah and Carly, a couple of big girls from the East wing," Lizzy said, concentrating on her food, "they'd been drugged. I was whacked with a metal broom handle, on my leg too."

"My God, what happened?"

"Broken arm, cracked ribs."

"You poor thing."

"Not me, them," Lizzy took another bite of the sandwich and gulped down some milk.

Diane shot her a worried look and was about to speak when she was interrupted by a rush of footsteps up the stairs and along the short hall.

The door swung open and Bill stood in the doorway. He looked worried, "Mum, she's already on the news. The forest is swarming with soldiers." He made an effort not to make eye contact with Lizzy.

"Okay, Bill, get the bike out, we'll be down soon." Diane turned to Lizzy," We'll have to hurry."

"You should see it, Mum, it's serious."

"Bill, I'll watch it up here, get your bike ready." Diane watched her son leave and turned to Lizzy. "What was that about?"

Lizzy shrugged.

"Did something happen with Bill?" Diane crossed to small flat-screen TV hooked up to a cable box on the wall.

"No," Lizzy thought for a second then said, "Oh, he came in

when I was dressing."

"Did he? Sorry about that."

"That's okay."

The cable box booted up and Diane switched to the news channel. The newscaster's voice spoke over the image of a fire truck and black van parked several yards from the burnt-out, blackened prison ambulance.

"… forensic team is hard at work identifying the remains, believed to be those of the three guards and the patient, who was being taken to the Neurological centre for surgery."

Someone handed the reporter a sheet of paper and the reporter scanned it then looked up. The face of Lizzy slid across to fill half the screen. "Reports are coming in that the remains are those of the prison guards. Police are warning the public that the patient survived the explosion and is at large. Lycus have issued this image of Elizabeth Francis, now wanted in connection with the murder of the three Lycus prison guards. Lycus warn she is a severely disturbed and dangerous patient. We've been asked to warn people that her magical powers caused the inferno that killed three prison guards. Having just escaped she may not be in full control of her abilities."

Lizzy glanced up at the screen, a sour expression on her face, then picked up the remains of her sandwich. Diane was now staring at her; Lizzy ignored her and bit into the sandwich as the newscaster continued. "Police and Lycus troops have arrived to close off Baron's Wood while a search takes place. The public are urged to call the police immediately if they see her or know her whereabouts."

"Murder?" Diane put the mug of tea down and muted the screen.

"It's a lie. I didn't murder anyone."

"Lizzy, what happened to that prison ambulance and those men?"

Lizzy pursed her mouth shut and stared at the half empty glass of milk. She took a deep breath and said, "I told you, I'm not a murderer."

Doors clunked shut in the yard below, and Diane crossed to the window. Down in the courtyard, Bill wheeled the motorbike out of the garage. "Can you remember anything?" Diane said, without taking her eyes off her son.

"I was drugged," Lizzy's gaze remained fixed on the glass of milk, a stony expression on her face. She wiped her eyes and shook her head.

"Lizzy."

Lizzy closed her eyes for a few seconds, "I remember lying down, strapped down. Then the straps came off my legs. Big hands, pushing me down, pulling my pyjamas, then there was fire everywhere." And the screams and smell of burning; flesh, fabric, plastic.

"My God," Diane said, "those monsters."

Lizzy shot her a look. Mum said you could never trust straights.

"What about the fire, Lizzy how did it start, did they knock something over?"

"I don't know," Lizzy bit her lip and avoided Diane's gaze. "It just happened."

"What do you mean it just happened? I know your kind can't lie, so—"

"My kind?" Lizzy snapped, and with anger pushing back tears, glared up at Diane.

"Lizzy, that's not what I meant. I—"

"You what?" Lizzy almost shouted. The air in the kitchen crackled and the image on the TV broke up into pixelated fragments. Thin lines of vapour rose from where her fingers gripped the sandwich.

They died because her magic came back while she was drugged out and took over her survival instinct. It wasn't her fault, she didn't want to kill anyone.

"I was drugged, I don't know how the fire started, okay?"

"Okay," Diane nodded slowly. "Okay." Without taking her eyes off Lizzy, she crossed to the door and pulled it open. "You should get going."

Lizzy glared down at the table while thin threads of smoke rose from where her fingers gripped the sandwich. Then she took one last bite and dropped the charred crusts onto the plate. She wiped the dust from her hands and pushing the chair back, stood up. She should never have accepted help from a straight. She finished off the milk then followed Diane downstairs. That safe house near Bristol, she'd find out where it was and get there herself; away from these straights, find other magicians, people who'd trust her, not turn on her for no reason.

Diane took a crash helmet from the side, "Take this, wait here," she said and crossed the yard to Bill.

Stony-faced, Lizzy waited beside boxes of fruit and vegetables. She grabbed an apple and ate it while Diane spoke to Bill. Bill listened and nodded, sometimes glancing over to her. Then Diane waved her over.

The old Suzuki 250 looked well cared for. Lizzy's dad had a Kawasaki; she helped look after it and they'd go on long rides.

"Bill will take you to his brother's place. There's a bus stop nearby. You'll go to the Bristol safe house from there on your own. Here's some money for a bus and some food." Diane held out two ten-pound notes and a slip of paper. "The bus numbers are on the paper." Something in Diane's voice, a sadness maybe, made Lizzy think of her mum.

"Thanks." Lizzy mumbled and took the slip of paper and money.

Their eyes met and Lizzy sensed that sadness again. Diane confused her in a way she couldn't explain, and for a moment Lizzy felt she'd miss her, which was strange.

"She'll need a jacket, Mum," Bill said, "what about your old one?"

Diane sighed then said to Lizzy, "Wait a sec."

Bill climbed onto the bike. "Don't worry," he whispered, "it's too small for her now."

Lizzy nodded and they waited in silence.

Diane came back with a black leather biker's jacket with tassels across the back, and handed it over.

"Thank you," Lizzy put the jacket on, zipping it up to her neck. She got the feeling Diane was losing something else, something far more precious than a worn biker's jacket. Straights and their meaningless stuff that meant so much to them. Still, "I'll look after it. I'm sorry."

"What for?" Diane said.

Lizzy shrugged, "You helped me, I got angry."

"I understand, Lizzy, don't worry," Diane said. "You'll have enough troubles to deal with." She leaned forward and whispered "You be careful."

Lizzy responded with a brief nod and put the helmet on then climbed onto the back of the motorbike, slipping her hands through the passenger handle.

Bill rode with a confidence that came with a familiarity of the narrow country lanes; the tall hedges became a green blur. In the fields either side, rows of people pulling small trolleys worked their way through rows of fruits and vegetables. Orchards buzzed with activity. Every so often they'd go through a village high street with telephone boxes dotted with advertising boards. Lizzy held on tight behind him and moved her head from one side to the other, watching him change gears, use the throttle and brakes; same as before, bikes still worked the same.

Bill pulled over in a lay-by beside a billboard once, and leaning round said, "Can you not move around please?"

"Okay." Lizzy said and they set off again.

They arrived at the cottage and Bill parked the Suzuki round the back. He took off the helmet and ran his fingers through his long, black hair. "This is where I drop you off," he said, stuffing the keys into the pocket of the jacket.

"Okay," Lizzy took her helmet off and Bill froze.

"What is it?"

Bill slowly raised a hand and pointed it at her head. "You.. you got hair."

"I know," She now had short, spiky golden hair. Lizzy climbed off the bike, "My magic's back."

She took in a deep breath and relaxed. It was a warm day and the air was alive with insects and birdsong. Tiny Amisra faeries flew around under flowers releasing mote clouds that swirled and ribboned around the plant stems, sinking into them then rising to burst out of the flowers in a cascade of colour, attracting the attention of bees and male Amisra.

Bill was still staring at her.

"What?"

"You... you really are a magician," he stammered. "I've never seen a real magician."

"Really?" Lizzy said, still distracted by the small, neat garden. It reminded her of the garden they had at home, the garden where she saw her parents executed.

"It must be amazing, to do magic." Bill waved a hand through the air in a mock spell-cast.

"It's not, they kill us."

"Oh, yeah, sorry." There was a short, awkward silence then he pointed in the direction of the occasional buzz of distant traffic, "You go straight down this road to a junction where it joins a main road. There's a bus stop on the right."

"Okay."

"Ozzy's place is the first house past a field after the White Hart pub. His house is opposite a church. I can't remember the name but it's uphill from a low wall and graveyard. The bus stop is just across the road from the house."

First house past the pub opposite a church on a hill. "Okay."

Bill responded with a nod and turned towards the house.

"Can I use the toilet?" Lizzy said, not looking at the Suzuki.

"I guess, but Mum said you can't stay around us, Lycus probably already started searching houses." He went round to the side of the house and she followed. A small utility room led into the kitchen. "The news said you locked the guards in the ambulance and set it alight."

Lizzy didn't look at him and Bill continued, "That's what Mum said, but…"

"But what?"

"Nothing. She worries a lot." He put his helmet on the side. "What kind of fire would incinerate a whole ambulance? I don't get it. Maybe you—"

"I what? Murdered them? Because we're all evil?" Lizzy snapped. "What do you want to believe?"

"No, what? Believe?" Bill stepped back, a look of fear on his face. "I… what do you mean?"

"Your news, your TV. All those adverts and logos. You straights are told what to believe every day. Have stuff or you'll be a nobody, be weird. No wonder you're all so scared of magic; it really does change things."

Bill gaped at her then lowered his head. Lizzy, shocked by her own outburst, fell silent.

"No," Bill said quietly, "I know, the way you got away, what happened, it was scary; we still helped you though, didn't we?"

He was right. Lizzy didn't say anything, and Bill looked up at her, "Mum told me to be careful but I knew you wouldn't hurt anyone." He took his jacket off and slipped it over the back of a chair. "You don't know my family." He pointed to a door, "Toilet's through there." He picked up a small wicker basket lined with scrunched-up papers and examined it for a few seconds, "I have to collect the eggs." He pushed the back door open, "Anyway, I know stuff is just stuff, it's just fun, that's all."

Lizzy gave a barely visible nod.

"Do you know about reavers?"

"Yes, they come out at midnight." she wanted to apologise, "thanks, Bill."

"Okay. Bye, good luck." Bill pulled the door shut and headed up to the small field where the chickens were. He stopped at the small gate, made sure no chickens were nearby, then quickly went through. The little wooden gate swung shut behind him with a reassuring clunk.

Lizzy hesitated for a second then grabbed the keys from his jacket pocket. She waited until Bill was at the far end of the field then swept up her crash helmet and rushed out to the bike. The engine was still warm and it started with the first kick.

"Hey!" Bill dropped the basket of eggs and ran down the field towards her, eggs rolling down after him. "That's my bike!"

Lizzy twisted the throttle and shot out of the yard, almost crashing into the telephone pole as she skidded round into the road.

Another twist of the throttle surged the bike forward. Lizzy gasped as the engine roared through the gears. The wind rushing round her, she snapped down the visor. Such simple movements, so much control. It was just like magic. She eased into the angle, tilt and balance as she took the corners and leaned forward on the straight sections.

There wasn't much traffic on the A4, only the odd delivery van or a car full of sharers. Lizzy kept to a steady 40 and let vehicles pass her. After a few minutes, her confidence grew and she tapped into fifth gear and shot along a stretch of dual carriageway, overtaking vehicles on either side. Then the road narrowed again and she slowed behind a small van roughly painted to resemble a slatted wooden box of vegetables. She tensed up when a Lycus military truck appeared round a corner and she remained behind the van as the truck passed.

A short diversion led her into a village and she stopped at the top of the high street; people going about their everyday lives. Lizzy toed the bike into gear and rode slowly along the high street.

Shops, most of them with faded façades lined both sides of the street. A few had been repaired with polished bare wood and reused bricks. These stood out from the rest. A second-hand book store; a grocery with prices for buying and selling fruit and vegetables; a bakery; a shop selling second-hand clothes. A department store on the corner had been turned into a multi-faith community centre. Large religious symbols painted in garish, bright colours covered the outside wall and reached to the roof. Two pedestrianised islands lined with benches, grassed areas and a few parking bays for bicycles ran down the centre of the road. Three bald monks in brown robes stood by one of the benches. Two held Bibles and read from them loud enough for people to hear over the hubbub. The third monk handed out little strips of bark and stones with symbols and prayers scratched onto them. A small group of people had gathered to listen and passers by would occasionally put a fruit or vegetable into a basket on the bench. The monks would nod and smile and continue reciting. Over on her right, an old man filled a battered Toyota pickup at a petrol station.

People wandered along with bags and baskets. It all looked so ordinary, so unreal.

***

Ozzy's house opposite the church was easy enough to find. The small grey stone building was set back from the road, with space out front for a couple of cars. A guy with a neat, thin-cut beard opened the door and pointed to a wide path leading round the house. Lizzy rode round past a small pond and parked up under a lean-to built beside an old barn.

The back door opened and the guy reappeared. Using his foot, he nudged a small grey stone against the door to keep it open, "You got some nerve nicking Bill's bike."

Lizzy shrugged and took the helmet off then with a swipe of a hand over her scalp produced a mess of golden hair.

Ozzy smiled and shook his head. "This way."

Coloured sketches of hot-air balloons, people on skateboards and aerial photos of the countryside lined one wall.

"Is this what you do?"

"The people I work for have a hot-air balloon," Ozzy said, nudging the stone with his foot so the door swung shut. "I take care of it and track it in a four-by-four."

"A hot-air balloon," Lizzy said to herself.

"What was that?"

"Oh, nothing," Lizzy put the helmet on a small pile of boxes full of electronic parts and circuit boards. "Sandy, the little girl I shared a cell with, she was a seer. She had a dream that rescue would come from the sky."

"No chance of that, the prison has its own small army. It's a miracle you escaped."

"I know," Lizzy followed Ozzy into a large living room.

She crossed the room and dropped onto the sofa. Ozzy stood staring at her.

"What?" Lizzy said.

"What happened," Ozzy said, "Why did you do it?"

"They told you didn't they?"

"I thought they'd just repeated what was on the news, but killing someone leaves a resonance other magicians can sense. You don't have it. There's something different, weird about what's coming from you. Tell me what happened."

Lizzy explained what the guards tried to do while she was drugged and barely conscious in the ambulance.

"You weren't conscious or in control?"

"I think it was my born magic protecting me."

"That would explain the strange resonance from you."

"Am I stuck with this now?"

"I don't know, maybe the elders can help. I'll reach out to them. It'll take a while, a few days at least. Nothing we can do about it until we know more. I'll put the kettle on."

Ozzy left the room and Lizzy got up and wandered around. A large flat-screen TV hung on the wall opposite the sofa. A scratched and dusty old PlayStation 4 Pro, wired into the cable router, rested on a small table below.

Lizzy had a smaller TV at home, along with an old cable box which they rarely used. The world of people on TV was so dull and linear.

Over to her left, boxes of old electronic parts, circuit boards, cables and tiny components, were neatly lined up beside a workbench. A couple of large studded collars lay on another tray on the corner of the table. A window faced the long garden, the far end of which was lined with a row of tall bushes and a few trees. On the opposite wall, a statue stood in the centre of a small table where an incense stick released a thin ribbon of scent into the air.

"He helps with meditation," Ozzy said as he returned, "and keeping this reality in perspective."

It reminded her of home; Lizzy responded with a glum nod.

"Are you all right?"

"I guess. What happens now?"

"I've sent a request for a meeting with Suzie."

"Who, why?"

"Suzie Emerson, the first New Sorceress. You're the only one to ever escape. Now we wait." Ozzy crossed over to the window facing the field beyond the small garden and pond. "It will be a fair shock to the system being out here again." He half closed the wooden Venetian blind then turned to Lizzy. "You will need time to adjust as your magic returns, learn to focus."

"I feel better already."

"No mood swings, getting sad, angry, upset?"

Lizzy shrugged, "Maybe."

"Maybe?"

"A little, I guess." Lizzy bit her lower lip.

"What happened?"

"I lost my temper, with Bill, and his mum. It just came out."

"Ah. Well, feeling guilty won't help," Ozzy said. "The outbursts means you are retuning, the turbulence will pass." Ozzy went across to the long table and picked up what looked like a large dog collar. "It happens with the guys too, the ones we rescue who've had the collar on for a good few years. They settle down in the end, start to see, think clearly."

"Collars?"

"Suppressor collars," Ozzy turned it in his hand. "It makes us powerless, flattens our potential."

"Is that what they do? We assemble them in Salem."

"Mm, that would make sense since the place is impenetrable."

"But we, I mean the girls in prison, don't wear collars, magic doesn't work in the Unit."

22

"Really? That is interesting." Ozzy looked at her hair, "I see you haven't wasted any time with your magic. You might want to think about toning it down a little, your hair's like strands of sunlight. No wonder it gave Bill a scare."

"Bill?"

"He phoned after you stole his 'zuki."

"'Zuki?"

"His bike, the Suzuki 250. Don't worry. He forgave you."

"What?"

"Cantata forgive, remember? It releases us from negative energy." He pointed at a bar stool by the workbench. "Here. I want to try something out."

Lizzy joined him at the workbench where the innards of old radios and mobile phones were sorted in different plastic boxes. "What is all this, what are you doing?"

"I make devices that disable the suppressor collars before we take them off, the problem is it hurts like hell. Here." he handed her a rectangular circuit in a metal frame

Lizzy took it, "We called this a part 4."

"Okay, see that tiny yellow-and-black scale just off centre?"

"Yes."

"That's the amplitude modulator, put the tip of your finger on the top and try to feel into it."

"Feel into it?"

"Yes, y'know the way your arm feels all spongy hollow when you cast a spell? Well just imagine that space spreading out into the modulator. You'll feel the ripples bouncing back."

"I'll try." Lizzy placed her finger gently on the little scale. "What am I supposed to feel?"

"I don't know, you're the one with the innate power to control energy, so you tell me."

"Why hasn't some other magician done this for you?"

Ozzy glanced at her hair then looked her in the eyes, "You do know you're a sorceress don't you?"

"What?"

You can cast spells that remain permanent as well as regular spells that fade after a while."

"What do you mean?"

"Spells cast my magicians don't last, the universe, some kind of laws of nature shifts things back to normal after a while; the spell wears off. Sorcerers can combine and cast spells that can be permanent; make magical changes that fuse with the stuff of this world. Your hair foe example, that has to be sorcery."

"Oh, so how have you been making these things up till now?"

"Like I said, I can, we all can, but the magic doesn't stay long enough to get rid of the extraction pain."

Lizzy examined him for a second then held her palm low over the box, an inch or so from the scaly circuit strips and closed her eyes.

"You don't have to close your eyes," Ozzy said through a smile.

"Oh." Something like a smooth caress glided down through her hand. She felt a soft trickle from her fingers and a gentle push back. "Like a little zippy pulse."

"Okay, now put your finger on the orange-and-green one."

Lizzy moved her finger across. Again, the same soft sensation through her hand, and another response. "That's different, like it's slower."

"Excellent," Ozzy picked up the box of circuit strips and handed it to Lizzy. "First incantation: the Nuyika hunting sprite."

Lizzy's eyes lit up, "Great."

"Say, 'Nuyika, guyllefi,' move your first, second and little finger like this to summon," he gestured. "Cast like this," he twitched a finger left, "to send out a spray of the tiniest magical sparks you can muster."

"You want me to call an incantation to remove something from each of the yellow-and-black ones?"

"You got it."

"You sure I can do this right?"

"Judging from what you've done with your hair, managing the kind of energy involved in these devices is right up your street."

"I'll try," Lizzy murmured and with the tips of her fingers pointing downwards, held her open palm over the box. Ozzy grabbed her wrist before she could speak the incantation.

"What is it?"

"Have you been formally attuned?"

"Attuned, what's that?"

"Okay," Ozzy took her hands. "What is your full name?"

"Elizabeth Francis."

"Is that all your names?"

Lizzy hesitated, "We never shared our inner names, not even in the Unit."

"I must know your inner name to fully attune you. You can trust me."

He wasn't lying, he couldn't, "Okay, my inner name is Seshat."

"Interesting," Ozzy took her hands in his and closing his eyes, took a deep slow breath. "Elizabeth Seshat Francis."

The sound of his voice resonated through her and Lizzy felt the vibrations flow in her hands. A sensation of something opening began in the centre of her chest and expanded to spread through her body like she was being filled up.

"The Word that resonates prior to all that arises, and whence all that exists arises, is what we were, are and will all return to."

Lizzy took in a deep breath, and whatever had filled her now surrounded her like a living ocean that breathed her. She felt a moment of falling and Ozzy quickly let go of her hands and gripped her arms to steady her.

"What happened?"

"All magicians have to be attuned by another so their magic is clear and always in harmony, with no chaotic or unexpected consequences. Now you are one of us."

"Who is us?"

"Each magician attunes to a Section with a particular resonance or harmony. When magicians of the same clan draw magic in proximity, the harmony of their magic is magnified. You are now part of the London Section, as I am. Now, with your attention on the components and the first feeling you had, the zippy one, try the incantation."

"Okay." Lizzy spoke the incantation, "Nuyika, guyllefi."

A thin layer of golden cloud teeming with glittering pinpricks of light grew from a point over the box. It spread out so Lizzy could barely see through it and when it covered the box completely, she shifted a finger to the left. The sparks of light glided down from the cloud to scatter and disappear into the circuits and the cloud dissolved away. All those incantations and spell-casting games she played with her parents weren't games any more.

"Excellent," Ozzy took a tiny circuit board out and slipped it into a slot on the side of a collar. The collar lit up immediately.

"Lizzy," Ozzy said, "this will help rescue a lot of collared magicians."

"Boys, not the girls though."

Ozzy went to say something then changed his mind. "I know, we haven't forgotten them, we just need to figure out a way to free them. Meanwhile, let's get to work and put together a new identity for you and find you a home."

"And then?"

"Then we wait for Suzie or one of her group to get in touch. The tea, I forgot, back in a sec. Here, try out the PlayStation." Ozzy picked up a controller, and turning the PlayStation and TV on, tossed the controller towards her. The room snapped into sharp relief as the controller slowed and arced across the room, trailing swirls like coiled air that twisted the reflections inside. It stopped to hover a few feet from her and Lizzy plucked it from the air.

Lizzy's eyes froze on the date on the top right corner of the screen. She'd been locked up twelve years. She was seventeen, not fifteen. Her thoughts lost in the past, she blinked back the tears and moved her fingers slowly over the controller.

Using the D pad, she tapped over to the Video menu then came across the BBC iPlayer. She stopped browsing when a documentary about the first High Security Prison highlighted itself in the main menu. She clicked play and sat back.

Photos and footage of wrecked houses and streets scrolled across the screen while the narrator spoke.

"The War on Magic was fought on three fronts: the first was the direct conflict with magician insurgents and their supporters. The second involved defending the Containment Programme of building prisons and research centres where young magicians could be held and treated. Many books and programmes have already told of the bravery of volunteers who helped Lycus scour the country for common and exotic materials necessary for the cells and restraints. Even more donated their silver and gold jewellery necessary to protect our freedom. The third front was the relentless pursuit of knowledge to develop better forms of detection and control. In the early days, extreme measures were necessary to contain some inmates and many criminal magicians perished along with some newly appointed prison guards. The hunting down and execution of the last elder magicians marked the beginning of the end of the War on Magic."

An arena-sized laboratory filled the screen. Silver-white cubicles with desks and computers surrounded slender pillars that carried power and data cables to each desk. Wooden tables were covered in leather restraining straps; thick metal mesh screens swung slowly on chains hanging from steel girders that criss-crossed the ceiling. "Today's story begins in this laboratory, where research led to the collar technology that resulted in these prisons being closed down and the elimination of scenes like this." Photographs scrolled across the screen: teenagers strapped down on operating tables, chained to metal grills, immersed in mercurial liquid, their bodies punctured by metal tubes or peppered with jagged metal runes.

Ozzy returned with a tray of red fruit tea and biscuits to find Lizzy with tears in her eyes. He put the tray down and turned off the television then passed her a box of tissues.

Lizzy pulled out a tissue and wiped the her face.

"They're scared of losing control, of their world falling apart. Here," he passed her a cup of tea. "They don't understand what we mean by 'everything is connected'."

Lizzy stared down at the hot drink, "How can the war ever be over when they treat us like that?" She took a sip, "It's sweet."

"Yeah, sorry, habit, I put honey in it."

"No, it's nice, I like it," she went to pick up the controller and Ozzy grabbed it first, sat beside her and offered her a biscuit.

Lizzy rubbed the thumb of her free hand across the tips of her fingers. Thin threads of light spun out and sparkled briefly then disappeared. She clenched her fist then opened her palm, turning her hand like she was examining a weapon, "I'm seventeen."

"Are you okay with that?"

Lizzy responded with a whisper of a nod.

"Good, now important things first."

"Like learning some more spells?"

"No, what do you think of my biscuits?"

Lizzy looked at him and took a biscuit, "What is it?"

"Shortbread."

"It's nice."

"Thanks." Ozzy clapped his hands. "I'll show you a spell to change your features to resemble any face you see in a photograph.

Then I'll see about getting you a new ID and finding somewhere for you to stay."

"Where?"

"I'll write to a few Cantata safe houses, see what's available. You might have to stay here for a few days, maybe even a week or two."

"Cantata?" Lizzy took another biscuit.

"Magicians and straight people, like Diane and Bill, people who support us. What?" he said, "don't you trust them?"

"They don't trust me," Lizzy gave the biscuit a quick dunk in the tea.

"No," Ozzy said, "I spoke with Bill and Diane. Yeah, they were shocked by how you escaped; but Diane's family are good people. She had a daughter, you know, born with the magic. Lycus took her away a month after she was born."

"I think I knew that, I got this feeling from her."

"I'm not surprised, girl magicians can tell if a woman has had a magician daughter."

"What was her name, the girl I mean?"

"Melanie."

"Melanie, I know her, she was nice, always with the little girls, looking after them."

"Melanie would have been around the same age as you. As a mother, Diane would have sensed the same subtle resonance in you that she felt from her daughter; that must have been very difficult for her."

Lizzy glanced over at the biker jacket Diane had given her. "She never said."

"Losing a child is not an easy thing to talk about, more so when you know where they are, what they are going through. I'll let her know about Melanie." Ozzy leaned over the side of the sofa and picked up a stack of old magazines. "Have a look through these, find a face we can work with and I'll show you the spell."

Lizzy flicked through a magazine and Ozzy said, "I'll show you a few more incantations later. Meantime, I'll start working on your new identity and ID card."

"Will it take long?" she said, scanning the pages.

"A few days, our hackers have been busy on other things lately. There are rumours about a rescue."

"Rescue?"

"A raid on the Secure Unit, free all the girls; can't see how though."

She threw the magazine aside and sat up, "I can help."

"It's just rumours, Lizzy, they pop up every so often; vague plans that just can't work. Lycus is powerful, and magic doesn't work in or around the Unit."

"They killed my mum and dad," she said and stared out at nothing.

Ozzy's eyes widened. He lowered the mug in his hands and turned to her slowly, "How could you know? Weren't you taken at birth, like all girl magicians?"

Lizzy shook her head, "I was five."

"Five? So you remember things, your family?"

Lizzy nodded, "I was born at home. We left London straight away and moved to Glasgow where I was raised as a boy." Lizzy chewed on her lower lip and gazed out of the window. "They called me Frankie."

"Lizzy," Ozzy put his hand gently on her shoulder, "you don't have to talk about it."

"It's all we did, told stories, about what they did to us in the labs, what we did together."

Ozzy sat beside her, sipping his tea, listening.

Lizzy gave him a small smile. "Attention is energy, right?"

Ozzy nodded.

"I always thought the other girls in the Unit were lucky, they arrived as babies; never had a family to remember.. or miss." She swallowed and continued, "They all loved Mei's stories about her family, life outside."

"Mei?"

"She was the only other one like me."

"She talked about her family?"

Lizzy nodded, "I couldn't. So I started to tell stories about a boy I knew: Chris. Our dads were old friends; they were always coming round." A brief smile crossed her face, "Our dads had motorbikes. We used to go on rides, to magical places. Chris didn't even notice the difference. He was a bit... he didn't understand much. I could tell, even though he was a year older than me, a magician too. What, why are you staring at me like that?"

"You said magical places." Ozzy stopped gaping at her, wide-eyed. "Someone knew how to open a Rainbow Bridge?"

"Rainbow Bridge, like Asgard?"

"It's not just Asgard that has a Rainbow Bridge, you know."

"Asgard is real?"

"In a way, but you've heard of the infinite universes theory, right?"

"Sort of, Dad drew me a picture book."

"There are billions upon billions of universes, new variations bubbling up every second." Ozzy gazed out of the window. "Each with billions more galaxies, stars and planets."

"I always thought the bikes were magical."

"Impractical, but anything, even a motorbike, can easily be enchanted. It would take a powerful Talisman to radiate a Rainbow Bridge. Is that how you learned to ride, from those journeys?"

"Yes."

"Do you have any other family, cousins, uncles, aunts; people you could trust?"

"Cousins, in the Enclave, they visited once."

"The Enclave. Lycus has built another wall round it; one infused with dark magic."

"What does that mean?"

"People can't get in or out so easily. I'll see what I can find out. Maybe you should try to get in touch with Chris."

"I guess." She gave him a sideways look.

"What? Oh, Chris never knew you were a girl?"

Lizzy shook her head and Ozzy smiled, "He could be in for a shock then."

Chapter Two

A heavy moon hung in a cloudless sky. Across the country, street lights silently switched off as the public grid shut down and generators in hospitals, supermarkets, police stations and prisons hummed into life. In North Finchley, Chris peered through the bushes at the dark, moonlit street. Every house had thick curtains drawn across the windows; many of them with thick wire mesh or reinforced steel shutters. The only light came from a small solar-battery-operated neon cross which glowed a welcoming soft green outside the entrance to a shelter.

Chris checked his watch again: fifteen minutes before midnight. Sunrise at 4:50; alarm set for 4:55, just to be safe. This was a bad idea. "Andy, we could make it to the shelter across the road."

"It's a shed with bunk beds," Andy laughed, "you chickening out, Chris? This was your idea."

"I was joking, this is craz—"

A blinding white spotlight swept across the houses down the street and the rumble of a large vehicle rolled up to the junction. The long, heavily armoured van with blacked-out windows stopped and idled loudly on the corner. Gears churned as the spotlight scanned the area from left to right, catching a lone fox in its sights. The fox stopped motionless for a second then disappeared down a path between two houses. With a loud hiss of hydraulics, the van took a right turn and the turret carrying the mini-gun let out a heavy clank as the van bumped the kerb and headed up the High Road away from Chris and Andy.

"Did you see that Chris? An M134D mini-gun; 3000 shots a minute. That thing could take out a whole rage of reavers just like that."

"We could be playing COD instead of being here."

"Yeah, but this is real."

"This is insane."

"No it isn't, we just don't have to look them in the eye. This is gonna be soo scary," Andy said excitedly, "come on." He sidled out from their hiding place and headed for the grassy area by the park's main gates. Chris glanced over at the shelter then joined Andy who was already face down on the cool grass, pulling the sleep mask tight over his eyes. Chris lay down beside him and positioned his mask over his eyes. Five hours, that's not so bad.

Andy broke the silence, "They say reavers can smell you from a mile away."

"Smell you maybe."

"Ooh, Andy, there's a shelter," Andy said in a mocking, whiny voice, "let's go hide there, it's nice and cosy. I'm so scared they'll eat me."

"Don't be a dick."

Andy giggled, "Hey, I know, let's join the Witnesses tomorrow, bring offerings to the priests and get a strip of paper with a prayer on it."

"Sh, what's that?" Chris hissed.

"What, what?" Andy said. "Did you hear something? Chris, are they coming?"

"So you're not scared?"

"Shut up."

A soft rumbling woke Chris from a half-sleep. The sound turned into a clattering like an avalanche of small rocks. "Oh shit." The noise slowed as it neared and was joined by low, coarse grunts. Chris swore under his breath and pressed his eyes shut under the sleep mask, "It's a rage."

The small avalanche of hooves rumbled across the pavement and thumped onto the surrounding grass, filling the cool night air with a sickly stench of rotten flesh. Chris gagged and almost threw up while stomps fell heavily around him. Snarls and coarse grunts blasted the hair on the back of his head as the creatures breathed in the smell of fear in his sweat.

Chris scrunched his face and fought the urge to get up and run. He shouldn't have come; he should have just let Andy go alone. Why the hell did he make such a dumb joke? He should have known Andy would go for it. He should have left that stupid idiot and gone to the shelter on his own.

Andy mumbled incoherently, his voice almost lost in the stamping and guttural noises around them. It actually sounded like the reavers were talking to each other. Was that even possible?

"Andy?" Chris panicked and raised his voice when Andy didn't respond, "Andy!"

Andy's mumbling came back louder; he was praying.

The night fell silent and after a while Andy let out a loud, nervous laugh, "We did it, they're gone, let's have a look."

"Andy, No. No way!"

"They're gone."

"Don't do it, Andy, it might be a trick."

"A Trick? No, man," Andy said, "how can reavers stay quiet this long? How would they even know to do that?"

"I think they were talking to each other."

Andy laughed nervously.

"Seriously, Andy. Maybe... maybe they're smart."

"Smart, yeah, right."

"We don't know, do we? We didn't hear them go."

"We were too freaking scared."

"Yeah but we'd still hear those hoofs, wouldn't we?"

Andy didn't respond for several seconds, then said, "Nah. I still can't hear anything. I'm going to have a look."

"Are you crazy?"

"Coward. Oh fu—"

A violent thick ripping and snapping cut short Andy's blunt, agonised cry. Chris groaned under the sound of flesh being gouged and torn; the snap and crunch of bones; squelching followed by heavy splashes falling over and around him. A frenzied stomping and the brutal cadence of ravenous slobbering and throaty breaths. Shaking violently, Chris pressed his hands over his ears and pushed his face into the soil.

Blood and globs of drool-soaked flesh splattered over Chris, spreading warm, wet patches across the backs of his legs. The horror seemed to go on forever.

Gradually the feeding subsided to cracks and snaps, The grinding and scraping of jagged teeth gnawing on bone was replaced by a gruesome sucking and coarse spitting. It all finally ended with a clatter of hooves over tarmac fading down the road.

Chris lay on the blood-soaked soil in a heavy silence surrounded by the stench of flesh and putrid residue of reaver aether. Another smaller rage arrived and snuffled around him, scooping up clumps of soil, licking and sucking the blood, spitting out stones and sprays of mud. Then they too scuttled away. Chris didn't move, not even when his watch alarm chimed at 4:55.

***

The door to the interrogation rooms opened and a policeman led Chris out to the waiting area by the station's entrance. The man towered over Chris by several inches, the bright logo of three different types of body armour brands over his right chest. "Here," he thrust the transparent bag of bloodied clothes at Chris and pointed to a row of faded blue plastic chairs bolted to the wall, "wait over there."

Chris grabbed the bag and it squished under his arms. A thin pool of blood and viscous liquid slid along the bottom and he grimaced, "Don't your CSI people want it?"

"CSI," the policeman snorted, "we're done with it." He couldn't have sounded more bored. "We know what happened." He jabbed a stubby thumb on the pad by the door. The lock clicked open and he returned to his desk.

Chris dropped onto a seat. The coarse, synthetic jumpsuit given to him after the harsh detergent and scrubbing, crackled and rubbed against his raw skin. Wincing, he stood up and moved his shoulders around to ease the scratching.

The policeman lowered his pen and pressed the button at the base of the microphone stand, "Sit down, Asten."

Chris sat back down and the policeman continued, "A miss Jessica Keats is coming to pick you up. Now be a good boy and wait quietly, unless you want to walk home dressed like that."

"I'm not a boy."

The policeman glared at him. "You want I should drag you downstairs and throw you in the scrubber again? Just shut it."

They usually called granddad, but he'd been away for the weekend. The old man was soft. Granddad would pick him up from the police station or the hospital; drunk, tuned out, or after a fight.

Chris leaned his head back against the wall and examined the noticeboard opposite. One half was covered with photographs of teenagers – all boys who'd ran away to avoid the string filament test for magicians. Some would turn back up with no powers, others would get caught, collared or shot, a few would disappear into the underworld or the Enclave where they'd join Cantata. Either way the posters would be removed after a few months.

The other half of the board had a jumble of Lycus notices about staying safe. A poster warned people about being enticed or tricked into making deals with magicians; the dangers of potion to physical and mental health. There were loads of notices about the severe punishments and death penalty for pretty much anything to do with magicians.

Someone had stuck a sheet torn from a notebook. It read 'No one shall be found among you who engages in divination, or is a witch, an enchanter, or a sorcerer, or one who casts spells, or who consults spirits, one who is a wizard or a necromancer.' (Deuteronomy 18:10–11.)

Other colourful notices presented the various benefits of being a police or Lycus recruit. In the centre of the board a Fed artist's version of a reaver's demonic eyes stared at him accusingly. 'Out after curfew? YOU WILL DIE.'

The door opened again and LX Lanks came out. Tall, athletic, dressed in the dark grey, urban combat patrol gear worn by the LX, Lycus Extra Forces Police. She had more brand logos on her chest and on her arms than the other policeman, sports brands as well as body armour and weapons. They probably sponsored her made-to-measure uniform; it perfectly displayed how fit she was. She fired a glare at Chris then turned her attention to the woman who followed her out.

The other woman, Carol, Andy's mum, looked awful. She wiped away thick strands of hair hanging over her face. She'd been crying for hours. Her eyes were red and she moved like she had barely enough energy to walk. Chris dropped his gaze when she turned to him and her face twisted in recognition. "Wu-why?" she groaned and fell back into a sobbing that ripped into Chris.

Lanks took Carol's arm and said something to her then walked her out of the station. Carol climbed into a waiting taxi and Lanks watched the cab drive off. She came back into the station and the door hissed shut behind her. "Asten," she scowled, "You really are scum. You've destroyed that poor woman's life."

Chris didn't look up. "He wanted to do it."

"Sure," Lanks tapped the bag with her foot, "you put him up to it, Asten. I know you."

Chris shook his head and said nothing.

"Run out of chat?" Lanks said. "Last week you steal your girlfriend's father's car and trash it and now this."

"She said it wasn't me."

"Her first call said it was you. But you got to her, didn't you, Asten?"

He couldn't deny that. Lanks was about to say something when the door clicked and the policeman from behind the counter came out and pinned a wanted poster to the wall. "LX Lanks," he said over his shoulder, "don't you have a victim report to complete?"

"Yes sir." Lanks leaned forward, resting her right hand on her holster. "Her son's death, his blood, is on you, Asten."

Chris tightened his grip on the plastic bag and stared hard at the floor.

"Filthy, lowlife punk," Lanks said as she stood upright and turned to leave.

"Lycus Bitch," Chris mumbled under his breath.

Lanks spun round, "What did you say?

"Nothing."

"You turn eighteen soon, Asten." Lanks sneered, "If you're not a magician I'll still get you. Your national service call-up is due and I'll make sure my name is on the recruit leader list. You might be going home, but not for long."

No; he was going home because Lycus and cops got bonus payouts for catching magicians; they got nothing for busting and processing people like him. He looked up at her and smiled.

Ten minutes later, a buzz on the outside door drew the policeman's attention from the screen he'd been staring at, to a tall, thin figure waiting outside. He pressed a button and Miss Keats came in. She lived in the same block as Chris and spent most of the day in her allotment behind the estate. She gave Chris a sympathetic smile and went over to the counter and showed some ID to the officer.

While the officer shuffled through forms in the filing cabinet, Chris examined the new wanted poster. Lizzy Francis, a magician girl wanted for the murder of three Lycus guards. Her face had an expression of angry defiance; and she looked good, even though she was bald; and she looked strangely familiar.

Miss Keats signed the release form with a pen linked to a small chain, took the envelope containing Chris's keys, wallet and ID, then turned to him, "Let's get you home."

Chris nodded and stood up. Miss Keats scrunched her face at the bag of bloodied clothes, "They gave that to you?"

Chris nodded again.

"Give it here." She took the bag and passed him the envelope of police papers along with the keys to her car. "Wait in the car, Chris."

Her old Skoda was parked outside. Bolts of eldritch lightning cracked noiselessly across the sky then split into shards that slithered and dissolved away. Traffic stopped; drivers waited and watched the shards fade into the distance. A policeman in the front passenger seat of an LX patrol car parked across the road sneered at Chris then turned and said something to the driver. The policeman behind the wheel looked over at Chris and laughed. Cars started up again and the policemen drove away.

A large, black cat sat on a garden wall across the road, watching him. It continued to watch Chris as he walked several metres to the car and get in. Chris slumped down in the small seat as far as he could. The cat suddenly bolted and disappeared just as Miss Keats came out of the police station.

Miss Keats settled in behind the steering wheel and glanced across the road to where the cat had been sitting. "Seat belt, Chris."

Chris sat up and clipped the belt across his waist and stared out of the passenger window. "Where's the bag with my clothes?"

"You really wanted to take that home?"

"No."

"I didn't think so." She started up the car and they set off.

They turned off Ballards Lane and the car wound its way through an irregular half-mile square of demolished streets and ruins of houses left untouched since the war. Cars and bikes wound through a surreal landscape where vines and weeds grew over and out of the remains of buildings. Bushes rooted deep into broad cracks in the side streets; ancient streams rose to reclaim their age-old routes down to the Thames. Children played in the wasteland and skeletons of houses; places where Chris used to play with Andy and Paul when they were all kids. Half of London was still a wreck, yet people were so dumb and scared they were still giving what little money they could spare to churches and Neighbourhood private security patrols run by Lycus.

"Why do you never talk about the war?"

"It was a terrible time, I lost a lot of friends."

"You never say anything bad about magicians, you don't even

hate them."

"Do you?"

"No, but you were around during the war, after magic came back."

"People were all the same before the CERN incident, Chris. Nobody asks to be born with the string filaments."

"Yeah but mages can mess with reality, wreck society."

"Fifty years Chris, who's done the most damage in that time? Magicians or the government who handed the country over to corporations and private military companies?"

Chris wished he'd never started this thread. He tried one more time. "Mages can trick you into promises; they opened the portal, let reavers through."

"Those are rumours. No one knows how the reavers first came."

"Tch," Chris tutted, "you don't blame anybody."

They emerged from the wasteland and traffic slowed again as they passed Victoria park. Across from the park, a long queue of people carrying offerings and gifts had already formed outside the church and stretched round the corner. People held bags of food or packs of frozen meat, lamb or mutton, for the priests. Someone had a cage with a couple of live chickens. The other side of the road, had been closed off for cleaning. A murder of crows blotted the nearby trees and park fence, cawing angrily, tiny eyes glaring at a team of six teenage magicians. Gaunt, scraggy hair, dressed in bright green overalls and zonked by the magic-suppressing dog collar round their necks, the teenagers cleaned the bloodied grass verge beside the gates. A short distance away, one of the guys scrubbed at a large Anarchist logo sprayed on the park notice board.

Two heavily armed LX policemen leaned against a red-brick wall covered in big ugly stains where graffiti had been bleached off. One would occasionally use the barrel of the rifle to point to a bloodied patch of grass. Someone in a green overall would slouch over and spray foam onto the ground from a canister on his back, then stare blankly as the bubbles dissolved away. Magicians were weird.

On the street corner, two zealots, bearded men in black suits and wide red sashes draped around their necks, waved Bibles over their heads.

"For has it not been written that the Good Lord Jesus said, behold, I am coming soon. Blessed is the one who keeps the words of the prophecy of this book. Worship God. Do not seal up the words of the prophecy of this book, for the time is near. Let the evildoer still do evil, and the filthy still be filthy, and the righteous still do right, and the holy still be holy."

The bearded man stopped speaking and nodded to the other man who began, "I am coming soon, bringing my recompense with me, to repay each one for what he has done. I am the Alpha and the Omega, the first and the last, the beginning and the end. Blessed are those who wash their robes, so that they may have the right to the tree of life and that they may enter the city by the gates. Outside are the dogs and sorcerers and the sexually immoral and murderers and idolaters, and everyone who loves and practises falsehood."

"Is that where it happened?" Miss Keats said.

Chris nodded.

Miss Keats didn't take her eyes from the road. "Andy made his own choices, Chris. He's been reckless before without your help. Wasn't he into train surfing?"

"I said it as a joke." Chris stared blankly through the window then suddenly punched the dashboard, taking Miss Keats by surprise.

She pushed her round, gold-framed glasses back up her short nose. "You shouldn't blame yourself. You didn't reach into his head and press a button."

He might as well have done. Chris slumped back and folded his arms.

The inmates cleaning up the park stopped when a group of Two dozen young Lycus recruits boys and girls, arranged in four lines, marched past. Dressed in grey uniforms, the backs of their jackets lined with various military supply logos; the Lycus ZT Logo emblazoned in thick white letters on their right arms. They all carried Smith & Wesson M&P15-22 rifles. The steady crunch of boots on tarmac thumped along the street and disappeared down a side road, heading for the squats.

Miss Keats turned to Chris, "So how did you both end up at the park gates?"

"He kept hassling me to go with him."

Streaks of iced lightning sliced the sky and all the cars stalled again. Miss Keats put the Skoda into neutral. She leaned forward slightly to look up through the windscreen. Her eyes seemed to follow something through the sky, moving across the flow of lightning.

Chris looked up and didn't see anything. He fixed his gaze on the shelter and let out a breath.

"To the park gates?" she said, following his gaze to the shelter. "Was that your idea?"

"Yeah."

Cars shuddered into life and started moving again. Chris laid his head back and closed his eyes. After almost thirty hours being awake, he fell asleep instantly.

***

The bumping over potholes in the road woke Chris and he sat up, rubbing his eyes. The entrance to the estate and tower block was a short distance ahead, beyond the four burnt-out cars and the bus shoved to the side of the road. The shells of the vehicles now a chalk-white sculpture covered in vines and weeds. A cat lay curled up on a thick mossy mound. The boarded-up convenience store covered in smoke stains was all that remained of the riot and looting kicked off by the fight between Cantata and Lycus.

Two Lycus vehicles with blacked-out windows had parked up either side of the short road that curved down to the estate. The Lycus logo, a shield of crossed swords over a serpent and some weird pretzel shape in the V of the swords, was plastered across the bonnet and both front doors. Two burly police officers in grey, lightly armoured, urban combat outfits, watched another two officers searching a couple of teenagers. One of the kids, a mixed-race teenager stood facing the wall with his hands above his head. A backpack lay ripped apart on the ground, the contents strewn across the pavement and gutter. A policeman was going through the guy's pockets and throwing down whatever he found. The policeman's partner used the muzzle of his assault rifle to pin the girlfriend against the wall and was spending too much time searching her.

Miss Keats took one hand off the steering wheel and moved her fingers about, "Arthritis," she said, smiling at Chris.

Across the road, the policeman searching the girls stopped and slapped a hand to the back of his neck then stepped back, moving his shoulders around as if something had fallen between his clothes and skin. The young woman watched him until he managed to gesture to her, "Go on, get out of here," he said to her and she rushed off.

One of the police officers pointed to Miss Keats and gestured to the kerb with his assault rifle.

Miss Keats parked the car and wound down her window.

"ID," the policeman snapped.

Miss Keats produced her ID and took Chris's from the envelope along with the release forms and handed them over.

"What's his story?" the policeman said, using the ID cards to point at Chris.

Chris went to respond and the policeman cut in, "I wasn't talking to you, boy."

"Officer," Miss Keats said, "this is a release form for my neighbour here who I picked up from the police station this morning."

"Uh huh." The policeman examined the ID cards. "Neighbour eh? Why'd you collect him?"

"He helps with my allotment," Miss Keats said, "pruning, pulling up weeds."

That was true.

"Wait there." The policeman took the ID cards and wandered over to the police phone box on the corner. He unlocked the panel and, taking out the phone, spoke into it, reading from the ID cards. He listened for a while then hung up, locked the panel and returned. He handed back the ID cards, shot a glance at Chris, took the release form and examined it. His eyes stopped at the 'reason for holding' section then finally looked at Chris. "You moron," he said, handing the form back to Miss Keats.

Miss Keats drove down and round the corner and the housing blocks came into view. A group of a half dozen Lycus recruits armed with tasers and stun batons stood guard outside the low-rise South Block. Wooden boards covered in various religious symbols and security company logos had been nailed over the windows. Twenty families of a penitent cult, seventy or so people, had committed suicide there just a week ago. They'd deliberately opened the windows and watched the reavers, putting their faith in their religious leader and with God. The rats and roaches had arrived after the reavers left and the whole block was now infested.

Miss Keats drove past in silence, both she and Chris avoiding eye contact with the recruits. Turning into the main courtyard, the 24 storey tower block where they lived, came into view One side of the block was patched with large steel plates; cracked concrete slabs covered in grey stains and clumps of moss spread over the North facing side, illuminated by bright sunlight. Three other long, low-rise blocks, where the older people and disabled were housed, spread left and right of his block.

Chris climbed out, "Thanks."

"That's okay," Miss Keats said through the open window. She passed him the spare key, "Drop it off later. Larry, I mean your grandfather, Mr Weston, should be back soon."

"Okay." Chris stepped away from the car and Miss Keats drove down the cracked tarmac ramp into the car park.

"Yo, Chris." Paul, the potion dealer, sat on the remains of a low wall, surrounded by his little gang of runners: Len, Poke and Reg. Simba, the ripped-eared monster of a dog, lay beside them. "What happened to your clothes, fam?"

Chris lowered his head and carried on walking.

"Chris," Paul called, "you seen Andy?"

Chris's stomach tightened. Paul and Andy were close; they all were. From the first day he moved to the estate; the three of them grew up and went to school together.

"Chris. I got something for him, and Mandy came by looking for him."

Chris gave him a sullen look, unsure of what to say.

"What?" Paul said. "You seen him or not?"

"Reavers got him."

Len and Poke, standing next to Paul, gaped wide-eyed at Chris. Reg, the crop-haired kid who liked nothing more than seeing animals suffer, let out a single, loud laugh and Paul punched him hard on the shoulder, almost knocking him over. "Serious? Jeez, Chris, that ain't funny."

Chris responded with a single nod, glanced at the other three kids, then slouched into the building. Behind him, the chattering increased then Reg ran off.

In the lobby, little Rosie stood beside Esther, her mum. A bag of vegetables filled the seat of her buggy. Chris joined them to wait for the one working lift. Rosie tugged her mother's hand and pointed at him. Esther ignored her and continued flirting with the engineer fixing the broken lift. The engineer looked up from the button panel in his hand, and seeing Chris in his yellow overalls, stopped working. Chris didn't wait for the other lift to arrive and hurried past them. He pushed through the door to the stairwell and the familiar smell of bleach and urine caught in his throat. He took a short breath and trudged up the narrow graffiti-covered stairs, Jessica Keats's words going round in his head. She was right: Andy did make the choice to go. Yet his thoughts kept coming back to the same thing– he said it first.

The machinery of the second lift cranked into life behind the wall and Chris went back down to the fourth-floor hallway. He pressed the lift button and waited, hoping no one would see him. The lift thumped to a halt and the door opened. The engineer inside heeled the open toolbox back and stepped sideways to lean against the wall by the buttons. There was a phone number, probably Esther's, written neatly on a piece of paper lying across the screwdrivers.

They went up eight floors in silence, avoiding eye contact. On the sixteenth floor, Chris stepped out and walked down the hallway. Someone, probably Nora, Dave's girlfriend, must have cleaned up. Twizzler mewed at him from the end of the hall but didn't move from the worn, yellow doormat. The door opened and Claire knelt down, picked the cat up, smiled at Chris and disappeared back into her flat.

Chris opened the door to the flat he shared with his grandfather, stepped over the small pile of letters, dropped the keys on the shelf and slouched into the living room. A large raven, sitting on the wall of the narrow balcony, looking in, cawed loudly and flew off. Too tired to notice or care, Chris collapsed onto the sofa and fell into a haunted, restless sleep.

Chapter Three

Lizzy woke slowly and stretched under the warm duvet, relishing the feel of soft fabric across her body. She lay for a few minutes staring at the motes of dust dancing in the shaft of light coming in through the thin gap between the curtains. The door was ajar and she could hear Ozzy in the kitchen downstairs. Noodles, the grey tabby cat, lay curled up at the foot of the bed. Getting out of bed, she stretched and rubbed her eyes then went over to the tall mirror and examined herself again, turning round to look over her shoulder at her reflection. The bruises and scratches across her body had all gone. She grabbed the towel and headed for the shower. Ten minutes later, with the towel around her shoulders, she went over to the clothes rail and checked her clothes. They were dry so she put them on and went downstairs.

Ozzy slid a couple of fried eggs onto two thick slices of toast from a home-baked loaf and looked up as she came in, "Up for a late breakfast?" Ozzy said.

"Late? What time is it?"

"Almost noon."

"Noon?"

"Well, we were still talking at one in the morning." Ozzy smiled, "Your ID is on the table."

A small van beeped outside, "Oh, excuse me," Ozzy left and a minute later crossed the yard with a sealed box full of hacked collars he and Lizzy had packed up the previous night. He shook hands with the driver and came back in. Lizzy was examining her ID card and driving licence when a bark from the garden door brought her back. She pocketed the cards and opened the door. Ben waddled in and looked up at Lizzy, wagging his tail. Lizzy bent down and scratched his head then went back to making a cup of tea.

"Ben," Ozzy said, "back already, you scraggy old mutt?"

Ben ignored him and ambled across to his bowl, sniffed the contents then went over to his basket and lay down.

Ozzy took his food to the table and Lizzy joined him. "So where were you?"

"The warehouse, met Ben's old owner early this morning. He'd come down from London last night. Wanted to talk about the balloon. I think he was hiding something?"

44

"Like what?"

"I don't know; it's rude to ask if a magician doesn't want to talk about something, y'know because we can't lie. He's a really nice, straight-up guy, old magician. Probably one of the first ones. Hadn't seen him since he brought Ben to me."

Hearing his name mentioned, Ben came over, sat down and rested his chin on Ozzy's knee. He didn't move when Ozzy gave him a crusty edge of bacon; he just swallowed and kept staring up at him.

"How about taking Ben out?" Ozzy said. "He didn't have much of a walk this morning."

"Sure, why not?" Lizzy nodded.

The phone rang as she was finishing the last of her toast and Marmite. Ozzy went out to answer it then came back. "Good news, Lizzy, there's a room in Hackney." He handed her a small sheet of paper with an address.

A broad smile spread across Lizzy's face, "I'll get my jacket." She looked down at Ben, "Sorry Ben."

Ozzy crossed the yard with a postcard in his hands as Lizzy wheeled Ozzy's Honda out. "This was in a letter addressed to me but the message is for you."

"For me? What is it?"

"A postcard."

Lizzy took the postcard. "Who else knows I'm here?"

"No idea, some seer magician I guess. The postmark said Scotland."

"That's weird." Lizzy read the message. 'Keep this. For when you have nowhere to go.' The other side of the card was blank. She read the message again and slipped the card into her inside jacket pocket then put on the crash helmet.

"Need the map?" Ozzy said.

"Very funny," Lizzy said then caught a strange smell, like burnt meat. "What's that smell?"

"What?" Ozzy said in alarm.

Across the street, a dense wall of black cloud rose out of the muddy soil in the field by the church. The cloud expanded in a bloom and rolled down towards the house.

Ozzy grabbed Lizzy's arm and pulled her close as the cloud blasted forwards and engulfed the house.

Ozzy curled his hand through the air, "Nerag Gulash Maruma," he growled and a small protective dome formed over him and Lizzy.

Ahead of them, the house imploded with a slow, deep, grinding rumble. The walls and roof spiralled and caved inwards; wood and stone crashing into each other. The mass of debris churned and spun, crashing around inside the black cloud which rose like a tornado, swaying in a widening circle and took the form of a giant serpent.

Ozzy shouted out another spell and silvery white spears peeled off from the surface of the dome and flew at the towering creature.

The monster pulsed and jolted as it was struck by the gleaming shards. The creature shook them away and then began to stab at the dome with a long forked tongue. With every hit, black shards bounced off and rounded back to smash down onto the dome. Cracks began to appear across the surface of the dome and a cold putrid stench rushed in

Ozzy swore under his breath and grabbed Lizzy's hand, "Did your parents ever tell you the story of Ghenol Bakam?"

"How did you-"

"Call him... now," Ozzy shouted.

"Ghenol Bakam" they both shouted as Ozzy raised his other hand and turned his attention to the remains of his house.

Behind the serpent, a flaming dragon rose from the rubble and slammed into the serpent which let out a deafening screech. The serpent swayed from side to side, spitting out black shards and more cracks appeared and spread along the dome's outer layers.

The dragon blasted the serpent with a torrent of flame that burnt gaping homes across its body. Ozzy and Lizzy held onto each other to keep their balance as the ground shook with a low rumble, threatening to crack open. The dragon and serpent crashed and fought sometimes striking the dome with such force that the air inside throbbed and jostled the magicians around.

Finally, with a high-pitched screech, the serpent slowed and swayed in a widening circle until it fell away from the protective dome. Bending back towards the smouldering rubble of concrete, wood, and tiles, the creature curled into a thick, churning, thundering cloud and exploded in a blast of fused and molten chunks of stone and metal that crashed down over the dome.

The dragon raised its head to the sky and let out a roar of victory then burst into a blinding flash light and disappeared.

Surrounded by a circle of rubble, Lizzy got to her feet and helped Ozzy up, "Are you okay?"

Ozzy nodded, "It kind of takes it out of you. Oh hell."

Figures in full black uniforms, all covered in an array of corporate brand logos, emerged out of the rippling air beyond the rubble and a hail of gunfire snapped and crunched against the dome. Most of the bullets melted into mercurial globs on impact and dropped to the ground, the rest sank a few inches through the cracks and weak spots and got stuck there.

"It's not going to hold for much longer," Ozzy shouted. He opened a small gap round to the side of the dome facing the Suzuki. "You should make a run for your bike. I'll hold them off."

Lizzy's eyes had turned an electric-blue "No!" she snarled and leapt out of the protective dome.

"Lizzy!"

She ignored his cry and clambered onto a mound of rubble. Before the soldiers could redirect their fire at her, she moved her hands and a wall of silvery flames took shape in front of her. Bullets sizzled and exploded while Lizzy swirled her hands around in wide overlapping arcs. A whoosh of rage-fuelled energy surged through her, starting from the centre of her chest and flowing down her arms. A second before she lost complete control, she clenched her fists, focussed her energy and snarled, "Ateshkan Jarn."

Ribbons of light shot out from her open palms, struck the protective wall of flame and shattered it into a shower of lightning flecks that crackled and swarmed towards the soldiers and converged onto their weapons, lighting them up. Soldiers cried out and dropped their burning hot assault rifles and guns.

Next, Lizzy touched a finger to her thumb, and moving her other fingers in a delicate movement, sent out another dense golden white stream of ribbons that curled around the soldiers' bodies. Their clothes dissolved into ashen grey flakes and drifted away in the wind, leaving the men and women raw and naked. The troops stumbled back, covering themselves with their hands while the ribbons formed an impenetrable ring around them. Exhausted, Lizzy dropped her arms and slumped forwards breathless, resting her palms on her knees.

Ozzy stood gaping at her. He took in a deep breath, pushed his shoulders back and, moving his hands through the air, chanted, "Hevadun Ruka." The domed shield of solid air protecting him slowly rippled and folded outwards, bending light, distorting and curling reflections of his surroundings. With an impatient shove, he broke the thick layers of solid air into powerful waves that surged towards the naked Lycus soldiers. Men and women scrabbled away in a panic and Ozzy charged forward, spread his arms out and leaped into the air with a cry of "Kuzai!" A wave of solid air lifted and surfed him forwards and up to around thirty feet off the ground. He glanced down, and with a scooping sweep of his hand drew up a mound of gravelly rubble. With a simple gesture he formed it into a dust cloud that fell on the soldiers.

Ozzy mumbled another incantation and turned in the air to drift gently to the ground beside Lizzy and fell to his knees.

"How," he took in a deep breath, "how did you do that..." he said, breathless, "... know that incantation?"

"I saw my mum do them." Lizzy sniffed and pursed her lips.

"You're a sorceress, undo the incantation."

"What?"

Ozzy leaned forward, hands on his knees. "You combined incantations," he said, catching his breath, "made something completely different, undo the spell or it will stay forever."

Lizzy looked over to ribbons of light circling the soldiers and with a gesture said, "Dimish." She turned to Ozzy, "are you okay?"

Ozzy nodded and raised a hand, "Took it out of me a bit. Just need to catch my breath. Good thing we harmonised." He straightened up and looked back at the dust cloud prison. "That'll keep them for a while. You okay?"

Lizzy nodded, "They killed Ben."

Ozzy swallowed, "I know." He took some keys from his pocket. "We should get away from here, I'll take the car, follow me on the bike, you'll need it." He opened the door of the large shed to reveal an old dust-covered, bottle-green Mini Cooper.

Lizzy took one last look at where the house once stood and got onto the bike. Ozzy drove out of the garage and pulled up beside her. "Stay close, I'll extend the crystal concealment around us."

"Where did they come from?"

"I'll explain when we're somewhere safe. Let's go."

An hour later, Ozzy turned off the road and along a narrow lane that led them to an old water mill. A tall, lean man with sinewy muscles under a short-sleeve shirt emerged from the mill, wiping his hands on a towel.

Ozzy went over to him and they shook hands then both turned to Lizzy.

"Lizzy, this is Sam, he's a Cantata supporter."

Sam gave Lizzy a nod and smile then turned to Ozzy, "I'll get your gear, Oz," he said. "You both need to keep moving." He turned and headed into the farmhouse across the cobbled courtyard.

"We didn't see them coming," Lizzy said, "how is that possible?"

"They used dark magic to open portals through the Outer Realm."

"How?"

"No human or magician can open that kind of portal. Some inhuman creature is using human sacrifice to open a shortcut through the Outer Realm." He grimaced.

"What?" Lizzy said.

"Torture; only the energy released from a magician's torture can open an Outer Realm portal."

Lizzy gaped at him, shocked, "Who would even do that?"

"A Shadow Fae," Ozzy said, a worried expression on his face. "Something with no regard for human life. If one of them is helping Lycus then we really are in trouble."

Lizzy gave him a fearful look, "So they can find us?"

"Find? No, just transport. They must have exact locations point to point. It takes a powerful spell to open a portal that big for so many soldiers to come through and create a deathstorm."

"Is that what that snake was?"

"Yes," His face fell.

"What is it?" Lizzy said.

"Doug, an old friend, he hasn't been in touch for a while. He knew where I lived. Lycus must have captured him."

"Oh."

Neither spoke for a few seconds then Lizzy said, "Could they find us again?"

Ozzy thought for a moment then looked up and off into the

distance, "It's possible, if we're not careful. I have a crystal that conceals me, and I never leave anything personal behind."

"I don't have one."

"You don't need it. I noticed your aura realigned each time you used your magic."

"My aura realigned? What does that mean?"

"It means a sorcerer cast a spell of concealment on you when you were a baby. Nothing you own or touch keeps a magical connection to you. Magic can't be used to track you with anything personal."

"Oh." Mum used to say she was the world's best at hide-and-seek.

"Did your innate powers show at all, before you arrived at Salem?"

"No."

"Good. Then our attackers can't be sure who you were back there. That was quite a show of power."

"I was scared, I could have killed them."

"You did good to keep control."

Lizzy looked down and sighed then straightened up. "What do we do now?"

"Split up. You should get to Hackney as planned, while you can. Lycus was not expecting anyone to be with me."

"Where will you go?"

"Another place, best you don't know."

Lizzy looked worried and Ozzy said, "Lizzy, your aura realignment is a powerful and permanent protection, and for now you're safer away from me."

"Okay."

Sam emerged with a small rucksack. "Your tools are all there. I've thrown in a few of mine to replace your crappy ones."

"Thanks, Sam."

"Don't mention it." Sam turned to Lizzy, "It was nice to meet you, Lizzy. I'm sorry it wasn't under more pleasant circumstances. But, you know where to find me now if things get bad."

A hiss and clunking came from the mill. Sam looked at it then up at the sky, "I should get back to work. You two should hit the road." Sam turned and headed back to the Mill.

Ozzy wrapped his arms round Lizzy and they hugged.

"Who's he?" Lizzy said.

"Sam, says he's a mechanic who dabbled in history. I think he's an alien, a few hundred years old. Definitely not human."

Lizzy smiled and shook her head, "Thanks for looking after me, Ozzy."

"It was fun, mostly. You take care, Lizzy."

She climbed onto the bike and put the crash helmet on, "I'm sorry for stealing Bill's bike."

"Sure you are."

Lizzy gave him a guilty smile and started up the Suzuki. "Bye," she said as the bike rumbled gently into life. She toed it into gear and with a wave, set off towards London, sticking to the country lanes.

Chapter Four

Chris had fallen asleep on the living room sofa and woke with a start. The neighbour on the right was tuned into some religious channel pumping out Gregorian chants with the bass turned up; his grandfather was speaking with a neighbour outside the front door. Chris rubbed his eyes and groaned when he saw the yellow overalls; it hadn't been a nightmare. He got to his feet slowly, weighed down by guilt and grief, and shifted his tired, heavy body, up the stairs to his bedroom. The chants died down and Chris was halfway to his room when Granddad, carrying a newspaper and an overnight bag, came into the short hallway, "Chris."

Chris glanced back and pushed his bedroom door open to a mess and faint hint of a tune, now slow and dismal, lingering in the air. He stepped over the scatter of comic and opened the window as far as it would go to let the sound out. He fell onto his bed just as his grandfather turned the landing at the top of the stairs. The old man put the overnight bag down by his bedroom door and took a step along the hallway towards Chris's room. Chris crossed to the door and grabbed the handle.

"Chris."

"What?"

"Do you want to talk?"

"No."

"Jessica called, she told me what happened. I came back as soon as I could."

The memory of last night twisted Chris's face into an expression of helpless guilt.

"Chris, you can't blame yourself for what happened."

"No!" Chris punched himself on the chest, alarming his grandfather. "It was my stupid idea. I got Andy killed, okay? Me. Don't try to change things. You always change things. You—"

His grandfather winced and turned his wrist, moving his fingers around, something he had a habit of doing.

The emotion faded and Chris struggled to remember what he was thinking. "Just leave me alone!" He slammed the door shut and tore off the thin plastic overalls, almost tripping as he kicked them away. His naked body, scratched and bruised by the scrubbing at the police station, stank of detergent and cheap plastic. He grabbed a towel and hit the shower, the hot spray stinging the scratches across his back. He turned up the heat and dared the water to burn him.

The shower's five-minute shut-out kicked in and Chris snatched the towel off the chrome towel rail and wiped the steam off the mirror. He pushed back the strands of long black hair, swore at the grim, dark face staring at him and went back to his room.

Wire, the puppy in Duncan and Maureen's flat upstairs was barking and yapping. Chris threw a trainer up at the ceiling and Duncan's muffled shout of "Wire, shut the hell up," made no difference. Duncan shouted at Maureen about her dog, then heavy footsteps stomped across the floor and a door slammed.

Chris dressed then went over to his desk, reached into the back of the drawer and took out the small plastic phial containing the last of his potion. He moved the chair to the open window overlooking the dilapidated estate of low-rise blocks, and popped open the stopper on the phial. The liquid inside dissolved into sparkling purple bubbles that drifted slowly out and burst softly in front of his face, releasing a whispering enchantment that sensed his mood and adapted the tunes mystical tone and rhythm. The soothing tune drew out and dissolved away his guilt and grief.

Beyond the high wall around the estate, London, covered in bruises of rubble dotted with scattered clusters of new housing projects and high-rises, spread to the horizon. Noon was approaching and the eldritch flashes had died away. In the distance, a dark plume of smoke rose from the Southbank. It tilted and bowed as if avoiding the clouds.

On the tarmac courtyard, Paul and his gang kicked a punctured football about. Wire, barking excitedly, ran after a ball and returned it to Maureen who stood with a bottle of beer in one hand and a roll-up in the other.

The tune faded into a whisper and Chris put the phial back in the drawer and kneeled down to pick up the comics.

"Chris," his grandfather called, "come down here please."

Chris's shoulders dropped and he swore under his breath.

"Chris?"

"All right." He walked out and slammed the door behind him.

In the living room, sunlight poured onto a table covered with stacks of paper and a box of essays where his grandfather sat over an open notepad. The TV was on mute, showing some documentary about the CERN incident and the first hours after every type of wireless signal across the world disappeared. A thin scrolling banner along the bottom of the screen presented a feed of disasters: aircraft crashes, satellite collisions and drops from orbit, military accidents, IT and phone companies in a panic, global financial market crisis, riots and looting. His grandfather crossed the room and switched the TV and cable box into standby.

Chris fell onto the sofa and picked up the newspaper. A picture of a police car next to bodies covered by thick white sheets had the headline– 'Nine More Magician Teenagers Shot Dead by Snipers' – in big bold letters underneath. He dropped the paper onto the coffee table and leaned back.

"Chris," his grandfather stood up, "we need to talk."

Chris looked up at him, "What?" he said in bored resignation.

His grandfather lowered his voice, "Your interview at the police station included a DNA swab didn't it?"

"So?"

"We have to leave before the results come back from the lab in Manchester."

"Why? It's just a stupid test."

"Not for magicians and sorcerers it isn't."

"Who gives a fu… what?" Chris blurted.

"Listen carefully." His grandfather slid open the glass door of the half-empty bookcase and muttered something as he moved his hand along the top shelf. The spaces below shimmered and filled with books. He took a small book and flicked through the pages as he spoke, "Your parents were descendants of The First Ones, Chris, sorcerers long before the CERN incident. They trod the Earth, this realm, lightly. It's why they weren't detected."

Chris gaped at his grandfather, almost shouting, "What the f—?"

"Shh!" his grandfather gestured. "Keep it down." He slipped the book into his coat pocket. "Your parents had a unique ability to deceive the test; hide their sorcery."

Chris's voice fell to a whisper, "Jesus. why didn't you tell me?" he hissed. "What the hell?"

"Try to stay calm, things are going to look different." His grandfather gestured, as if wiping away smoke, "Ephphatha."

Something lifted from Chris's mind, like a thick fog fizzling away in bright sunlight. Chris rubbed his eyes. His vision had sharpened; reality seemed deeper, filled with rich, intricate detail, patterns that undulated gently. Everything in his peripheral vision had turned to superfine foam. He felt a gentle shunt and firming-up as if he'd been dropped into a better fitting body. At the same time, the usual cascade of thoughts rolling through his mind separated and smoothed out into clearer, more distinct streams. "What's going on?"

"Clarity. You pushed reality away when you lost your parents, turned your grief into anger. That wasn't safe and I..." His grandfather hesitated. "I did what I could to help."

What was the old man saying, had he put a spell on him? Jesus; Chris leaned forwards and buried his face in his hands, "I can't deal with this," he said and rubbed his eyes again, "I'm tripping out. My eyes are fuzzing."

"That is the uncertainty principle in action; it's what makes magic possible; as a sorcerer you have more choices about the reality you wish to shape."

"Oh Jeez," Chris said, not lifting his head.

"The swab Lycus took from you..." His grandfather finished cleaning his wire-frame glasses and put them back on then ran his fingers through his thick grey hair. "They'd take you apart while still alive, slice you down to your DNA."

"Sushi, brilliant," Chris murmured while the room momentarily pulsed and crowded round him. Details clamoured for attention, to be made real. "I feel sick."

"That will be the hyperthymesia."

"The what?"

"You do know magicians remember every single thing they see and hear, right?"

"Yeah," but he never believed it. "Brilliant," he murmured as one of the streams of thought in his mind considered this. That meant a lot of memories would come back; it also meant he'd start taking in more too; and that he'd start processing stuff in some kind of more complicated way. "Fan, bloody, tastic." he said dryly.

"It's all in your mind, yours to control, so take control."

"Fine." Chris moved the streams to the back of his mind; and they slid back out again to crowd his attention. "Can't do it, I feel sick."

"Try this short incantation, it will calm the mind, and stop the nausea too. Repeat these words."

Chris looked up at his grandfather, "You want me to say a spell? Jesus." he shook his head. "Okay what is it?"

"Akil tam uy Ghuz."

Chris sighed and repeated the spell. The nausea subsided instantly, his breathing steadied and the pounding in his ears stopped. The superfine foamy background smoothed out and his eyes focussed more easily. "Wow, it worked."

"Of course. Now, we have to think about leaving town, today."

Chris fell back into the sofa, "Why can't I stay, dodge the test, like Mum and Dad did?"

"The test has changed, Lycus are using some form of arcane energy."

"So what's the basic magic I'm meant to have? That's right isn't it, magicians are born with a core power or two?"

"Have you ever wondered why no one ever pressed charges for all your crazy stunts?"

Chris shrugged, "Lucky I guess."

"No one is that lucky, you have a way of getting round people. I've seen you do it. You can be a real charmer when you have to."

"So that's it? Great."

"That's simply your minor innate ability. Your core innate power will manifest when you need it."

"What is it?"

"I have no idea."

Chris leaned back on the sofa. Charmer? He thought of Terri, his girlfriend. Did he do something to make her like him? What about Andy? Did he—

"Chris."

"What?"

"I said have you ever looked at these books?"

Chris glanced over at the bookcase. More books had appeared. "Course; all kinds of science and 'ology stuff. Nothing to do with magic." Maybe he could help out Andy's mum in some way. Can magic change what ordinary people think and feel?

"... parents learned of a world exactly like ours where magic is a fiction. They were... Chris, stop drifting off."

"What? I can't help it. There's too much to process."

"Fair enough. The main thing is that your tests result will be back in a few days. Go pack some clothes; I'll do the same. Then we'll have a quick bite to eat and leave."

Chris went to his room and pulled an old rucksack from the top of the cupboard and knocked the dust off it. He threw his denim jacket in there along with a bomber jacket then went to his chest of drawers and grabbed clothes from each drawer and stuffed them into the rucksack and went downstairs.

His grandfather was already in the kitchen. "Tidy up the table please, Chris."

Chris scooped up the science books and dropped them into a pile on the end of the worktop. They looked too messy and he tidied them into a neat stack. It was then he noticed the photo of him and his parents at the Nine Sisters Stone Circle. His parents were standing in the middle and he was kneeling beside Benjy, their Tibetan Terrier. For the first time in years he remembered being happy. He had a different life; they had a house, a dog.

"What happened to Benjy?"

"He went to a good home."

Chris pulled a chair out and sat at the table. The sights, colours and sensations were all more intense; even the feel of the table under his fingers and the odours in the surrounding air were more real; yet at the same time it was all somehow connected and...

His grandfather was speaking, "... an energy in life, this realm we live in. Left alone, the reality we know carries on as normal. It works, right from quarks and electrons inside atoms, right up to the stars, everything in between and everything beyond."

"That's physics, not magic." Spots of grease covered the wall behind the cooker and wall unit sides. The faint odour of cooked food and detergents hung in the air. The place had a stronger feeling of... what was it? Of course, home.

"Sorcery is just physics beyond borders," his grandfather said, "it helps to understand both, that's why your parents read all those books."

"What happened to them?"

"Lycus found out about them and I helped them escape. But Lycus sent Shadow Fae, powerful creatures, after us. We split up. I took you. Your parents also gave me some magical items and this."

His grandfather reached under the collar of his shirt and took out a teardrop crystal pendant. "It's a powerful concealment. It even hides me from other magicians."

"They're gone?"

"Lycus must have caught them." Steam rushed from the kettle's spout and it clicked off.

They were really gone, dead. Chris continued rubbing his eyes. "Chris?"

"Yeah, my eyes. Do I need glasses or something now?"

"No. This reality is just one layer of many," his grandfather said. "That blur you see in your peripheral vision, the corners of your eyes? Those are probabilities that become fixed only when you look at them, leaving behind new realities from the choices we don't make."

Whatever that meant. Beyond the kitchen window, it was another bright day, but sharper, ultra hi-def sharper. A large bird burst out of the clouds and glided across the sky. Chris leaned forward and squinted to get a better view. Golden-green scales glinted softly in the bright morning light as the dragon swooped up and, with an elegant flick of its long, serpentine tail, disappeared into the clouds.

Chris jolted back and almost fell off his chair.

"Chris, you okay?"

Chris pointed to the sky beyond the window.

"A drag…" the words caught in his throat, "a drag… a dragon," he whispered.

"Ah, yes," his grandfather said in a matter-of-fact way, "I forgot to mention, those other universes, realms, they're closer than you realise. Some creatures occasionally take shortcuts through ours."

Chris gaped at his grandfather.

"You'll get used to them."

The phone in the living room started ringing. "Ignore it," his grandfather said and nodded to the window. "They can't affect this reality." He went back to the kitchen worktop and took a couple of mugs from the cupboard. "They are all quite harmless, like a film."

"A film," Chris said in a daze. "Except they're real."

"Relatively." The phone stopped ringing. His grandfather dropped a teabag into each cup. "Only to our eyes."

Chris nodded slowly, and returned to scanning the sky.

"There are ground creatures too, you know, Chris."

"Yeah?" Below them, around the overgrown mess of community garden, bushes hung heavy over the borders surrounding the uneven, patchy lawn. Wire ran around being chased by a couple of kids. In the far corner of the garden, bottles and takeaway boxes of different shapes, colours and sizes piled up against the recycling bins. The world looked a tangled mess. Beyond the high mesh fence stretched the allotments. Jessica Keats had around four of them, hers and three she 'bought' from other people who couldn't be bothered to use them. Her herbs and flowers stood out from the rest. The stuff she grew seemed to fit, as if they belonged together; and no one went near them. A flash of light caught his eye. Chris pressed his head against the window and squinted. Tiny figures trailing bursts of yellow light, gold, jasmine, saffron, sunglow, danced along the ground between the plants and shrubs, then disappeared.

"Are those fairies?"

"The yellow lights in Jessica's allotment?"

"Yeah."

His grandfather nodded, "Elves, the Aureolin Clan. Jessica has an arrangement with them. They feed on minute streams of plant energy in return for protecting her garden from other clans. Elves are tribal, very territorial, military."

"So it's not just doing magic then?"

"No, it's your whole reality; this world, your entire life, will be different."

His grandfather poured the hot water into the mugs. He looked so ordinary, just a sixty-something-year-old guy, teaching at the college, marking essays, reading; doing all the normal stuff a guy does; while all these weird creatures flew around.

Chris stared out of the window, "So they're real?"

"What?"

"Those creatures, but only we can see them?"

"Yes, mostly they are reflections, sometimes they do cross over. Girl sorcerers can speak and interact with them, even allow them agency, influence. It's their special thing." His grandfather took some butter and milk from the fridge then took down two plates.

"Her allotment looks kind of, I dunno, right, how it should be."

"That's the underlying symmetry. Jessica imbues herbs and

plants with magical properties; it's a rare gift. Perhaps when we meet her again she'll explain."

"Explain what?"

"How those other creatures fit into our world. As I said, all those universes, infinite realities; none are truly separate from any of the others."

"Everything is connected," Chris said.

"Precisely. As a Mystic Gardener, Miss Keats grows plants which draw from the natural energies in these other realities. She understands the sublime ways the biology of realities are connected and affect each other."

"So what about magic?"

"Magic is the ability, I mean the decision, to choose the reality you want to shape."

"You what?"

The toaster popped up the bread and his grandfather transferred the thin slices to the two plates. "Reality is a matter of choice, something perfectly normal and acceptable in one reality would, in our reality, break all the rules, appear to be magic. Magicians can reach into those other realms and pull objects, creatures, even energies, back."

"How?" Chris said. "We don't have wands and amulets and talismans or other magical stuff like Doctor Strange."

"The Sorcerer Supreme," his grandfather smiled. "We are mostly space. If…"

"Space?" Chris crunched into the toast and examined it while chewing.

"Everything is. We're made of atoms. If the nucleus of an atom were the size of a football, the electron orbiting it would be ten miles away – ten miles, Chris. That goes for all the atoms in our body too. The strings inside magicians and sorcerers have a stronger entanglement with the other realms. By speaking incantations and moving our hands in a particular way we trigger a chain reaction that resonates down to the very strings inside us. Those spaces behave the same way an amplification chamber of a guitar amplifies the sound made by the string vibrating."

"Okay," Chris said.

"It's what CERN was secretly doing, working on opening a portal to those other dimensions, replenish Earth's dwindling resources; perhaps even find another Earth-like planet."

Chris almost dropped his toast and gaped at his grandfather.

"As magicians we are anchored here to Earth, it's why we'd rather take care of this one. We resisted from the start. That's how the war began, when we refused to sell out."

"So we're Anarchists?"

"You're getting the picture. The important thing is," his grandfather continued, "that with the right talisman, sorcerers, unlike magicians, already have the ability to travel across to other realms. That's how your parents discovered an Earth where magic was a fiction."

Chris remembered the bedtime stories his father told about strange lands and magical creatures. The phone started ringing again and Chris's grandfather took a sip of his tea and stood up, turning to head for the phone in the living room. He stopped at the kitchen door like he'd hit a wall.

Chris gave him a strange look and his grandfather turned to him with an expression of horror that made Chris shudder, "Granddad, what…?"

The kitchen pulsed and sucked the breath from his lungs. Everything blurred for a second then snapped back into sharp focus and Chris found himself inside a bubble, beyond which time had stopped in a perfect sphere of destruction. The blasted remains of the tower block hung around him; time had slowed to a barely visible crawl. Fragments of sky shone through the motionless storm of debris and small clouds of pink dust laced with shreds of fabric. Off in the distance, beyond the chunks of concrete and shattered remains of what used to be his kitchen, the sun gleamed across the ruins of Alexandra Palace, and the patchwork streets of London shone in a bright June morning.

Chapter Five

Lizzy filled the bike, parked it up and went into the café. The TV was halfway through a ten-minute advertising break enticing people to buy all kinds of meaningless stuff, when a stout guy wearing a grubby apron emerged from the kitchen.

The woman behind the counter looked at him in surprise, "Dennis, is everything okay?"

Dennis ignored her and tuned the cable box to the News Channel. "Dennis," the woman said, "what's got into you?"

"Mage terror attack, Becky, look," Dennis said in an unfamiliar accent and pointed at the screen.

The newscaster sat in the studio; a screen with the image of a tower block hung on the wall behind him. "We hope to have a live feed direct from Barnet in a short while as soon as our team can link up to a working cable box close to the scene. Initial reports are saying that an explosion destroyed the top half of the tower block. With over eighty homes in the blast area fatalities will be high as it was a weekend and many people would have been at home. Lower housing blocks have also sustained damage from falling debris, which is hampering access to ambulances and fire teams. Rumours are spreading that this was a Cantata attack although no statements have been made."

"Of course it's Cantata," someone behind Lizzy said, "it was only a matter of time. I mean, we lock them up, shoot magicians on sight, take away their kids. What do you expect?"

Lizzy turned to see two men halfway through the all-day breakfast. "What?" the other guy said, "You taking their side?"

"Course not, Joe, I'm just saying. It's a kind of racism, innit? What would you do?"

"Not kill hundreds of innocent people for one thing," Joe said. "Besides, they can do magic, mess up the way things should be."

"Way things should be?" the other guy said. "That went down the pan before we were born."

"Brian, will you two keep it down," the woman behind the counter said, "I'm trying to hear what's happening."

"Okay, Becky," Joe's friend said, then addressed Lizzy. "What do you reckon?"

Joe nudged him, "Let the girl finish her food in peace, Bri'."

Brian ignored Joe and looked to Lizzy.

"I don't know," Lizzy said, "have they done this before?"

Brian turned to Joe, "She's right, they've never attacked innocent people."

"They melted the bloody Shard and turned the Gherkin into a giant tree," Joe said.

"Nobody got killed though."

"Well," Joe took a gulp from the mug of tea, "Lycus are going to lock down London, that's for sure."

"The Fence?" Brian said. "No way."

"Yes way," Joe nodded, "I bet you ten quid they'll set up checkpoints; block the A roads and motorways and just shut off all the other roads." He raised his open palm to shake hands with Brian and seal the bet, "Come on."

Brian was about to take Joe's hand when Becky said, "You'd lose, Brian."

The two men looked up at the screen where a metal fence rolled out of a tall, broad tower standing on the corner of an M25 junction.

"Damn," Joe slapped the table and shook his head. "Well, least I was right."

Lizzy finished eating, paid for her food and headed for the Suzuki, wondering where she should go now London was too dangerous. Zipping up her jacket she felt a tingling over her left breast. Reaching into the inside pocket, she took out the postcard. The blank side now had a photograph of a beach front with the words, 'Greetings from Brighton'.

She stared at the image for several seconds then putting it back in her pocket went into the shop to look at a map.

Several miles later, she slowed when the road ahead filled with pilgrims. They looked like an army of tramps, burdened with rucksacks, tents and sleeping bags, which they carried on their backs or in wheelbarrows. Even with her helmet on and visor lowered, their musty smell made her grimace. They emerged in ragged clumps out of a field, a few of them leading goats, some tilting their heads from side to side, thick strands of matted hair swinging across their faces as they chanted.

Behind them in the field, flags with brand logos or religious symbols, flapped lazily in the breeze. Scattered around the symbols, pilgrims were loading up barrows or filling large rucksacks.

The crowd on the road shuffled to the verge either side, and Lizzy gave them the occasional wave of thanks as she passed. Those at the front carried tall, narrow banners with images of saints; robed men with halos over their heads and illuminated books in their hands.

"Join us," one of them cried out as Lizzy passed him.

"Come with us to Canterbury."

"We will pray for you."

An hour and a half later, she arrived in Brighton and drove slowly through town looking for magicians. A skinny, balding guy, a magician, strolled out of Wilmington Way convenience store. Dressed in dark chinos and a loose, short-sleeve shirt, he looked like a friendly vicar. With one hand on the small backpack slung over his shoulder, and a bag of food in the other, the guy walked slowly beside an old lady pushing a shopping cart. The old lady chatted away while the guy nodded and smiled. Lizzy parked the bike up in the direction they were heading and watched them in the side mirror.

The couple stopped at a corner and after speaking for a few minutes, the old lady disappeared and the guy continued towards Lizzy. Knowing he'd recognise another magician, she took her helmet off and waited.

A flash of shock crossed his face as he approached her.

"Hi," Lizzy said, as he approached.

"Hello," he said, cautiously. Looking up and down the street, he muttered an incantation under his breath then relaxed. "Okay, we're safe."

"I'm Lizzy, Lizzy Francis." They were now both speaking in low voices.

"I know," the man nodded, "I recognised you. I'm Simon. What are you doing here?"

"I need somewhere to stay."

"Shake my hand," Simon held his hand out and they shook hands, Simon tapped a spot on her wrist and a ripple of energy, like the rush of warm water, ran up Lizzy's arm and faded. Simon mumbled an incantation then pointed down the street and a thin green fluid thread appeared in Lizzy's sight. It stretched down the street, a few feet off the ground, and disappeared round a corner.

"Can you see the trail?"

Lizzy nodded.

"It leads to our house. Patsy's at home. Say Simon sent you, she'll understand."

Lizzy tried to ignore the small group of sylphs who materialised to surf and swim along the trail, and followed it to the house. Parked up in the driveway, she took her helmet off and rang the bell then turned to see the trail dissolve away, leaving several disappointed sylphs floating in mid-air.

A woman with long, straight blonde hair and black-frame glasses opened the door. Seeing Lizzy, she gasped and almost dropped the open book in her hand.

"Hello, I'm—"

Patsy gasped, grabbed Lizzy's arm and pulled her in then quickly shut the door. "You were on the news non-stop until the explosion," Patsy said. "My God, you're the first person ever to get out of Salem."

"Simon told me to come here." Lizzy wiped away the face of Maria Jennings then put the helmet on a shelf by the door. A small painting of Jesus giving the Sermon on the Mount hung above the shelf. Lizzy unzipped her jacket. "I didn't kill anyone, it was an accident."

"Don't worry about that, you can tell me later," Patsy said. "How do you know Simon? How did you find us?"

"Rode around until I saw another magician," Lizzy said, rubbing her neck. "Can we sit down somewhere, I've been on the road for hours."

Patsy nodded and led her into the living room where Lizzy fell onto a sofa and stretched her legs out. Patsy sat on the sofa opposite. "Where have you been these last few days? You escaped a while ago."

"Ozzy's."

"You met Ozzy?"

"I stayed with him when I first got out of the Unit. He gave me the Maria Jennings ID."

"Good," Patsy said, "that's the biggest problem out of the way. How is he?"

"Lycus blew his house up, we only just got away."

"What?" Patsy blurted in alarm. "Is he okay?"

"Yes," Lizzy said, "I don't know where he went."

"Thank God, I'll try and get a message to him through Naz, let him know you're okay."

"Naz?"

"Naz Ra-Udin, an old friend. A religious teacher in the Enclave."

"He's a magician too?"

"One of the best."

"You got a picture of Jesus." Lizzy gestured to the hallway. "Is that your cover?"

"Not at all, we're Followers of Christ."

"Christians."

"No, purely the teachings of Jesus, his spoken words, nothing else."

"But he used the Old Testament in his teaching."

"Yes, as part of his teaching. He understood his audience and how to properly instruct and awaken them."

"But we're magicians."

"Makes no difference. In Luke chapter 17 verse 21 it is written that Jesus said, 'The Kingdom of God is within you'. We can only realise that truth if we conduct ourselves each moment as if we reside there, with compassion, selfless humility and service to others. The better we become at doing that, the more resonant with grace our interactions will be, the more powerful our magic. The meek shall inherit the Earth and that is how it will be done."

"So was Jesus a magician or a sorcerer?"

"Far, far more than that. His connection to the Unconditional Creative Force, within which everything that exists arises, is unparalleled in humanity. Sorry, it sounds like I'm preaching."

"Yeah, a bit," Lizzy said. "Those leaflets on the table. You work at a shelter?"

"Yes," Patsy said, "homeless people and collared magicians no longer able to work. But we're getting better at removing the collars and giving people new identities."

"Simon said London. What about the super-fence?"

"The fence is just fake reassurance for straights and only keeps them in. There's a waypoint in the woods right of Whitehill Lane."

"It feels like another war is starting," Lizzy said.

"I doubt anyone wants that," Patsy said.

"But that block blowing up, and all the raids, It's really serious," Lizzy said.

"There was a raid on the farm last year," Patsy said, "that was a big event for us. Lycus used dark magic that day. People even said the Blind Man would return."

"Who?"

"A sorcerer who helped us organise, establish Cantata when the purge against us began. Then he just disappeared. No one knows where, or why."

"Ozzy said the attack on his house used dark magic."

Patsy's eyes widened, "My God, and you both got away?"

Lizzy nodded, "He said shadow fae were helping them."

"My God," Patsy crossed the room and muttering an incantation, slid her hand along the wall. A bookshelf materialised and she took a book from the far left side. The bookshelf became a hazy mist and disappeared as Patsy returned.

"That's a big bookshelf," Lizzy said. "We only had a small one, less than half the size."

"It took us a long time and we had a lot of help from Naz. Here, chapter five," Patsy said.

Lizzy found the chapter and read while Patsy went to her desk and continued writing into a thick notebook.

Several minutes later a bark came from the garden and Patsy looked up. "Come on, I'll introduce you to Hiro. We'll tell people you're our new live-in nanny and dog walker while we work. It'll be a relief not to take turns coming back for lunch-time walks."

Lizzy followed Patsy out to the hallway and down to the kitchen.

"So the CERN incident drained all the energy from the realm of Light, the Silent Fae world, and turned it into a wasteland?"

"Not all, most Fae still live there, but it's not the paradise it used to be, not by a long shot."

"It's our fault."

"Not at all. Some magicians refuse to cast spells but it doesn't make any difference; the energy is in our universe now and some of us are born tuned into it. There's nothing anyone can do."

"So, what are the Shadow Fae doing here?"

"No one knows. But we do know they're helping Alumbrados."

"Are we safe here?"

"Very much so. There are magicians and supporters in the system making sure there isn't a whiff of magic in Brighton." Patsy opened the garden door and a furry rust-brown dog scampered into the kitchen and jumped up at Patsy.

"How did you manage to escape?"

"Me or the dog?"

"You of course," Patsy smiled.

"I don't know," Lizzy said. "I woke up really early feeling strange and then – I think I flew up and hit the ceiling."

"You flew?" Patsy checked her watch then took out a cardboard box of dried dog food. She poured some into Hiro's bowl and Hiro tucked in.

"I guess so," Lizzy said. "Everything was upside down."

"Perhaps I can help, come with me." Patsy led her into a study and closed the door. A desk stood under a window, to the left was a bookshelf and to the right a whiteboard covered in the sketch of a stage plan, with arrows.

"Take a seat." Patsy pointed to a small red sofa and armchair against the far wall. Lizzy sat down and Patsy took the armchair beside it. "There's a spell called Siblica that only works between magicians. We use it to share memories of past events, to share spells. Now, take my hand. Okay, we close our eyes after I say 'Tesh gel efdi'. You say, 'Gel ela aklim'.

"Then what happens?" Lizzy said.

"You visualise the event and I'll be there, seeing what happened."

"All of it?"

"No, it's like a story, you can start and end wherever you like. Just let go of my hand when you want to stop; but let me know first."

"Okay." Lizzy took Patsy's hand.

"You won't see me," Patsy said, "but I'll be there. We'll be able to talk. Remember you can stop anytime."

***

Patsy found herself in a small prison cell illuminated in a pale pinkish-grey hue by sunlight fizzling in through a small window. Across the room, Lizzy lay in her bed, awake and staring at the bunk above her.

"Patsy?"

"I'm here Lizzy, tell me what's going on."

"A funny smell woke me up, sharp, like lemons." Lizzy's voice was faintly hollow in the back of Patsy's mind, "I knew something wasn't right."

Lizzy expertly put on her pyjamas under the sheets.

"You know to sleep naked?" Patsy said.

"Yes," Lizzy said, "I told the others too." She peeled back the thin duvet and swung her legs off the edge. She wore pale orange pyjamas: prison-issue trousers and a T-shirt a couple of sizes too large. Placing her feet gingerly on the cold ground, she winced a little at the chill across the soles of her feet. She put on her slippers then rubbed her eyes and stretched. Lizzy looked around the cell, then realised the block was eerily silent.

"It's very quiet," Patsy said.

"I know, that's strange, there's usually this never-ending low hum that leaks through the walls and ceiling. You can hardly hear it but it's always there. If you press against the wall you start to feel dizzy and sick; and the longer you stay there, the worse you feel. The bullies and wardens use it as a type of punishment or a way of forcing you to do things you don't want to."

Lizzy stood up, her expression of discomfort turning into fear. "That's little Sandy in the top bunk."

Patsy smiled at Sandy's soft snoring. Lizzy put on her thick woollen pullover and, still shivering, crossed her arms and wandered over to the window. "I can feel this weird tingling inside me." Her breath misted the glass and she wiped it away with her sleeve. "I felt strange, like big bubbles going through my whole body. I knew if I told anyone, I'd be taken away and be 'treated': experimented on with drugs and surgery. In the labs they do what they like with you." Lizzy shuddered and the fear rippled through Patsy's mind.

Beyond the window, a light rain fell over the abandoned military airfield the prison had been built on. "The weather was always cold, and most of the time, it was foggy or raining. Have a look outside."

Patsy went and stood beside Lizzy and looked out of the window. Lights on tall poles glowed in the haze. Soft dawn sunlight glimmered over rusty, rain-soaked swings, broken basketball posts and the remains of a small climbing frame in the exercise yard. Several clear plastic shelters, covered in graffiti scratches, had been erected not far from the climbing frame. CCTV cameras stood on the corner of each shelter and more were scattered around the yard. A field of razor wire spread out and disappeared into the fog. Patsy sensed another painful memory. "Did someone die?" she asked.

"Three little girls froze to death last winter. We always get thrown out whatever the weather. They don't care, leaves space for new girls."

Lights blinked on in a building beyond the twenty-foot high fence around the yard. "That's the staff block," Lizzy said. A thick metal door on the side of the block opened and a group of men in grey-blue uniforms emerged. A few of them lit up cigarettes and hurried to join the others, already walking along the caged pathway. The group made their way towards the block where the local research and treatment laboratory was housed on the lower levels. They were halfway across when the door opened again and another group of people came out pushing gurneys, all with short poles supporting pouches with tubes running into the bodies under the white sheets. Lab technicians and 'experimenters', wearing thick, long black coats over their white lab gear, marched through the cold drizzle.

"If we ask what's happened to them, the whitecoats make out one of us is ill, but it's just an excuse to pick someone to experiment on."

Lizzy rubbed away another misty layer on the window. Another day, another race through breakfast for a chance of getting out quick and into one of the shelters before they filled up. Hopefully one, maybe even two of her gang would be there to help hold a spot. If not for her friends, this place would be totally unbearable.

Going to the door, she pressed her face sideways against the glass. "I'm looking to see the clock in the security guard's office at the end of the hall. It was just past six in the morning. Look up in that corner, there's a motion-activated camera, it's probably tracking me now."

A faint buzz came from the camera mounted in the corner of the ceiling. In the guard's room, the little screen with the feed from her cell would now have a bright green dot under it. "I can see two nurses just outside the guard's room, standing over a trolley, preparing the daily medication, taking pills from bottles and putting them into little plastic cups. Look, this is where it started."

Lizzy returned to her bed and lay down. She took a few deep breaths. "I felt so light, like there was a glow inside me. I thought my magic was returning."

Terrified, she got under the thin duvet and pulled it up over her head. She lay, fists clenched, eyes shut tight, trying hard to control her breathing. "Got to calm down," she murmured to herself. Repeating the words seemed to work and the sensations subsided, her breathing steadied and she started to relax.

Patsy felt something like an electric shock jolt Lizzy so hard she rolled off the bed and thumped heavily onto the floor. Somewhere down the hall an alarm went off.

"What was that?" Patsy said.

"I don't know. There was a floating feeling and I remember looking down at Sandy; she was still fast asleep. The room looked upside down."

The door slammed open below her and two nurses and security guards rushed in. Somebody grabbed her arm and yanked her, then the sharp jab of a syringe stung her neck.

"Everything went black and I felt so heavy I thought I was going to die. But then the feeling faded. I think whatever they'd given me began wearing off way too quickly." Lizzy kept her eyes closed and remained limp as she was lifted into a wheelchair and pushed out of the cell.

"Lizzy, Lizzy," Sandy cried. "Leave her alone, put her in bed, leave her alone. Lizzy!"

"Shut up and stay in that bed," an angry woman's voice said. There was a slap followed by Sandy crying out, then her weeping.

Footsteps shuffled to the side of the wall and the clipping of metal-heeled shoes approached and stopped beside her. An unfamiliar voice said, "She's on the priority list. Bring the ambulance round. She's going to the Central RAT centre."

"Great, another zombie."

The vision faded and Patsy felt the weight coming back to her body and she opened her eyes.

Neither of them spoke for a while then Patsy said, "That's how you ended up in the ambulance, your magic started to come back?"

"I think so, it has to be. But that never happened before. There's never, ever been any magic in the Unit, ever."

"Do you think that smell had anything to do with it?"

"Maybe. I'd smelt it before."

"Really?"

"Yes," Lizzy nodded.

"When?"

"The nights Sandy spoke in her sleep," Lizzy said and pursed her lips. Sandy said Lizzy would die alone under a Yew tree.

Both women looked up to the sound of the front door opening. Simon came in and put the bags down by the living room door.

"So I presume everything is okay?" Simon said and went to the window where he stood looking up and down the street.

"Lizzy's met Ozzy, she's got ID, Maria Jennings," Patsy said.

"Excellent," Simon said. "Ed said over a dozen people came through the waypoint this morning, some of them badly injured." He picked up a set of car keys. "Let's go to the shelter and help out."

Chapter Six

Gravity kicked in and Chris dropped to the ground; not hundreds of feet to his death, but a few inches onto soft, damp ground. The devastation had disappeared along with the daylight and all of London. It was night and he was in the middle of a stone circle. Beyond the stones a dark, barren moor stretched into the distance. A full moon hung in a sky illuminated by a vast constellation of stars scattered around the Milky Way.

Several feet away from him, his grandfather fell heavily to the ground and didn't move. Chris staggered back against one of the stones. Either side of him, rising from the murky moonlight, eight more stones formed the ancient circle. His grandfather struggled to sit up, a hand clasped to his neck, blood seeping out between his fingers.

"Granddad!" Chris ran and knelt beside his grandfather as a familiar noise rolled out of the night. The rumbling became louder, and darkness clumped into jagged, lean shapes that hurtled towards him. Snarls and screeches tore through the gloom while blotchy slap of leathery wings stained the silent sky.

Reavers, a massive, full-on rage, charging straight at him. He'd made eye contact. Chris was as good as dead. This was the last thing he'd see. Creatures that no camera could capture, that no person had ever seen and lived to describe. They stood upright on feet that ended in long hoof-like claws, three front, one back; long, rat-like faces. Their skin was an ugly, morphing mush of fur, scales and hide, as if reality couldn't decide what it should be. Whatever it was that covered their bones and flesh, it barely covered them and looked like it would rip open if they moved the wrong way Long gnarled fingers tipped with stubby, sharp nails stretched from stubby, muscular wrists deformed by oversized knuckles. Moonlight glinted off polished metal gauntlets that covered their forearms. Some wore metal chest pieces, thigh and shin guards. It was armour, covered in rows of rivets, some of which blinked the same dull red as the creatures' eyes.

His granddad groaned and the creatures went wild. They angled their heads up and howled out of grotesque long, dry throats and the sky echoed back the cries. Winged reavers spiralled round and down to hit the ground with ugly crunches, as if pain was alien to them. They folded their leathery wings and leaned forward on arms that reached to the ground so they walked on all fours. Their shrill shrieks joined the snarls, grunts and howls of the ground reavers now pacing around the stone circle. They stamped on the ground, throwing up their arms and jerking their heads to stare at him with blood-red eyes. Large, vertical irises reflected oily colours, dilating and contracting as they absorbed and filtered the entire spectrum of visible and invisible light, revealing secrets only they could see.

Chris dropped to his grandfather's side and folded his arms over his head, unable to stop himself shaking with fear. The waves of howls, screeches and stamping continued but didn't come closer. What was going on? He shouldn't even be alive by now.

Chris slowly looked up, The rage were there, just beyond the stone circle, mad as ever; they stomped, punched the ground, pounded their chests, but they stayed outside the circle. They pushed and shoved each other, growling and tearing up clumps of grass and moss; slapping it into their own gaunt faces disfigured even more by fury and frustration.

Chris almost jumped when his granddad reached up and grabbed his arm. A cold shiver ran through him. He could feel his grandfather's life slipping away and an eerie void seeping out from somewhere to fill the space, as if death was a thing that abhorred the vacuum left by fading life.

The brutal clamour around him became a distant roaring and the whisper of his grandfather's voice was clear in his mind. "Alumbrados, they did this... for the book... fourth... book. They'll kill for it... You... you... tree... take.. protect the Key" His hand dropped and a key fell from his palm. "Find... Frankie, Brighton."

"What?" Chris moved to take his grandfather's hand other from his neck but the old man resisted and Chris's hand came away soaked in blood. His grandfather kept his hand pressed on his neck, a steady stream of blood pulsing out between his fingers.

"My crystal... take it... Go." His grandfather's voice was a feeble whisper in Chris's mind. "Don't let them find you... find Fran.. key."

A wave, heavy, dark shadow seemed to pulse through Chris. His grandfather was dead. Beyond the stone circle, the reavers' howls rose to a deafening frenzy.

"Shut up!" Chris screamed. "Just shut up!"

The reavers jerked their heads around violently and stomped angrily around the circle. They pushed and shoved each other, spitting and flicking out long, broad tongues. They drooled thick strands of saliva that hung from their jaws until cast away with a violent shake.

The uncontrolled movements, noise and drooling settled after a while and their noises sounded like they were speaking. The creatures prowled around, growling with intelligent, angry eyes.

Chris jumped up and went to the edge of the stone circle. "What?" he shouted through the tears. "Can't stand it, can you? I'm right here, right here and you can't get me." He stopped, wiped his eyes and stared at them. "Yeah, right in the eye. Right in your stupid, fat red eye and you can't do a thing about it. Nothing! Take a good look at what you're not going to get, you filthy—" Chris jumped back when a reaver thrust its arm towards him. Flesh sizzled black and red and dripped off the bone like melting wax. The creature screamed in agony and staggered back. The reaver fell to its knees still screaming wildly while those around it watched in silence, heads tilting like curious dogs, edging forwards towards it while shooting glances at each other.

The injured reaver swung out with its good arm and bared its teeth with threatening growls and clawed at the other creatures until its head dropped with a resigned groan. Before any of the surrounding reavers could pounce, a winged reaver swooped down in a low arc and snatched up the injured beast, hooking its long talons into its back. The reavers on the ground howled in protest as more sky reavers swooped in, grabbing and tearing at the reaver's flailing limbs as it was lifted higher into the night sky.

With nothing left but bones, the reavers turned back to Chris; coarse, angry snarls ripping from their throats. After a while he stopped hearing them. He could see them going through the motions, mouths moving around but no sound was coming out. It was weird; like he'd seen on TV. Remains of people, mostly homeless guys or drunks who'd lost track of time, would be found in a street and the people living right by the feed would say they never heard a thing.

Chris went and sat by his grandfather and waited for dawn.

Finally, a thin grey line broke through the trees along the horizon and the first streaks of cold lightning gashed the sky. The reavers vanished, leaving an eerie silence as the moor emerged out of a fading twilight. Dawn summoned a thin, misty shroud across the bleak landscape. It spread through the circle to lie over his grandfather's body while more shards of cold, silent white lighting ripped across the sky.

Off in the distance a solitary cottage stood off the one tarmac road that snaked through the moor. An old car was parked up on the grass outside. A few minutes later the first glow of sunlight struck the stones and cast pale shadows that stretched around Chris and his grandfather's body.

He touched his grandfather's ashen face and pulled away from the cold, unresponsive skin. The old man really was dead. Chris got to his feet, knees stiff from hours of sitting, and looked down at his granddad who had brought him up for twelve years.

"Bye, Granddad." So many people dead. Granddad, Miss Keats, little Rosie and her mum, old Harry upstairs with his comic collection. Phil's family.

Brighton, his granddad had said, find Frankie, his childhood friend. "Okay."

Chris knelt down and took the keys by his grandfather's body. A keyring with the key to his car, the house key and an old mortice key. Chris pocketed them and stood up. He had to get away from this place, far away. He checked his wallet, two five-pound notes; he needed more cash. Grimacing, he went through his grandfather's pockets. The small book, a wallet with two twenties, a ten and a five. He took the money, along with his grandfather's old pocket watch, and put the little book into the pouch of his sweatshirt. He was about to stand up when he remembered his grandfather's words about the crystal. He removed the bloodstained chain along with the pendant and wiped it as best he could on the dewy grass. Swallowing his grief, he touched his grandfather's hand and walked away. He stopped twice to look back then hurried towards the cottage. Another long line of lightning fractured and fragmented into shards to slither across the sky.

The thick curtains over the windows made it impossible to tell if anyone was home or awake in the cottage. It him took less than a minute to break into the small Honda parked on the verge by the front gate. He eased down the handbrake and with the door open and one hand on the steering wheel, leaned his shoulder into the door frame and pushed. The car rolled slowly down the lane and Chris clambered in, holding the door with one hand and steering with the other. He closed the door with a barely audible clunk as the car rounded the first corner just before it crossed a small stone bridge. He could see the house up the hill to his left and almost steered off the road when three demons, the height of children, ambled round from the back garden. They chatted and gesticulated animatedly, laughing as they came into view along the path that led down the side of the house. The demon in front took a quick look around then lifted the latch on the front gate and pulled it open, the other two demons followed, laughing and shoving each other as they crossed the road and headed onto the moor.

Chris started up the engine, looking back up the road to the house. No movement of curtains, no lights came on. He relaxed and drove away. The narrow road curved round the hill where his grandfather lay in the stone circle then turned away. It felt wrong, leaving his granddad up there. It could be ages before someone found him. He wiped his eyes as he drove, wishing there was something he could do, to show that he cared. Maybe he should find a phone box, call the police or someone. No, they'd know where the call was coming from.

He pulled over by the first signpost, 'Stanton in Peak' and 'Darley Bridge', and flicked through the map. "Brilliant," he groaned; he was in the Peak District National Park. Frankie and Brighton were hundreds of miles away and the petrol gauge was broken.

The second time he almost fell asleep and drove off the road, Chris pulled over and opened both front windows. He drove the rest of the way yawning, shivering and cursing every time streaks of cold lightning stalled the car.

The car shunted a couple of times and stopped completely a couple of miles from the Manchester bus station. He swore and slapped the steering wheel. Chris dropped his head back and sat for a few minutes then jolted himself awake and climbed out of the car. Slouched over, his hands in the pouch of his sweatshirt, Chris walked along the quiet streets. The sight of a strange half-man, half-lizard creature crawling up the side of a church wall stopped him dead. For a second he thought it was a reaver, but this thing wore a pair of baggy shorts and what looked like a roughly woven short sleeve top; not the armour worn by reavers. The creature turned its long neck to stare at Chris through fishy sea-blue eyes, the slit opening and closing, breathing in the light. Their eyes locked and Chris got the strangest feeling the creature had somehow recognised him. Then it scuttled sideways along the grey stone wall and sunk down through the stained glass window as if it were liquid.

People began to fill the streets, heading for work. Bicycles and low-powered mopeds buzzed past him. Not a single Dawn Patrol vehicle, which was strange. Turning a corner he stopped when he saw the news vans, interviewers and camera operators crowding the street ahead. People huddled in small groups watching neighbours being interviewed by State TV and radio journalists. Cables from microphones and cameras snaked across the pavement to vans from where thicker cables connected to cable access boxes, allowing a live feed. Chris stopped a man; somehow he knew the guy was a magician. The man wore a suit, and was hurrying away from the crowds, a soft leather shoulder bag slung across his back.

"Hey," Chris said, "what's…"

A rippling in the air over a rooftop snapped his attention to a small group of gold-skinned teenagers, dressed in nothing but loincloths. All seven of them, three boys and four girls, chests and breasts bare, had shimmering, translucent wings neatly folded one over the other, behind them. They sat watching the activity on the street and talking amongst themselves. They were the most beautiful people he'd ever seen.

The man followed Chris's gaze then gave him a knowing look. One of the girls saw them looking and waved. Chris went to raise his hand to wave back and the guy nudged him, "Don't," he hissed

"What's going on?"

"Police and Lycus operation. They're coming down heavy. Raids all over the country." There was fear in his voice.

"Raids?"

"That explosion in London yesterday morning,

"Yesterday morning? He'd lost a whole day.

"Yes, they're saying Cantata have started to attack civilian targets."

Streaks of lightning broke into fragments across the sky and activity in the street stopped while the news channel equipment shut down.

"Cantata? That's just crazy," Chris said.

"The country's gone paranoid. Be careful." The man checked his watch, turned abruptly to cross the road then stopped and looked back. "Good luck," he said and strode across the road, disappearing round a corner.

At the coach station, Chris tried to look casual as he went to the ticket booth and passed the money and ID through the slot under the glass partition. The ticket officer swiped the ID card and glanced at the screen, his bored expression remaining unchanged. Chris took his ticket and went into the lounge. The half dozen people there were watching the TV up on the far wall. He recognised the wreckage; it was a live feed from the block where he lived, or what was left of it.

With the volume muted, subtitles appeared along the bottom of the screen. 'News is coming in of dawn raids on premises of suspected safe houses and Cantata sympathisers in cities across the country. We are getting reports that up to a hundred suspects and sympathisers have already been arrested. Deaths resulting from people resisting arrest have also been reported. It is not known how many of these were magicians or sympathisers.'

Sooner or later someone would look at the bowl shape left by the explosion and figure out his flat was slap-bang in the middle of where the explosion happened. Hopefully he'd be reported dead, along with granddad. Then they'd find his body and it would all kick off.

He headed for the London bound coach. The thick night-shutters were raised and there were around a dozen passengers already on board. He stepped onto the coach and greeted the driver, "Hi."

"Morning," the driver smiled back.

Chris's neighbour, Dave, was a driver. He had a nice place, massive CD collection. Chris hung out with him sometimes. Drivers owned their own coaches and worked as self-employed contractors.

A few of the passengers glanced up as he passed them. Apart from a couple towards the back, the others all sat alone beside empty seats.

The driver picked up the mic and untangled the wires leading down to the console.

"Good morning, my name's Steve. We'll be setting off to London in around five minutes, when the lightning finally dies down." Steve started the engine and put the air conditioning on to get rid of the smell of detergents and polishes. He rummaged through a book of CDs and slipped one into the player. Easy-listening jazz played softly through the speakers.

Chris settled back and fell into a deep sleep invaded by short, intense dreams. He was a kid back at home and both his parents were somewhere inside. A dog came running out onto the garden porch but it wasn't Benjy; it was Spyro, the staffie from the Tooting squat. Then he was inside his old home, sat on a sofa with Lizzy Francis from the wanted posters. She had a head of blonde hair, cut short. "Remember me, you twit?" she said and shoved him. The shove coincided with the shunt of the coach setting off and he woke up.

The coach pulled out of the parking bay and Chris relaxed back only to be thrown forward when the coach braked suddenly. The other passengers around him were panicking. Chris looked out of the window to see what was going on.

A policeman stood at the exit ramp with his arm raised. Chris decided to get out of there, fast. Looking back, he saw two black four-by-four Lycus Jeeps rumble in and park up in the passenger drop-off area and he began to scan for another way out.

Police with assault rifles got out of the first vehicle followed by burly, heavily armed Lycus soldiers. The police headed for the ticket office and the soldiers went into the waiting room and took positions either side of the double doors. Two more Lycus soldiers got out of the other Jeep and headed towards the coach, signalling Steve to open the doors.

"Sorry everybody," Steve called over his shoulder and the door opened with a hiss. Chris panicked, looking up and down the coach for the emergency exit as the soldiers slipped the rifles from their shoulders and unclipped the safety. The scrunch of their heavy boots echoed through the car park.

Several yards from the coach one of the soldiers shouted, "Everybody out and against the side of the coach."

As the other passengers got out of their seats and began to pick up their bags, the sound of rapid gunfire from the street echoed around the underground area. Chris and all the other passengers dropped to the ground or cowered in their seats.

Nothing was hitting the coach and Chris climbed slowly across his seat and peered out of the window.

The four Lycus soldiers and two policemen were now running across the car park towards the exit ramp. Beyond the ramp, lights came to life inside the multi-storey car park across the road revealing rows of tents, old camper vans, transits and makeshift homes spread across each level. A gang of teenagers ran towards the car park and away from gunfire. Some older people leapt forwards in long strides, all but flying.

The magicians swarmed up the side of the car park like it was nothing more than a steep hill, and clambered into cover behind the short walls. Seconds later a hail of bottles, planks of wood, wooden boxes and small barrels rained down onto the Lycus soldiers below. Sirens wailed in the distance and someone shouted commands over as loudspeaker, "Continue the assault" Soldiers continued firing up at the car park as they charged towards the building, dodging the missiles and shouting loudly.

A loud 'woomph' resonated through the air then ice-blue sheets of liquid poured out of the upper car park levels. Soldiers stumbled back or ran for cover as the liquid crashed onto the street and spread across the ground, turning into a thick, icy sludge. Soldiers slipped and slid into each other while others slammed into vehicles and walls. Parked Lycus trucks and cars lost their grip and skidded into each other; several crashed through shopfronts setting off alarms. The ice sheet quickly spread and began to pour down into the exit ramp and towards the coach.

"Bloody hell!" Steve had fallen back into his seat. He yanked the gearstick into reverse and the coach shunted backwards and bumped over the kerb of the pavement. Steve stamped on the brake before the coach hit the wall. "Dammit!" He made a grab for his sandwich box as it flew off the wide dashboard, and miraculously caught it, then gaped out of the window towards the street.

The noise of people shouting and wail of alarms joined the deafening chaos of gunfire. Magicians stepped out over the car park walls and glided on waves of solid air over the soldiers. The first line of magicians moved their arms in wide arcs and pulsing blasts white mist rolled out, repelling bullets. A second stream of magicians followed the first, curling their hands and filling the air with a harmonic chorus of incantations that, for a moment, swept away all the other noise. Showers of ice-blue lightning balls flew downwards then morphed and stretched and snaked through the air, striking soldiers and bursting into a blinding, sticky white foam that clung to them, making them look like puffed-out snowmen.

More military trucks arrived and lost control on the icy ground. They crashed into the vehicles already rammed up against each other and buildings. Soldiers stumbled out, lost their footing then clambered onto the roofs of cars and vans and began firing wildly towards the magicians. Deflected bullets smashed into concrete pillars and walls behind the magicians who responded with a storming deluge of water that thundered down and hit the ground with a deafening roar, the surge carrying soldiers and vehicles back. The wail of a siren blasted out and the soldiers still able to move took cover in buildings or retreated down the coach station exit, still firing wildly.

More sheets of icy liquid appeared from nowhere and crunched into each other and slid towards the coach stations behind the soldiers who had retreated down the ramp. Soldiers, coaches and other vehicles nearest the exit slid and collided into each other and against the pillars.

Cheers rose from the magicians floating in the air behind their shields.

"My bloody coach." Steve shouted.

"The entrance," Chris cried and pointed over to where coaches entered the station, his hand knocking onto the windscreen.

Steve's eyes widened. "On it!" He shoved the gearstick and spun the steering wheel. Passengers scrabbled and fell into the nearest seats as the coach skidded into a turn and shot out of the station the wrong way up a one-way street. Steve scrunched his face and tightened his grip on the steering wheel as the coach bumped over the speed humps. Taking a left turn and steering onto the right side of the main road, Steve breathed a deep sigh of relief and glanced up at Chris. "That was quick thinking, thanks, mate."

Chris nodded, still shaking from the adrenalin rush. He made his way back to his seat while the other passengers murmured and shifted nervously around him, occasionally looking back. There was nothing to see. The streets outside slowly filled with people setting off for work, cycling, sharing drives or waiting at bus stops, no idea of what had happened over on the other side of the station.

Half an hour later the coach hit the motorway. Chris fell into a sleep full of haunting dreams and flashbacks of the past two nights; dreams that kept scaring him back into consciousness until he gave up on sleep and took out the book.

Written in pale blue on a slate-grey background was the title, *The Atlas of Elegance*. Why did his grandfather take a guide to the 'Realm of Elegance' board game from the bookcase? Chris and his granddad drew up the map, and Miss Keats helped design the meadows, forests and jungles. Each double-page spread had a detailed replica of different parts of the board map. He knew his way round the map like the back of his hand; Granddad made sure of that.

Elegance was a medieval present-and-futuristic Earth-like planet with all kinds of terrain: deserts, tundra, wetlands, canyons, caves, plains, glaciers, forests, mountains, lava fields, lakes. Across these were dotted castles, villages, farms, mills, towns, ports and inns, docks, airports, spaceports, roads, lanes, paths, canals, railway lines, monorail lines. Every route was beaded with small red, yellow, green or blue waypoints with arrows showing the way to turn. Each finely drawn route also had an incantation written in fine, elegantly curved lettering along it. This had to be read out to ensure safe passage through any obstacles or threats on that particular route. Some waypoints – portals to areas not linked to any path, road or canal – had a map coordinate in them. Waypoints led to places like caverns, underground lakes, old mines and mountain caves, or hideaways where individual challenges were faced in reward for powerful, time-limited magical spells. Players moved little avatar models along the lines and paths: Horus, Osiris, Seth, Anubis, Thor, Loki, Sif, Baldur, Shiva, Ganesh, Vishnu, Krishna, Sid Raguel; and his favourite, Zen, the podgy demon.

Chris put the book away and took out the crystal pendant. He hesitated for a second then slipped the chain with the crystal over his head; nothing happened and with some relief he checked his wallet. Having paid for the coach he had thirty quid and change. "Brilliant," he muttered. How was he going to stay on the run with that? Spyro; of course. He'd just thought of where he could get some more cash.

The coach arrived in London and the doors hissed open. Chris stepped out onto the bright, busy streets of Golders Green. A tangible tension hung in the air; Granddad was right, no one paid any attention to people he could see were magicians.

Everyone looked worried. A small gang of witchfinders, all wearing brown leather gloves stood on the corner. Some shouted slogans while others handed out leaflets. A couple of Lycus police stood by the entrance to the Tube station, and a Lycus truck was parked up under the bridge.

Two Lycus police officers strolled out of a shop and almost walked into him. One of the policemen grabbed him by the neck and pushed him up against the shop window. Several passers-by stepped back and the woman behind the counter inside the shop cried out in alarm.

"Jackson!" a voice snarled from several yards away. "What the hell do you think you're doing? Our shift ends in two minutes. Bust that kid and you'll have half an hour's paperwork for Chrissake."

The policeman thought about this and was about to let Chris go when he noticed the book in his pocket. "What's this?" The policeman pulled the atlas from Chris's pocket and flicked it open. He glanced at the map images and glared at Chris, "What is this?"

"A board game," Chris said, hiding his fear.

"I ain't never seen no game like this. Looks all over the place."

"I made it myself."

"Gamer nerd, eh?" The policeman grunted and slung the book aside. He let go of Chris's collar so he almost fell, "Watch your step, boy."

Chris nodded and, picking up the atlas, continued along the street and past the remains of a block where a month ago, a fight between magicians and armed police had killed everyone involved. People say a stray shot blew up an oil tank while others blamed magicians. Either way, the buildings had melted into a broad, thirty-foot high mound of ugly rubble covered in weeds and waste. Several Gorfels, creatures Chris recognised from the *Atlas of Elegance*, scuttled over the mound, their bright blue snouts twitching. Sunlight shimmered through their double pairs of delicate, transparent wings. All that stuff in the atlas was real. These were the same creatures that in the game he followed through the Forest Maze of Durkhem.

Chris crossed the road to the market, a collection of stalls and trailers scattered around the half-cleared rubble of what used to be a row of shops and houses. He lifted a pair of sunglasses and moved to another stall selling gloves; the guy had hiked prices up to over three times the usual price. The jerk had a prime location facing the pavement and had three guys watching the shoppers. Chris was about to pick up a glove when a tangible rise in tension rippled around him. Several magicians disappeared down side streets.

Traffic had pulled over to one side of the road and a pair of Lycus ZT patrol cars moved menacingly in his direction. The vehicle in front was a black saloon car, the bonnet and side driver doors emblazoned with the Zero Tolerance logo. The filament scanner rotating on the roof of the four-by-four behind pinged a sickly blue-green. No one knew whether they actually worked and Chris didn't hang about to find out if they did, or if the crystal round his neck would protect him. He stuck his hands in his pockets, kept a steady pace and headed away towards the tube station and the Northern Line.

Chapter Seven

Chris slept through the journey and almost missed his stop. He jumped when an automated announcement said, "This is Tooting Bec; the next stop is Tooting Broadway." He'd fallen asleep at a funny angle and the sudden movement sent a slight stinging ache up the side of his neck.

He stepped out of the station and, with his sunglasses on, set off down the quiet side streets to the squat his old school friend Jim had moved into with his girlfriend. It was Monday afternoon, so the house should be empty. Brian, Nora and Jim should be at work, and Spyro's owner, Sean, would be at the 'shop', an abandoned warehouse where stolen goods were traded.

Chris ducked behind a parked van. Sean was loading boxes into the back of an old Volvo estate. Ian, Sean's brother, came out of the house with Rufus the Boerboel and opened the back passenger door. The dog clambered in and Ian climbed into the driver's seat. Sean slammed the boot shut, swore at his brother then closed the front door before getting into the car which immediately drove off.

After a quick look around, Chris strode up the side path to the back of the house, banged on the door and waited. Spyro appeared in the kitchen, and seeing Chris, barked and jumped up at the door. Luckily, the beast of a dog, Rufus, had gone with the brothers. Chris had never liked the Boerboel and it didn't like him, in fact, the mastiff didn't like anyone. Chris found the key under the plant pot and let himself in. Spyro greeted him with happy yelps and began chasing her tail. "Hello, Spyro," Chris gave her head a stroke, "come on then."

Spyro trotted ahead of him up the stairs to wait by the door to Sean's room. The Yale lock on the thin pine door broke with the first kick. Spyro ran in, sniffed around then settled on the sofa while Chris went to the fireplace where Sean stashed the money he made from burglaries and selling potion. He found a little over three thousand pounds tied in rubber bands in a small shoebox. The crook was probably saving for something; too bad. Sean's car keys were there too, along with a couple of ancient mobile phones and a charger. Why did people even bother to keep this junk? He pushed the old phones aside. Inside an old envelope was a wad of petrol coupons; excellent.

He took the money, coupons and car keys then washed the soot and dust from his hands. Spyro was waiting for him when he came out of the bathroom. Sean would kick the crap out of the dog once he'd found his stuff gone. Would Sean guess it was someone he knew? Screw him, who cared? "Come on, girl, let's go for a ride."

With Spyro curled up on the back seat of Sean's old Ford Escort, Chris hit the M23 to Brighton.

He stopped to fill up with petrol at the first petrol station. None of the other customers could see the half dozen Gorp monkeys sitting in the branches of the trees behind the shop. The wind and sun rippled through their bright golden-brown fur while the creatures used their long, broad tails to balance as they groomed each other. The younger Gorps gazed around in wonderment as they opened and closed their mouths rhythmically in big gaping smiles.

The line of cars moved forward slowly and when it was Chris's turn, the guy behind him stared as Chris fed one coupon after another into the pump. "Been saving months for this," he said and snapped the petrol flap shut.

He arrived in Brighton and abandoned the car it in the most run-down part of town he could find. He left the windows open, door unlocked and keys on the front seat. He walked through Withdean Park to have a look at the crater left by two satellites that had collided and fallen out of orbit. A natural footpath had formed round the crater and Chris followed it, throwing sticks for Spyro to chase. After a while he started looking for somewhere out of the way to stay, not connected to the system or anywhere they'd ask for ID.

The single house stood at the end of a bombed-out terrace where a battle had wrecked all the other buildings in the street. The faded 'B&B – Room available' sign barely clung to the peeling, yellowed tape on the inside glass of the weather-worn front door. Chris knocked and waited. He was about to knock again when the door opened.

"Yes?" an old man squinted at him through thick glasses and scratched a wrinkled, unshaven face. A limp, lifeless, half-smoked roll-up hung from the corner of his thin lips. "What?" he rasped, scratching his round stomach through an old Arsenal shirt two sizes too small.

Chris leaned back from the smell of stale urine and tobacco.

This was worse than he expected. He made to turn away then changed his mind. It would do for a couple of days, "I'd like a room, please."

The old man reacted with a surprised expression then checked himself and pointed at Spyro, "That a dog you got there?" He coughed and cleared his throat, "No dogs."

"You're kidding."

"You're wasting my time," the old man swung the door and Chris slapped his palm against it.

"I'll pay for her as another person, she's house-trained, I'll give you two nights up front."

The old man eyed him suspiciously. "Let's see your money then."

Chris had split the money and peeled off five twenties from the small wad in his pocket. The old man watched him count, then took the notes and stepped aside, "Upstairs to the right, white door." He cleared his throat, "No refunds."

Chris edged past him into the narrow hallway and headed up the stairs; Spyro ran up ahead.

"Dog better not mess in my house."

"Don't worry, she won't. What time is breakfast?"

Shuffling down the hallway, the old man grunted a short laugh, "When the café down the road opens."

"I thought this was a B&B?"

"Bed and Bugger off. Besides, you'd eat a breakfast made by me?" the man said over his shoulder and chuckled to himself.

The room was pretty clean; it had a double bed facing a dressing table on top of which stood a cable extension box beside a small TV. A narrow wardrobe stood between the bed and window on the far wall. Outside, beyond the window and back garden stretched a narrow alley, thick with weeds, hosting a couple of old shopping trolleys, a burnt-out motorbike frame and some rusty bicycle parts. The street was visible over on the left. Chris flopped onto the bed and lay back to stare up at the ceiling and was asleep in minutes. The noise of a TV playing loudly downstairs woke him a few hours later. Spyro was curled up on top of the duvet at the end of the bed snoring in little grunts.

Chris reached across the small gap between the end of the bed and the dresser and switched on the TV and cable extension box.

The TV didn't have its own cable tuner but displayed whatever the old man had tuned into downstairs. The evening news was on and Chris gaped at the carnage left after the Manchester battle. After that came a sickening edit of raids that had happened across the country. A lot of them included shots of bodies covered in tarpaulins lined up in front of houses. The piece finished with a 'Where it all began' article which replayed the footage from the wreckage of where he lived. The camera was around a hundred yards from the block. Ambulances sped up and down the street, passing rubble and debris pushed to the kerbside by diggers now parked up alongside emergency vehicles. Paul was making the most of being interviewed by a guy from some other TV channel. Lanks was talking to a couple of guys in suits holding notepads and pointing at the remains of the building.

Jessica Keats sat in a wheelchair with a drip leading into her arm. She was with a group of other people around a table beside a St John's Ambulance van serving tea and biscuits. She looked into the camera and seemed to stare straight at him. Chris sat up. The footage was a day old but her gaze caught his attention like she knew he was watching. Could magicians do that? No, that was crazy, wasn't it.

The newscaster's sombre voice continued, "With Police on high alert and supported by additional Lycus Units…" The image changed as the old man downstairs flicked through the channels and finally tuned back into the same News Channel. "…178 people have so far been unaccounted for and that figure is certain to rise. Most of the victims were mothers with young children, the elderly and disabled. Police, Fire Service and Centauri Community support teams are still working at the site. A spokesperson said they have identified the exact epicentre of the explosion and the flat where it happened. We are expecting an official statement in the morning. It seems there may already be a suspect and he may have survived the explosion. Traffic in the area…"

The epicentre, yeah, that would be his flat. Any policeman with basic geometry could figure that out. They'd probably already found Granddad up in the Peak District by now – well, his body. Next, Lycus would find his fingerprints on the stolen car and then his face would be all over the papers. Brilliant. If only he knew how to do magic. Chris turned the volume down and continued watching until he fell asleep. Spyro licking his face dragged him to the border of consciousness. His hand felt heavy as it pushed her away and he turned away from her.

Spyro's whines kept prodding into his sleep and he hauled himself up and fell back to lean against the headboard. "Bloody hell, Spyro, just one night's sleep, that's all."

Spyro paced up and down by the door and Chris swung his legs off the bed, "Oh all right, come on then." Putting his trainers on got Spyro all excited and her pacing sped up. Chris sighed, "Might as well grab some food while we're out."

It was another warm evening and Chris bought a can of dog food for Spyro, and fish and chips for himself. They went down to the promenade and Chris sat down on a bench to eat. Spyro wolfed her food down then dashed onto the beach, chasing after gulls. Chris finished eating and followed her, throwing a stick that Spyro would return and drop at his feet. As the sun set, Chris returned to the bench and took out the old key. Whatever door it opened, it had to be pretty old. Maybe the fourth book was behind it, or maybe the fourth book told him where the door was. And what was the tree Grandad talked about? That could be anywhere.

He was staring out to sea when two teenagers came by, their eyes glazed, nodding their heads slowly, obviously tuned out on potion.

"Yo, guys." Chris pocketed the key and stood up. The boys stopped, annoyed at the interruption. "Where can I get some of that?"

The taller of the two gave him a sour look and pulled a thin cylindrical phial no bigger than an AAA battery from a hidden pocket inside his jacket. Glowing silver threads of smoke swirled in spirals inside the phial. "A tenner."

Chris barely stopped himself laughing, "For that skinny tube? You're joking, fam. There's not half a tune in that."

The guy shrugged and turned away.

Chris stopped him, "Okay, I'll take two."

The guy gave the phial an angry look as if it should have told him to charge more, and handed over two phials.

Chris took the phials down to the beach and sat on a blue plastic milk crate a few feet from the shore. Facing the soft-rolling sea, he lifted one phial at a time to his face and pinched off the plastic stopper. The shimmering fumes swirled up over his face and streamed along his cheek to his ears. His ears tingled as the fumes slipped in and the eerie, comforting tune played through his senses. The tune, his breathing and his heartbeat synchronised with the ebb and flow of the waves, accompanied by the tones created by the breezes drifting around him.

Chris took in a deep breath and almost in response the wind picked up. The slow beat of waves gathered and rolled over each other with a sensual, irregular rhythm, rolling forwards to slap and slide back. The symphony of a million differently shaped stones rolled under the hissing caress of soft foams. Together, it was all alive, like lifeless molecules making an organic cell. What the hell kind of tune was this?

A pang of guilt ran through him. It was hard to believe Granddad was dead, and now here he was at the edge of the country, tuned out and with no idea how to find Frankie. What the hell was he supposed to do now? The tune around and inside him changed as Chris's attention shifted to absences and spaces between the sounds.

Stretching out to the darkening horizon, the sea undulated far beneath the evening sky. All that space but still the colour of the sky in the water. His thoughts drifted to the spaces between things, between strings, inside magicians and probably out there too, in everything, even the stars and the spaces between. All those creatures under the sea, every living thing, all those bacteria and enzymes and stuff in his gut and his blood. All the things he knew were there but didn't know about, nothing but strings vibrating. Was that how it worked? Those string filaments, connecting everything, across realities? Movement of stuff in spaces? Everything wasn't connected, but it was all... symphonic. Things were just instrumental in something bigger.

Maybe this was how magic worked, yeah. The strings, the weird magic ones inside him, retuning and reaching beyond him and everything out there, pulling stuff back from other realities? All he had to do was figure out how to get the strings to do that and somehow find Frankie.

Spyro came up and panted happily into his face, breaking his thoughts, and he pushed her away, "Get away, dog breath." Spyro gaped at him with a big grin on her face. "Crazy dog," he smiled back at her, "what do you care?" Spyro responded with a few short piggy grunts.

Closer to the shoreline, a bedraggled guy in a shabby, long brown coat shuffled along the beach. The ends of his ill-fitting trousers dragged through the sand and sucked up water to form dark stains. Even from this distance, Chris spotted the collar round the guy's neck. A burnt-out magician, unable to even work. The guy moved slowly in a perfectly straight line, scanning the sand through a wispy curtain of scraggy long hair. A thin layer of sand puffed away from wherever he looked. Poor guy, Chris shook his head, he'd rather die than end up like that. He flicked the tubes into a bin and watched the guy disappear down the beach.

The wind died away and clouds slowly dissipated to reveal a sky crammed with stars. Chris strolled along the shoreline behind the burnt-out magician, lost in thought while Spyro ran up and down. How did he grow up to be such a jerk? Disrespecting Terri, trashing her dad's car, treating everything like a joke; even got Andy killed. He jumped back several steps when a shallow wave splashed inches from his foot. He remembered playing on the beach with Frankie. It was like part of him had just stayed seven when he should have grown up. Frankie though, that was one weird kid, always sneaking off to secretly start little fires. "For the elves," he would say. How was Chris going to find that nutcase without magic? He could be anywhere.

Church bells rang the ten-thirty warning and people along the promenade quickened their pace, "Come on Spyro." Chris headed back to the B&B; finding Frankie would have to wait till tomorrow.

The lights were still on in a Chinese takeaway; an old man slowly wiped the counter. Above him, the TV on the wall was tuned to the China Today channel, piped through undersea cables that stretched from China to servers in America then across the Atlantic to here. A group of men and women danced in the dark, their bodies barely visible. Some held small torches; others had long, fluorescent ribbons curling and following the hand movements. Strings that resembled the fine lines in the atlas. Maybe he was more tuned than he thought. Trained in Tai-Chi and Kenpo, Chris recognised the moves. Seeing it through his mildly tuned mind, the dancers reminded him of the spin and orbit of atoms and electrons, energy and forces being exchanged. He started thinking about all the other ancient dances: Shaman, Hindu, Native American, Dervishes. Unaware his fingers were twitching, he struggled to piece ideas together. What was it he was thinking about strings earlier?

Some knobhead from a local witchfinder gang swaggered past him into the restaurant and pulled out a knife and started to shout and wave it about in front of the old man. A couple of witchfinders in tight-fitting T-shirts stopped outside, laughing and goading their friend at the counter.

Things were getting nasty and Chris was about to walk away when he caught a glimpse of movement reflected in the glass. Some instinct made him lean to one side just in time to dodge a punch aimed at his head. Chris dropped into a defensive roll-back, avoiding the swing of a baseball bat, and was on his feet in time to block a kick from a burly witcher.

Adrenalin kicked in and everything snapped into focus. He stepped sideways, whipped his fist into the side of the guy's face and followed up with a sharp kick, landing his heel in the guy's stomach. The witcher stumbled back into the two guys at the window who seemed too tuned to notice what was going on behind them and the three of them crashed through the takeaway window, setting the alarm off.

Chris bounced up to a combat stance and raised his fists, "Aw, gimme a break," he groaned as the rest of the Witchfinder gang arrived and bunched up, heading straight for him. The restaurant alarm rang out across the street, and three Chinese guys, two in white chef jackets, emerged from the back. An old lady with a walking stick hobbled out after them. The old boy waved his hands, shouting in Chinese at the old lady and chefs. The expression on the chefs' faces turned from shock to rage and, lifting the counter, they crunched over the broken glass, heading out towards the gang. Three of the gang members ran off and Spyro took after them. The fattest and slowest clambered onto the top of an SUV and Spyro ran round the car barking and snarling up at him. The alarm on the SUV joined that of the takeaway and the noise, coupled with the shouts of the gang, brought lights on in the houses up and down the street.

A wiry witcher yelled and jabbed a ling blade knife at Chris.

Chris blocked, grabbed the hand and forearm, and with a quick twist, snapped the guy's wrist. At the same time he slammed the back of his other fist into the side of the guy's face. The guy's head snapped sideways, and with blood streaming from his mouth, he let out an agonising scream and stumbled into the road, wailing at his disfigured hand.

Two more guys came at Chris and he jumped forward, twisted sideways, kicked out and broke the nose of one with the heel of his foot. Without lowering his leg, he snapped out another kick and whacked the other guy in the side of his face, feeling the jaw give way.

A second pair came at him, one swinging a baseball bat up over his shoulder, directing it into Chris's face. Before the bat connected, Chris threw the knife he'd taken off the skinny guy. It embedded itself to the hilt in the guy's shoulder and he dropped to his knees, screaming. Chris snatched up the baseball bat and held it over his head in a Kenpo stance when one of the chefs ran at the other guys. The chef sent the thug staggering into the road, just missing a car that had slowed to watch the fight.

In the takeaway, the smaller chef had another witcher against the wall with a cleaver pressed against his throat. The old man was on the phone, gesturing wildly as he spoke.

"Spyro!" Chris shouted over the alarms and cries of injured witchers and ran down the street with four witchfinders after him. People had come out onto the streets and Chris dodged around them as he ran. Few of the gang could keep up with him and the stragglers at the back soon gave up.

Chris lost the crowd and slowed to a fast walk and looked around to get his bearings. He was in a residential area, houses and blocks of flats. His best chance of getting back to the B&B was to walk along the beach until he got to where he was eating. He'd know his way back from there.

He'd just got his breath back when a car crammed with witchers squealed out from the side road, followed by a white van which braked first and several witchers tumbled out. Chris started running again and took a right turn as the four passengers jumped out and joined the gang. Chris found himself heading down a dark alley to a dead end. Someone behind him laughed.

Armed with baseball bats and knives, the gang lumped up

around the entrance to the alley and started to edge forwards, shouting and taunting him, goading each other forwards. Behind them, the car and van arrived to block the end of the street. Chris knelt down and clipped Spyro's lead on.

Lights flashed on in windows up and down the alley and cast a pale glow.

"Hey, leave the kid alone," someone shouted.

"I'm calling the police," a woman called.

"Shut up, bitch," a younger voice said, "go on, guys, waste the mage scumbag."

"Timmy Austin," the same woman called, "you wait until your mother gets home."

"Slapper won't be back till morning."

"Keep it down, people are trying to sleep."

Spyro pulled on the lead and Chris dug his heels in and pulled her back. Ahead of him, the crowd parted and an older, overweight witcher pushed his way through, slapping a baseball bat against a fat palm. He took a couple of steps forward and stopped when a light flashed on over to his right. He wore a tight T-shirt with a Union Jack that had a crucifix in the centre. Ugly faded tattoos covered his arms. "You and your dog are dead meat, mage." He spat out a heavy globule of phlegm and smashed the baseball bat against a bin, which set Spyro barking and snarling as she pulled against the lead.

Chris gripped the lead and backed away. He might land a few punches, but there were way too many of them. The big guy continued his advance and the gang followed slowly behind. Chris backed up against the commercial bins along the back wall and raised his hands.

"Watch out!" someone cried.

Chris moved his hands about and the gang backed off, their eyes fixed on him. He stepped forward and the gang stepped back. The big guy eyed him suspiciously and an ugly grin spread across his face. "The jerk doesn't know how to do the magic. C'mon, get him."

The gang exchanged uncertain glances and moved forwards again.

"Poor darko, mage," the big guy mocked, "won't have a chance to do your first magic."

Chris shifted to a Kenpo defensive stance and the big guy sneered, and shook his head, "You got no way, mate."

A way! That's what he'd been thinking. Those Tai-Chi moves, all those ancient dances; Morris, Native American, Hindu, African Shamans, witch doctors. Their hand movements followed similar patterns to the winding paths and streams you moved along in the Elegance game. Was it really that simple?

Spyro bared her teeth and snarled at the goon with the baseball bat. Chris dropped the lead and stepped on it. He just had to do the right spell, but which bloody one? He knew them all and every one of them now crowded his thoughts.

Chris fixed his gaze on the gang and reached out, flexing his fingers. If this didn't work, he'd be well and truly screwed. "Gorumek," he said, and the word resonated deep into him. For an instant he felt hollow, and wind swept through him, leaving a strange tingling that gathered and rippled along his outstretched arm. The energy condensed into a tension pushing at his wrist. This was probably what a cola bottle felt like after a serious shake. He scrunched his face and struggled to hold his hand steady. He instinctively lowered his two middle fingers to his palm, pushing them down with his thumb to hold the energy in.

Lights in windows sparked and blinked out and he ignored the shouts of people around him. It was working; well, something was happening. His eyes widened in astonishment and the rabble ahead of him stopped and looked around, mistaking each other's hesitancy as the effect of a spell. Then the big guy shoved the person next to him so hard he fell against his friends, almost knocking three of them over. "You morons," he snarled and swung the baseball bat in a figure of eight, "here's my magic."

Chris, his face tight in concentration, slid one foot back and shifted his weight to a 60-40 stance and swept his hands through the air. "Duerma yolichidem." He moved his fingers in a slow sequence, careful to lift and lower the right ones in the right order, like he was playing a tune, then thrust out his palm. Flashes of yellow, red and gold light sparked and bloomed around him, lighting up the alley in a cascade of colour. The gang panicked and took several steps back with fearful cries.

Everything went quiet for a few seconds then an expanding sensation rose in his chest and poured rapidly out across his body and down his arms. It felt like each arm had been thrust into a gushing stream of pure, bright, feather-light water.

"Stay, you idiots, it's just bloody party lights."

"Yeah, you wish," Chris said and narrowed his eyes. Moving his fingers he attuned to draw down, mould and direct the energy he was reaching out for, and found it. Again he punched out, palm open, "Schymn-di!" he shouted. A different energy; this time it gathered around his hand and the release felt as if someone had yanked a glove off him. At first, nothing happened and the gang relaxed, a few laughed nervously. The big guy and another older guy stepped towards him, this time a little more cautiously, glancing at each other.

Chris swore under his breath and kept his Kenpo defensive stance, ready to block the first few punches, and at least take a couple of those thugs down with him. Then, a soft, hollow 'boom' filled the alley and a pulsing bubble of swirling shadows the size of a basketball formed several feet above the ground between him and the thug. The alley fell silent and the bubble expanded.

"Is that it?" the big guy snarled. "Party lights and a bubble? Some magician you are. Man, are we gonna beat the crap out of you."

"Nah," Chris said, "I don't think so."

The bubble pulsed and sent soft, warm waves of air rippling around the alley and grew to the size of a car. The gang took a step back, swearing and pointing at the globe which expanded again to the size of a transit van, almost reaching from one side of the alley to the other. Lightning flashes burst and curved across the surface of the orb as a light shower of rain began to fall and sink into it, slowing to a syrupy crawl.

A woman at one of the windows above screamed, then more frightened voices rose from the buildings either side of the alley; then objects hit the ground around Chris. Bottles and cans – still heavy and full of food – mugs, flowerpots, anything people could get their hands on. Metal objects landed on the orb and exploded into crackling shafts of white light that snaked up into the night sky, lighting up the alley. Chris lifted his left hand and muttered, "Nefarishm," and the contents of the exploding cans spewed out over the gang members.

Shouts filled the air; 'Murderer, killer, demon, terrorist filth, mage scum.' A bottle hit his shoulder. Chris swore and waved a hand over his head, feeling again the ripple of smooth energy along his arm. It was impossible to tell which came first, the incantation, the spell or the feeling. Magic seemed to be timeless and it was only his mind putting it into sequence, "Kafaqudma," he said and a wide, translucent shield formed several inches above his head and spread to form a wide circle. Objects struck it and shattered into sprays of electric red light, drawing gasps and more angry shouts.

The bubble settled on the ground and rolled slowly towards him. "He's screwed it up," someone shouted someone above him. The big commercial bins behind Chris rattled on their wheels. Cans and glass from the broken bottles shuddered noisily across the wet tarmac. Chris scooped Spyro up in his arms, "It's okay, Spyro." He stroked her head and Spyro calmed immediately.

Street lights and shop signs refracted and curved through the turning orb, bouncing a surreal, twisted glow around the alley. Chris pushed a hand towards the bubble and an indentation appeared in its smooth surface; then the thing folded into itself until it had turned inside out. The gang watched mesmerised until it started to roll towards them.

Half the gang turned and ran, almost knocking the other guys over. The big guy with the baseball bat swore as he pulled out a pistol and fired at Chris. The bullet hit the bubble and slowed to a syrupy crawl inside, trailing a long, thin, spiralling tail.

"You wankers," the guy bellowed, "you scared of a poxy slow-mo bubble? Get around the bloody thing and waste that filthy mage."

A wry smile crossed Chris's face, everything on the map, in the atlas, now made sense. Curling his fingers, he waved a hand through the air, faced his palm down and made a sweeping motion, "Yolisil." The bubble floated upwards, pulsing like a monstrous heart while rain streamed over it like curling veins then sank into the pulsating sphere.

The gang laughed and jeered while the orb continued to rise up above the rooftops of the block either side of the alley. They rushed forward and Chris slapped his hands together then opened them, palms down, spreading his arms out. His fingers moved in a precise, elegant motion as if playing a piano. "Schym dyg Baush La," he sang out and high above the gang, the bubble stopped beating and plummeted down; the mixture of accumulated rain and debris crashing down over the gang.

The gang cowered under the shower, swearing and crying out in fear. Chris smiled as the bubble's jellied remains pooled around their feet like thick glue. "Kokuruma," he said and twitched his fingers. Fumes rose from the sticky gunk and the trapped thugs grimaced and covered their mouths at the awful stench. Almost all of them threw up, covering the front of their t-shirts and jeans.

Chris folded his arms and nodded at the helpless gang, "Witchhunt your way out of that, girls." Another bottle missed his shoulder by inches and smashed on the floor; the umbrella spell had faded and more objects fell around him. Chris waved a hand over his head, "Buyaseniste." The household missiles slid round through the air and fell onto the gang. Ignoring the shouts and screams, he gripped Spyro's lead and jogged past the gang and out of the alley.

Chris dropped Spyro's lead, grabbed the baseball bat, hopped onto the bonnet of the gang's car and stomped around on it, clambering onto the roof and jumping up and down on it. Swinging the baseball bat, he smashed the windscreen of the van, then with another couple of swings, sent the wing mirrors flying. Finished with wrecking their car, he threw the baseball bat at the gang and jogged away. With Spyro running along beside him he ducked into a dark doorway when he heard sirens. Three police cars screeched round the corner into the main road, sirens wailing, blue lights flashing in the drizzle. The cars shot past and skidded to a halt at the end of the alley.

With more confidence, he grabbed Spyro's lead and pictured his room in the Bed and Breakfast. He took a deep breath and gestured, "Evjarimiq." Again, electric colours flashed around him and for an instant he was falling through darkness, then he reappeared in the bedroom of the B&B. Spyro yelped and crawled under the bed.

He felt strangely calm, almost as if the teleporting from one place to another somehow left behind whatever he was feeling at the place he'd just left. Then his face broke into a broad grin, "Oh... my... God," he said slowly, "this is totally awesome."

Spyro crept out and jumped up at him and Chris knelt down and stroked her. With the big grin still on his face, he lay back on the bed. "I did it, Spyro," he whispered, "I'm a sorcerer. If only..." His voice fell away and he leaned back against the headboard. If only Granddad could see what he could do.

The TV was on downstairs and the old guy had turned the volume up "... is coming in of a major magic incident in Brighton, for so long believed to be the safest place in Britain since the deadly purge thirty years ago. Now, the seaside town has become the latest to witness a conflict involving a magician and members of the public. Lycus military forces have been mobilised and are converging on the area."

Chris punched down on the bed, "Oh crap!" How the hell was he going to find Frankie now? Spyro sensed his anxiety and nuzzled him for comfort. "It's all right, they don't know where we are. We'll stay here and get out of town in the morning, eh?"

Downstairs the old guy was grumbling about something.

Chris switched on the cable box and TV. People in suits and smart clothes sat round a curved table, a few were chatting. Chris left the sound on to drown out the mess in his head. "... audio evidence that strongly suggests reaver presence is increasing, and patterns are beginning to emerge in their routes. Some experts believe their movements are becoming more organised. In the light of events earlier this evening, we discuss the increasing calls for more investment in magic detection, containment and research. On our 'Truth be Told' panel tonight is Professor Isabelle Cross, from Bath University, a renowned historian and researcher of magic and magicians. The professor is also a major donor and patron of the Give Blood charity." The presenter smiled at the professor and said, "No pun intended, professor." A ripple of polite laughter rose from the audience and the professor smiled back and nodded.

The presenter continued. "To her right is the acclaimed journalist and documentary film maker Danny Inglis. Over on my left is the Lycus UK director of Magicians Assessment, Registration and Sentencing Unit, and Government advisor Boris De Gruer. Beside Mr De Gruer is retired general and member of the cross-party advisory panel on reaver containment, Lord Brian Gascoigne; and finally we have with us tonight The Bishop of Worcester, the Right Reverend Alistair Cooper. His recent publication, *Do Magicians Have Souls?*, caused some controversy in political circles."

Chris drifted in and out of sleep through the panel discussion, then the news. "Three hundred and fiftieth satellite... Atlantic... his grandfather for the past twelve years, explosion... 208 people ... Three guards... prison van... fire... Lizzy Francis, aged seventeen, escaped from secure unit... still at large after two weeks. Possible sighting in Brighton. Raised as a boy until her capture..."

She what? Chris sat up. Behind the news presenter was the same photo of Lizzy he'd seen in the police station. "Police warn the public not to approach her but to call the police immediately."

The photo of Lizzy with her shaved head filled the screen. Chris leaned forward. He peered at the image and his eyes widened. Frankie?

The camera switched back to the newscaster. Someone handed her a sheet of paper. "We have an update on the major magic incident in Brighton. Reports are emerging that Christopher Asten, wanted for questioning about yesterday morning's major terrorist attack, may be involved. Police want to remind people he is extremely dangerous and urge the public not to approach him but to dial 999 immediately. It's 11:30, now for the local news and weather in your area. Remember, keep your curtains closed and whatever you hear, don't look out."

Something pulled at his attention and Chris turned to the window. He switched the light off and edged along the wall and peered out. A small gang of half a dozen teenagers and men armed with baseball bats, crowbars and knives strode past, swearing and shouting threats. They disappeared round the corner, and seconds later the shadows in a doorway rippled like a stone dropped into a pool and a black woman with a short Afro stepped out onto the pavement. She watched the last of the gang jog round the corner and seeing no one was in sight, turned her attention to the window where Chris stood. A soft wind swirled around the room and gathered in the corner and a woman's voice said, "They're coming for you, the old man saw your face on TV and called Lycus. Get out, now." The woman lifted a hand and moved it around her head as she stepped back into the dark. Again the shadows rippled like liquid and the street fell silent and empty.

"Crap." Chris grabbed his jacket and stuffed everything into his pockets. "Here Sypro!" he clipped her lead on. He imagined

Lizzy's face and moved his hands, speaking the incantation. "Evjarimiq Ghelyor Sahami," he said as the door crashed inwards.

A strange calm washed over Chris as a blinding flash and thick smoke flooded the room. Thin beams of red targeting lasers cut through the smoky room as it quickly curled into a bubble and shrank away.

Chapter Eight

Lizzy woke up hungry, showered, dressed and headed downstairs. No bicycles in the hallway: that meant Patsy and Simon had already set off for work. With the house to herself, Lizzy turned the cable box and television on and the screen filled with a crackling grey haze. It was early morning and cold lightning was still messing up electrics everywhere; that explained why the street was quiet. She went into the kitchen and made herself a bowl of cereal and sat down to eat. Then she grabbed Hiro's lead and went out to the garden to find Hiro sitting under the tree trying to stare out a large raven perched on one of the lower branches. Cracks of lightning slid silently across a bare sky and the raven flew off.

"Fancy a walk, Hiro?"

Hiro looked over his shoulder, seemed to think about it, then trotted over to her, wagging his tail. "Come on, then," Lizzy said, and looked back to make sure he was following as she headed back into the house.

Mrs Wilson, the neighbour, was at the upstairs window and they waved to each other.

The lightning faded as Lizzy and Hiro returned from their walk in Withdean Park. A few houses from home, a mother came down the path, pulling a child in tears, "I don't want to go, Mummy, the mages might get me."

Lizzy stopped to let them pass and watched the woman lift the screaming child into the car, while the boy kicked against the door frame. The woman looked apologetically at Lizzy. "The attack last night," she said, "it's got him terrified."

"What attack?" Lizzy said.

"Magician attacked a Chinese takeaway and a group of people who tried to stop him."

"Why.."

The child continued to resist and the woman gave Lizzy an apologetic shrug. "Sorry," she said, strapping the screaming child into the seat and closing the door. She then got in and, yanking the door shut, drove off.

Why would a magician attack a takeaway, and who would be stupid enough to try to take him on? None of it made sense. Lizzy quickened her pace home.

Closing the front door, she unclipped Hiro's lead and removed the harness then rushed into the living room to switch on the cable box. While she waited for it to boot up, Hiro sat looking at her, willing her to give him his breakfast.

"Hiro, I know they fed you first thing this morning, go and lie down."

Hiro skulked over to his basket and flopped into it to stare at her with doleful eyes. Lizzy tuned in to BBC news and a photo of the wrecked Chinese restaurant. The headline read, 'Magician battles gang in Brighton. Police and Lycus special forces concentrate search for terrorist suspect. Coming so soon after the explosion in London and the riots in Manchester, security forces are increasing their presence in all major cities.'

Lizzy jolted upright when the phone rang. She stared at it for several seconds then picked it up, "Hello," she said, nervously.

"Lizzy?" The voice was barely a whisper.

"Simon? Where are you? Have you seen the news?"

"I'm at the hostel. The whole building has been locked down. A Lycus mobile test lab is outside. They're testing everyone with the new tech, staff too. We can't get out. There are cops and Lycus everywhere. People are panicking."

She could hear the faint sound of murmuring and people crying. "Can't you use magic to get out?"

"I can't leave, I'm not alone. People need me. Lycus are killing anyone who tries to run or avoid the test. Leave. Try and get to the waypoint in Whitehill Lane. Get out and lie low for a couple of days then go to London and head for the portal in North Finchley, Lodge Lane. Find..." A smashing of wood and glass then the rapid snapping of gunfire drowned out his voice. Then someone swore,

"Nobody move. Don't let him get away."

Screams shouts and the rush of footsteps was followed by silence as the line went dead.

Shocked, Lizzy dropped the phone. She ran to the hallway, flung her jacket on, grabbed her helmet and stopped just before she yanked open the front door. She took a deep breath and opened the door slowly, stepped out, turned, locked up, then casually walked over to the motorbike.

Mrs Wilson, the neighbour, stood at the front door, chatting to the neighbour on the other side.

"Hi, Mrs Wilson," Lizzy said. "How are you today?"

"Hello, Maria," Mrs Wilson replied. "Isn't it terrible, that magician terrorist hiding here. Who knows what he was planning?"

"It is awful," Lizzy said. "I can't believe anybody could be so cruel."

"Oh, I know, I was just telling Mrs Siddiqui. Where are you off to?"

"It's such a nice day," Lizzy said. "Thought I'd go for a ride, get away from this awful news."

Mrs Wilson nodded, "I don't blame you." She touched Mrs Siddiqui on the arm lightly, "Look at that girl's hair, it's so beautiful, like it's made of light." Mrs Wilson turned to address Lizzy, "Maria, you really should let it grow you know."

Lizzy smiled, "I might give it a try, Mrs Wilson."

Mrs Wilson smiled back, "Mind how you go."

"I will, thank you," Lizzy was about to set off but stopped. "Oh, Mrs Wilson, will you keep an eye on Hiro for me please?"

"Hiro?" Mrs Wilson said. "Why I'd love to, he's such a darling, loves my roast chicken he does."

"That's great, thanks ever so much." Lizzy unhooked the side door key from her key chain and gave it to Mrs Wilson.

Mrs Wilson took the key and waved it in front of Lizzy's face, "I've got a good mind to keep the little dear."

"I bet he'd love that," Lizzy said. "Thanks again, Mrs Wilson, bye, Mrs Siddiqui." Lizzy put her helmet on, breathed a sigh of relief and set off, sticking to narrow country lanes. Only once did she stop, at a crossroads, where she pulled in against an old wooden gate behind some bushes. Seconds later a convoy of Lycus armoured trucks and combat vehicles rumbled past.

An encampment of witchfinders had settled in the field where the portal stood. Visible only to her, it appeared as a hazy oval in the line of trees and bushes that marked the edge of a wood beyond the field. The portal shimmered around fifty yards from where the bulk of the witchfinders had gathered. Lizzy slowed along the narrow road to the field. A woman dressed all in denim and smoking a roll-up waved her over.

Lizzy lifted the visor, "Hi, what's going on?"

The woman took the foul-smelling roll-up from her mouth, "Rumour is there's a magic door around here somewhere. Filthy mages were using it to come here from London. We reckon they might try to escape this way."

"Good thing you're here," Lizzy said.

"Bloody right, girl." A man had approached her from the side. Like the woman, he wore blue denim jeans and short denim jacket. He held a rifle, which he turned and admired while he spoke, "Can't wait to shoot some mage scum."

"Seen any mages?" the woman asked Lizzy. "People acting suspicious?"

"No, sorry," Lizzy said.

"Nice bike," the man said, "where you heading?" He eyed Lizzy suspiciously and the woman nudged him.

"Lay off the girl, Col, since when did mages need motorbikes?"

"Well, they might."

"They might my arse, give over." The woman tutted knowingly at Lizzy and shook her head.

Lizzy pointed east, "I'm going to Lewes, got friends there."

The woman nodded. "Makes sense; if those mages and Lycus face off, who knows what'll happen."

Lizzy rode off, worried about the witchfinders. She had to do something. Any magician who came through there was going to get lynched.

After a short distance, she spotted a disused barn and headed for it up a tarmac lane cracked by tree roots and overgrown with weeds She rode in and managed to lift the broken door and lean it against the opening, blocking the gaps on the side with old wooden and cardboard boxes.

A window on the upper platform of the cast a long beam of dusted sunlight across to the opposite wall. Climbing the ladder, she stepped gingerly across the rotted platform to close the window. The field of witchfinders were visible in the distance.

With all the spells she learned as a child now fully recalled, she opened the window, summoned the heavy wind and climbed out. She drifted slowly to the ground and with a curl of her hands and slight twitch of her fingers summoned a Swift-dancer, something she often did as a child. The slender being, now half the size of Lizzy, had golden skin and radiant black hair. She smiled up at Lizzy through fiery glowing eyes and unfurled her six, long gossamer wings.

"The big oak tree please," Lizzy said, pointing towards the field, and held out her hands. The Swift-dancer grabbed Lizzy's hand and the two girls leapt into the air laughing.

The wind sang as it rippled through the Swift-Dancer's wings with a rapid, flute-like sound and the creature sang with it, her voice in perfect harmony. With a laugh, Lizzy joined in.

It took them less than a minute to arrive at the Tree. The two girls bowed to each other then the Swift-Dancer disappeared.

Lizzy took in a deep breath and strode towards the gate that led into the field.

Most of the tent flaps were now open and there were more people wandering about, many had rifles and shotguns. They'd shoot at the shoulders and arms of magicians, preventing them from being able to cast spells.

The couple Lizzy had met earlier smiled as she approached them. The man had the rifle slung over he shoulder.

"See," the woman said, "I told you she was one of us."

"I'm not going to lie to you," Lizzy said, "because I can't."

Her words stopped the couple in their tracks.

"You bitch," The man said, attracting the attention of several people nearby as he swung his rifle down to point it at Lizzy.

"She's a witch, a mage." Shouted the woman and similar cries rose from the field around them.

Lizzy was close enough to simply step forward and, grabbing the barrel of the rifle twisted it away from her while the fingers of her free hand danced across the surface, "Slahals, hep siatesh." she said, loud enough for everyone to hear. A ripple of warm, sky blue liquid quickly spread across the rifle and instantly all the other weapons in the field took on the same hue. Painful cries and the clunk of weapons falling to the ground spread around her.

Guns, rifles, machetes, crossbows all turned into solid, lumps as they hit the ground.

The man dived at Lizzy and she stepped to one side and whacked him on the back, sending him face down on the floor. The woman stared at her fearfully then stepped back.

Lizzy raised her hands into the air and with a deep voice called "Usooree maash, hevalusha." A howling storm of glowing ribbons swirled across the field, gathering up the tents. Occupants were tipped out onto the wet soil. The witchfinders ran for cover against the hedges while the tentacles ripped and twisted the tents into an ugly knotted pile in the far corner of the field

When it was all over, Lizzy stood in the centre of the field, moving her hands and guiding the ribbons through the crowds huddled in small groups around the outside of the field. The ribbons glided over clothes, slicing and cutting without touching skin but still raising fearful cries. Then the ribbons turned and flowed towards Lizzy and wrapped around her so for a few seconds she looked like a mummy; then she disappeared.

She stood there for a couple of minutes while, one by one, people peeled away from the hedge until the field filled with people foraging around for the few possessions not tangled up in the pile of tents and camping equipment at the end of the field. Others had made their way to the enormous pile and began pulling at ropes and poles while looking over their shoulders. Some people swore and kicked at the lumps of metal that used to be their weapons.

Lizzy left the field and walked back to the barn started up the bike and headed for the portal again. A simple spell shattered the gate and she accelerated through and rode straight to the portal.

Going through felt like being both sucked and squeezed by a strong wind. She came out in a copse in Forty Hill near Maiden's Brook and braked inches from a fallen log. A narrow track led to a road which after half a mile reached a junction of a main road and more traffic. Spotting a café, she rode over to it and parked up.

People sat at plastic tables eating sandwiches and large rolls, drinking from big mugs of tea while a CD player in the corner played country music. She ordered some tea and scrambled eggs on toast then sat at a table and took out the postcard. A photograph now appeared on what used to be the blank side. An empty car park with a couple of vans parked against the far wall. Down one side of the postcard was printed the hours and parking fees for Lodge Lane Car Park, Barnet. Then the image shifted to a tiny concrete block with a stubby building on it stuck in the middle of the ocean. The last place she wanted to be. Lizzy hated the sea, hated boats. Chris always teased her about it.

The waitress, a middle-aged woman with thick straw hair tied back in a bun, brought Lizzy's food, put it down and said, "Do you want to borrow a pen?"

"What?" Lizzy said.

"A pen, you've been staring at that blank postcard long enough to write a book."

"Oh," Lizzy said, realising the woman couldn't see the picture. She put the card away. "No, I'm okay thanks, I'll do it later." She looked down at the food. "This looks good, thanks."

Lizzy finished eating and headed for the Finchley portal, passing allotments set up on old battlegrounds along the way. Arriving in North Finchley, she turned off the High Road and drove the short distance down Lodge Lane to the car park and pulled over. She locked up the bike and leaned against it, surveying the car park for some clue as to where the portal might be. Then she spotted a magician, a couple of years older than her, come up the alley into the car park. Lizzy gaped in astonishment as the man walked along the side of the wall behind some vans and didn't reappear. Lizzy took a quick look around then headed to the same spot.

Behind the van, an old wooden door with a faded brass handle and mortice-lock stood in a wall. Lizzy took hold of the handle and turned it. A powerful gust of wind swept her forwards and she leaned back and threw her hands up only to find herself in a big, circular room. Around the room, thick windows overlooked a churning sea.

Lamps hung from a low ceiling, lighting up tables covered in maps over which shapes shapes moved slowly. Groups of three or four magicians, all with weary expressions, pored over the maps.

Two people approached her. One was a grunged-out African woman; ripped jeans, check shirt, Doc Marten boots; and beside her a big, broad, red-bearded guy in dungarees and cowboy boots, a baseball cap pulled down over long, ginger, scraggy hair.

"Haven't seen you before," the woman said.

Lizzy gaped speechless at the woman magician; a dozen questions caught in her throat.

"Baz, Kathy," a voice said behind them and they both stepped away to stand either side of an older woman in a wheelchair. She wore a pair of army fatigues and a loose-fitting green T-shirt. On her hands was a pair of black workout gloves with a red lining. Her upper body strength was clearly visible, neck and arms firm and developed from wheeling herself around and whatever else she had to do to get by on her own. She had piercing blue-grey eyes and a head of red hair. "Get rid of the guise spell, please," she said in a Scots accent.

Lizzy rubbed a hand over her face, revealing her true features but kept the spell that gave her short, blonde hair.

"That'll do," the woman in the wheelchair said, "I'm Suzie Emerson, this is Kathy and Baz."

"Suzie, Ozzy mentioned you. He said you were the very first new magician."

Suzie dismissed the comment with a wave of a hand, "I've heard about you too." She looked from the bearded guy to Kathy, "Baz, Kathy, thanks, I'll handle this, you can get back to work."

Lizzy followed Suzie between the tables placed in lines around the room; she couldn't help but stare at the other girl magicians, all older than Lizzy. So many of them. How did they not get detected when they were born

"The other girls – I don't understand."

"They were born in the Enclave."

Suzie bumped the wheelchair over the power and network cables and stopped at the laptop placed in the middle of the long desk.

"What's going on?" Lizzy said.

"Normally this is a place of learning, where magicians share spells, learn about the fundamentals of how magic came from other realms, the war on magic and choose which group to harmonise with. Our plans for a rescue of the girls from Salem have all been put on hold since the explosion in London and the raids. Now we're looking for magicians who have managed to not get caught or killed by Lycus. The events of the last few days have forced everyone into hiding and wrecked our plans."

"For the rescue?" Lizzy said.

"Aye, that's right," Suzie nodded.

"Do you think it was one of us that blew the block up?"

"Media says a magician, Chris Asten, is the prime suspect." Suzie shook her head, "I don't believe it."

"Chris?" Lizzy said, visibly shocked.

"You know him?" Suzie said. "How is that possible?"

"From when I was little, our families were friends."

"So you weren't taken away to Salem at birth?"

"No. How do you know it wasn't him, or his granddad?"

"I knew his grandfather." Suzie paused and a sad look briefly crossed her face. "I sent a team to retrieve his body before Lycus got there and made all trace of him disappear."

"Can they do that now?"

"These past few years Lycus have been using some strange dark magic; a kind we've never seen before. Someone or something is helping them."

"Ozzy said vampires or Shadow Fae."

"That would make sense. We just need proof."

"What about Chris, can you find him?"

"Kid seems to be travelling around causing trouble everywhere he pops up. A car stolen a few days ago was found in Manchester. His fingerprints were all over it. He's not being careful."

"Do you know where he is?"

"Not yet," Suzie gestured to the room, "we're still searching. My guess is he's using a crystal to conceal his whereabouts." She pointed to a large canvas map contained in a dark wooden frame. Shapes moved around it, sometimes a tiny creature, dragons and other magical winged creatures Lizzy didn't recognise, would rise up and sweep across the surface of the map before sinking back into it. "Our priority is rescuing our own people. We bring them here. Most of the rooms are full of injured magicians or sympathisers who evaded the Lycus raids."

"We're in the middle of the sea."

"No Man's Land, in the Solent. It's the safest place for magicians, thanks to sea reavers tearing into anything not made of wood and pitch." Suzie pointed to a table where Kathy and another grunge teenager, a young Asian woman, stood over a map. The young women gave them the thumbs-up. Kathy took the Asian woman's hand and the two women disappeared.

"What... how... where did they go?"

"It's called folding. Kathy and Angela have left to bring some people back. Those girls are the best, lose only an hour at most."

"Folding?"

Suzie picked up a sheet of paper and put a dot at each end then gave the pencil to Lizzy. "What's the shortest distance between the two?"

Lizzy drew a line from one dot to the other.

Suzie shook her head. "For straights, maybe." She folded the sheet so the two dots touched then jabbed the nib of the pencil through both holes. "Folding," she said and put the pencil and paper down. "You're welcome to stay."

Lizzy looked out across the wild waves surrounding them and shook her head. "No thanks."

"We have portals to all parts of the country too," Suzie added.

Before Lizzy could reply, two men, twins, both wearing denim jeans and leather biker jackets covered in zips, came over. "Suzie, a word," the bald one said while the other brother scowled at Lizzy.

"Excuse me," Suzie said and wheeled across the room to a drinks machine, the twins following either side of her. They spoke for a while then Suzie gestured to Baz and Kathy and they joined her. Suzie, Baz and Kathy left the room and the twins went over to their table and, seeing Suzie leave the room, came over to Lizzy.

One of the twins eyeballed Lizzy. "No one's ever escaped," he said, "and there's a treatment centre in the prison. So why did they decide to move you?"

"They were taking me to the RAT centre."

"Why should we believe you?" the bald one said.

Lizzy let out a laugh that made the other people in the room look round, "Seriously?"

"Yes," the other twin said, bluntly. "You could be working for them."

Working for them, the people who killed her parents. Lizzy clenched her fists. "You don't know what you're talking about."

"We know all right," the bald twin said.

"You shouldn't even be here," the other added.

"Yeah?" Lizzy's eyes flashed angrily, "what are you going to do about it?" She raised her fists. Alarm shot across the twins' faces and they quickly stepped back. Baz appeared from somewhere and grabbed Lizzy's wrist. "Easy, kid."

Lizzy looked down to see crimson sparks sizzling out from between the fingers of her clenched fist. She opened her palm and glowered at the twins, her eyes a cold electric-blue.

"Lizzy," Suzie had arrived with Kathy, "We're all under a lot of stress, let's just slow down eh?"

Lizzy nodded and stepped back.

"Let's not start suspecting all newcomers. Paul, Dexter, get back to work please, I'll deal with this."

The twin glared at Lizzy then went back to their table.

"Come," Suzie said, "we can talk in my office."

"What's their problem?"

"Anger, it's too soon and they haven't forgiven their parents' killers, it's understandable but their grief and anger is stifling their capacity to attune."

Lizzy glanced back at the twins and thought of her own parents.

"Some don't want to let go," Suzie said, "it defines them. Did you see much of Salem, could you draw a diagram?"

"Yes."

"Excellent, I'll get you some pens."

Lizzy had drawn the outline of the pentagon-shaped prison when there was a knock on the door. It was Baz. "Suzie," he said, "sorry to interrupt but you should deal with this." He nodded beyond the open door to where a group of people had gathered around Suzie's table outside, the twins were in the centre.

Suzie sighed and shook her head. "Baz, wait here with Lizzy."

Suzie wheeled out and Baz closed the door, "Sorry about this, kid."

"It's the twins stirring things up, isn't it?" Lizzy said.

"It's been hell for them, they lost their whole family, gunned down."

"Not like they're the only ones," Lizzy said, her voice cold, "they should be old enough to deal with it."

"You mean forgive, understand what hate is doing to them?"

Lizzy said nothing and Ben put a hand gently on her shoulder, "Don't let their pain rub off on you. They're still hurting." Baz glanced down at her, "A lot of us are."

"I guess," Lizzy said. Waves crashed over each other and smashed into the walls beyond the window.

"Hey," Baz said, "don't beat yourself up over it. Besides, it's not a bad thing to show you don't scare easily. Most of the girls took your side."

Kathy came into the room, smiled at Lizzy and whispered something to Baz. Baz nodded. "Come with me," he said to Lizzy after Kathy left.

"Some magicians have weird ideas about our phrase,

'everything is connected'. They think Alumbrados arranged for you to escape. Some even think they brainwashed you, put some kind of instructions in your head."

"Well that's just stupid," Lizzy said, "how is that even possible with people like us?"

Baz shrugged, "Even magicians don't always think straight when they feel threatened or under stress. Like I said, the raids and killings have hit us hard, there's a lot of vulnerable people here, most are too scared to leave."

"Fine, they can stay, I'll leave. This is worse than the Unit."

Baz gave her a startled look, "Hey, slow down, we're all magicians here, we'll sort it out."

"People are turning against each other because of me. I started this vibe, it'll be easiest if I leave. I want to go anyway."

"Are you sure? The boys will probably see sense after a few days."

"I'm sure, tell them I get it, besides, I don't feel right here."

"Okay, sorry about this, Lizzy."

Lizzy took Baz's hand, "Thanks," she said and pointed to a misty door shape in the wall several feet from where they stood. The car park and vans were visible as a hazy image, "Is that a way out?"

"Suzie's waypoint." Baz sighed. "Your disguise and ID are perfect, but watch your back, trust your gut feeling. Listen, there's a hideout not far from here on the high street, an old boarded up bookshop. There's a sign like this on the bottom of the metal plate over covering the door."

He traced the sign on her palm and Lizzy nodded, "Got it, thanks."

They hugged and Lizzy stepped through the portal to reappear behind the vans and went back to the 'zuki. She rode down to the High Road. Passing a row of closed-down shops, Lizzy double-checked the small 'hide-out' mark on the door of the bookshop. She turned the corner and then up the alley between the rear of the shops and ruins of what used to be a housing block. Steering slowly around and over the debris, trash and clumps of tall weeds, she pulled up outside the bookshop. After clearing away some rubble she opened the back door then went over to the delivery entrance, slid up the shutter and wheeled the bike up the narrow ramp and into the dusty, bare delivery area. Large boards covered the shopfront windows and door, blocking out all the light. She closed the shutter and sent the shop into darkness.

Lizzy took off her helmet and muttered an incantation. Again the spaces between realms opened up along her arm. She moved her fingers and a spark appeared and grew to a golden, golf ball sized orb. The tiny Sun floated upwards and filled the room with a soft light. Constellations of fine dust, raised by the bike being wheeled in, hung in the air around her. Lizzy muttered another spell and a soft burst of light bloomed from the sun, dispelling the dust. Stepping around a couple of cardboard boxes, Lizzy went further into the shop. The ground floor was a mess of boxes and damaged books. The tiny sun followed as she headed up the stairs; it floated a couple of feet up behind her head and cast a light shadow ahead of her.

An old cash register and phone stood on a counter by the stairs. Narrow ply-boards covered the windows at the far end of the gloomy room. Thin shafts of light cut through the cracks between the boards and fell onto a single mattress leaning against the wall. A short exploration revealed a small storage room, a toilet and a small kitchen. A torch, several cans of food and a couple of bottles of water stood on the counter by the sink. She went back out and, taking her jacket off, pulled the mattress from the wall so it fell to the floor. The sound of children laughing rushed past outside. Lizzy sat on the mattress and picked up the book resting on a thick cardboard box: *Science in Service of the Global Community* by Ray Ruya. She threw the book across the quiet, bare room and began to cry.

Chapter Nine

Chris and Spyro flew through a void filled by ghostly spheres soaked in vague shapes and pale colours. It felt like a water-slide. The current carried them forwards, curving round the spheres until, in the distance, one particular sphere lit up and took on a more solid form. As Chris got closer, the sphere came into sharper focus than the others and a room took shape inside. When it looked like they were going to crash into it, Chris raised his arms to cover his face and found himself standing on solid ground in the middle of blinding cascade of colours and flashes of light. Spyro pressed herself against his shin and he knelt down to comfort her. The lights quickly faded and a shadowy figure rose slowly from the ground several yards away.

***

The subtle shift of aetheric energy woke Lizzy to what looked like a shower of shattered rainbows. She got to her feet and stepped back from the flashes and raised her palms to the figure now standing several feet from her. She concentrated and drew her left hand back, moving her fingers to leave glowing traces in the air then she thrust her open palm forward, "Xirillima." and a spray of white sparks flew out

She gasped when the person swept his hand up and say "Dibashilim." The sparks struck an invisible wall and splashed out across the surface then dissolved away.

"Effele zunesh," she said and a golden orb formed a few feet above the guy's head. The man arced his hand up, and the shield extended over his head but the orb didn't move. It hovered above him like a spotlight sun, shining a white light over him whilst keeping the rest of the room in darkness.

"Chris?" her face broke into a broad smile.

"Yeah," Chris raised a hand over his eyes. "Get this light off my face, will you?"

"Wait." She had to be sure. "What was my pet snake's name?"

"Your snake? Sif, it was a corn snake. Now will you switch this bloody light off?"

The beam shrank back into a soft, glowing sun, and hovered above his head. He'd grown too, slightly taller than her; with the same golden-caramel skin that reminded her of the cupcakes Mum used to make. She eyed him warily from the darkness, listening for sounds of anyone else; there were none. "What are you doing here?"

"Yeah, it's good to see you too," Chris said, squinting under the light, "oh, except I can't."

"How'd you get in here?"

Chris rubbed his eyes, "Magic, I teleported."

"Teleported? This isn't *Star Trek*, you mean folded."

"Folded?"

"Like when you fold a sheet of paper so the far ends touch." She gestured and another small sun drifted up to hover above her and cast a warm glow. The globe over Chris's head crackled with a quiet menace and spat out blue-white sparks.

"Wow," Chris said, awestruck, then became aware of the threat. "Hey, what is this?"

"Protection, just in case it's not you. When did you attune as a magician?"

"Sorcerer, not magician." Chris said, looking her up and down. "You got blonde hair. I thought you had black hair."

"Magic," Lizzy replied, "why are you looking at me like that?"

"I thought you'd be skinny, you know, from being in prison. But you got a figure. I mean... you look good," he stammered. "No, I'm not trying to... oh crap."

Lizzy smiled, it was Chris all right. "Don't worry, I know what you mean. They kept us older girls well fed so they could take blood from us."

"Well that's gross."

"I know. Show me your folding." She gestured and a thin beam swirled gently out of the little sun and stretched across the room to splash against an open door. "Fold in there and walk out."

"What's through there?"

"It's a small, empty room and a kitchen. Oh, and leave out all the clubby dance lights."

"I thought they were part of it."

Lizzy shook her head, "Not if you do it right."

"Oh, okay." Chris put Spyro on the lead. "Here," he said and Spyro ran across to her. Lizzy glanced down at her and didn't move.

"Look, just take the lead, all right? I don't want her close and getting hurt."

Lizzy knelt down, let Spyro sniff her hand then picked up her lead. "It doesn't work like that, but fine."

"Okay." Chris lifted his arm to gesture and Lizzy stopped him.

"Wait, you haven't been attuned have you?"

"You what?"

"Made sure your magic is always in tune."

"What are you going on about?"

"Those weird colours shouldn't happen with folding."

"Yeah, you said, I get that."

"No you don't, come here."

Lizzy took his hands, "Close your eyes."

Struck by an uncomfortable, shadowy feeling, Chris froze for an instant.

"What is this, some weird initiation?"

"No, just do it."

Chris tutted and closed his eyes. Lizzy closed her eyes and, just as Ozzy had, took a deep slow breath. "Christopher Asten," she said from deep within her stomach, and felt that same space opening up inside her and spreading through her body. Chris's hands twitched and tightened a little around hers.

"The Word that resonates prior to all that arises, and whence all that exists arises, is what we were, are and will all return to."

Chris stumbled forwards and she stepped aside so he almost fell.

"What just happened?"

"Harmonised you, put you in tune so you can use magic properly."

"Like being in tune with the rest of the band."

"I guess, now try folding into the room."

Chris gestured, being more careful with his finger movements. He found himself in the bubble zone again. This time the bubble of a dark room quickly rushed up and engulfed him. This time there were no flashing lights and he reached out into the dark with his hands as his eyes became accustomed to the dim light.

Lizzy waited for a minute then sat down with Spyro and stroked her head. Spyro nuzzled up to her and licked her face. Lizzy gave a short laugh and eased her away, "What's your name little girl?" She slid her hand round Spyro's collar and found the name tag with Spyro's name roughly scratched out in capitals on one side, "Spyro?" Spyro looked up at Lizzy, mouth half open in what looked like a mad grin. Lizzy smiled back and glanced up at the door. Chris still hadn't come out and she felt a twinge of worry that something might have happened to him. After several minutes a quiet thump came from the small room; then Chris came out.

"Five minutes," she said. Spyro had rolled over onto her back and was leaning against Lizzy while she stroked her tummy. Spyro turned her head to Chris but didn't get up. Lizzy smiled down at her. "That's really slow."

"Eh?"

"You were gone for at least five minutes."

"No way, I folded in there and walked straight out. It was less than a minute."

Lizzy shook her head, "Five, easy. It might be instant for you but it's not. The further you go the longer it takes, especially if you're a beginner; and from what I hear, you have to know how to get around the other side."

"But I got here really quick."

"This is London. I got out of Brighton first thing two days ago; thanks to you."

"What's that supposed to mean?"

"The two people I was staying with in Brighton have disappeared. I'm scared Lycus might have got them. They helped me a lot."

"That's bad," Chris said, "really bad."

Lizzy gave him a look and said nothing.

"Hey," Chris said, "I was attacked by a gang of witchfinders, okay? What else was I supposed to do, let them beat the crap out of me then set me alight?"

"The news said you attacked them."

"TV? Yeah right. I steamed in soon as I saw them, didn't I? Course I didn't start it. They came at me as I was going past the Chinese."

"Okay," Lizzy said. "You know, Cantata could do with your help."

"You trying to get rid of me?"

"No, I'm just saying, Cantata do need people who can fold."

"That's their problem."

"We're magicians too, we *are* them."

"So why aren't you with them? Or did they kick you out?" he joked.

The soft glow of the orb dimmed and an awkward silence filled the room. Lizzy gazed down with a distant look in her eyes.

Chris bit his lip and looked around the room, as if the right thing to say was somewhere out there. Then he smiled. "Hey... last time I saw you, you burnt my towel when we were on some weird beach. Was that your magic?"

Lizzy responded with a sad smile, "I was trying to warm it up." She was about to explain the beach, how it was in another realm, but stopped herself. "That was a long time ago, we were different then. You lived in a big house up in Glasgow, not that tower block in Barnet."

Chris nodded, "We played in the garden."

Lizzy gave him a sideways look and sat back down on the edge of the mattress. "What are you doing here?"

Chris fell into an old armchair, "You were on TV. I need to see a place or someone before I can fold there."

"Okay, but why did you come looking for me?"

"My granddad said I should..." Chris stopped and his eyes glazed over. "I still can't believe this is real." He looked up at her. "They killed my granddad."

Chris had the same expression the older girls had when they were brought back from the laboratory. "I heard they found his body in the Peak District."

"Yeah." Chris stared blankly into the distance.

"Cantata found him before Lycus took him away."

"Did they?"

Lizzy nodded.

"Doesn't matter,"Chris shrugged, "What difference does it make now?"

"He's your grandfather, the only family you had left; it matters."

Neither of them spoke for a while then Chris said, "He told me to find you; just before he died."

"Really, why?"

"He said Alumbrados were behind the explosion and to give—"

Lizzy jumped to her feet, "What?"

"I – what?" Chris sat up. "What's going on, why are you freaking out?"

"You said Alumbrados."

"Yeah, so?"

She peered at him, "You don't know about Alumbrados?"

"Never heard of them. What are they, some kind of criminal gang?"

"Worse. They've been around hundreds of years, even before the CERN incident. They're really bad, use dark magic."

"You're kidding, right?" Chris slumped back, "and they're out to kill me? Great, just great"

"Seriously. They control Lycus from behind the scenes, might even be tied up with the government."

"Bloody hell!"

"Exactly. They think they're gods, collecting ancient artefacts, killing anyone who gets in their way. Alumbrados are behind everything being done to us."

"What do you mean, everything?"

"Executions, experiments, girls disappearing from Salem."

"Salem?"

Lizzy sighed, "The Secure Accommodation Laboratory for the Extrusion of Magic. Salem."

"Brilliant," Chris murmured.

"Please, Chris, just fold somewhere else. It's too dangerous for us to be together."

"To be around me you mean."

Reavers clattering down the street interrupted their argument. Lizzy and Chris fell silent until the noise passed. Chris gestured in the direction of the street. "Where do you expect me to go? It's the middle of the night."

"You must know a building somewhere. Think of somewhere you've seen."

"This is crazy. Besides, no one knows I'm here. Come on, Lizzy. I thought we were friends. What happened to you?"

Lizzy gave him a cold stare, "Thirteen years locked up."

"Oh, right."

"Chris, if they don't kill us first, they'll take us in and cut slices out of us while we're still alive."

"Jesus!" Chris grimaced, "that's gross."

"It's true."

"Yeah but, come on, gimme a break, Liz, I've been moving around for days with all kinds of crap going on. Look, I'll go in the morning, okay?"

Spyro snuggled down beside Lizzy and nuzzled her arm. Lizzy stroked the dog's head for several seconds then looked up at him, then past him to the boarded-up windows, "Okay. I guess the night is safe. But you go first thing, okay?"

"Soon as I find somewhere."

"Thanks. Sorry, Chris." She was doing to him what the twins had done to her, but what else could she do? No wonder magicians couldn't organise, they were all too scared.

Spyro looked across to him, then rested her head back on Lizzy's lap.

Lizzy stroked Spyro for a few minutes, lost in thought. Pale shadows occasionally drifted across the face of the small sun over her head. She took in a deep, slow breath and when she breathed out, her sigh stirred an echo of grief inside of Chris. She lay down and turned away from him, the little suns dissolving into a fine mist that disappeared and sent the room into darkness.

Chris's eyes slowly adjusted to the dark. Sometimes a shape, half human, half animal, moved in the shadows. He somehow sensed they were no danger, just strange passers-by from a nearby realm. The shapes left rippling shades of grey as they appeared and disappeared. He shifted his attention to the little atlas in his pocket and the figures faded away.

Holding the atlas brought a lump to his throat. He glanced over at Lizzy, right now the only friend he had, or thought he had.

Lizzy interrupted his thoughts, "Never thought I'd see you again."

Her words lifted him out of the worries and a faint smile crossed his face, "Remember when we used to sleep over?"

"Yes, so don't start that talking, you could talk all night."

"No, that was you."

"Just stop."

"How do you know I didn't blow up the block?"

Lizzy turned and leaned on her elbow. "Have you ever been near a magician who's murdered someone?"

"No, how would I know?"

"Oh you'd know. They are really, really creepy, and it gets worse the more they kill. You just don't want to be around them, not even in the same room."

"So you didn't kill those guards?"

She gave him a sideways look and ran a hand through her hair; it glowed momentarily. "G'night, Chris. It was good to see you." She lay back down, pulling the small leather jacket up over her shoulders.

"Yeah, g'night."

Silence filled the darkness. The sound of Spyro's breathing while she slept reminded him of Benjy.

Lizzy breathed deeply, already fast asleep. It seemed that she, like him, could nod off within minutes if she wanted to.

Lizzy's nightmare woke him. She turned from side to side, still asleep, pushing with her hands, bending her legs and kicking out. Chris thought she'd wake any time but she didn't. There was a look of fear on her face as she spoke, "No, stop, get away from me." She pushed and kicked like she was trying to keep something or someone away. "Please, stop, don't, I don't want to." Flashes of light burst from different parts of her body then she cried out, "No, stop!" and a burst of heat from her made Chris jump up off the armchair and back away. As quick as it came, whatever hellish nightmare had invaded Lizzy's dreams, ended; she curled up into a foetal position and, her features relaxed into a calm sleep.

Lifting the corner with the wheel that squeaked, Chris moved the armchair slowly to the far end of the room and sat back down to quickly fall asleep.

***

Lizzy woke to find Chris, slumped in a deep sleep, on the far side of the shop. His head tilted sideways, and snoring. She slipped her jacket on and went over to him and was about to wake him when she saw several notes in one of his jacket pockets. She lifted the money out and headed for the stairs. Spyro looked up at her from the end of the mattress and followed her down. A quick check in the bike's mirror to make sure her straight face disguise was good and her hair looked real enough, she inched open the back door. No one was about. She clipped Spyro's lead on and stepped out into the alley.

A loose crowd of people milled about outside the church further down the street. It looked like the first service had ended and the new arrivals were meeting those leaving. People exchanged hugs and smiles, children were having their heads patted and men greeted each other with handshakes. In the opposite direction, a quiet procession of people clad in long brown robes and unified by a low droning chant, walked slowly and solemnly down one side of the road. The procession stopped at each open shop where one of the monks would go inside to berate the owner for trading on a Sunday. Meanwhile, another two monks took positions on either side of the door to drone some more and swing bowls full of incense on chains. Other members of the brotherhood carried plastic buckets with cut-out images of saints glued to the sides. They drifted through the passing pedestrians, asking for donations.

One of them approached Lizzy as she passed them on the way to the baker's and their eyes met. The guy was a magician.

He leaned forward and whispered, "They know, they help protect us." Then, lifting his head, he cried out, "And he said to them, 'Take care, and be on your guard against all covetousness, for one's life does not consist in the abundance of his possessions'."

The man shook the bucket in front of Lizzy. She kept a twenty and put the rest into the bucket. The man's eyes lit up and he gave her a big smile and walked away calling out, "Do not lay up for yourselves treasures on earth, where moth and rust destroy and where thieves break in and steal. But lay up for yourselves treasures in heaven, where neither moth nor rust destroys and where thieves do not break in and steal. For where your treasure is, there your heart will be also."

Lizzy smiled to herself, hopefully that wasn't all the money Chris had on him.

She struggled to keep poor Spyro calm as she hooked her lead through the ring on the wall outside the bakery. The smell of bad eggs and rotten food left by the incense wafting out didn't seem so bad now she knew what those monks were really up to. Going in, Lizzy almost laughed at the sour expressions of the three girls behind the counter.

She bought the sandwiches and a couple of bottles of water then went next door to the newsagent's. Spyro almost got away as she unhooked her. The two of them waited outside the pet shop while the owner emerged from the back, tucking his shirt into his trousers and putting on a fleece with the pet shop's logo. After rubbing his eyes with his knuckles, he fumbled through a set of keys and opened up. Spyro, already excited by the smells inside, pulled her in and headed for the counter at the back.

"Slow down," the man yawned.

***

Thin lines of sunlight sliced in through the cracks in the boarded windows and lit up the room, Chris woke, bleary-eyed and weary, to the noise of some religious nut shouting outside. For a second he wondered where he was, then it all came back. Rubbing his neck, he sat up and looked around. Half a dozen cardboard boxes were stacked up against the wall beside the door to the storeroom. Lizzy was gone. She must have really wanted to get away from him. Wow, was he that much of a liability?

Traffic rumbled past outside, then a dog barked. Spyro! He couldn't believe it: she'd gone off with his dog. Oh what the hell, maybe Spyro had a better chance with her. Stretching his arms and back, he went over to the windows and peered through a crack in the boards. There was an estate agent's across the road. He's wait until the street cleared before midnight and run across, find an empty building and fold there. If there was nothing, he could always come back here before the reavers showed up.

He dropped back onto the armchair. Was this going to be his life now? Hopping from one abandoned building to another while the feds, Lycus, Alumbrados, witchfinders, every bloody magic hating, god-fearing citizen in the country hunted him?

Too right Lizzy ran off with Spyro, he couldn't blame her, she had enough on her plate staying alive herself. He almost jumped out of the armchair when Spyro scampered up the stairs. Lizzy followed behind carrying a bag of food and a Sunday paper with all the magazines.

"Morning." She seemed more cheerful. Keeping the magazine section, she dropped the main paper on his lap then casually reached into the bag and tossed a wrapped egg mayo sandwich at him. "Breakfast; I thought I'd get you some pictures to choose from." She dropped onto the mattress and peeled the wrapper off

125

her own sandwich.

"Thanks. How come you're not kicking me out?"

"The latest news says you're hiding out in the Enclave."

"Are they raiding it?"

"Attack thousands of magicians? I don't think so." She began reading the paper and caught him looking at her and eyed him suspiciously, "What?"

"Nothing."

She raised her eyebrows and kept her gaze on him and he started to feel uncomfortable, "I can see auras, you know," she said. Her cheeky smile didn't completely hide the shadow behind it.

"No you can't."

"How would you know?"

"Yeah, whatever. You were having a nightmare last night." Chris said. "It looked like you were fighting someone off. There were these flashes of light coming from your... from your body."

She shrugged and looked back down to the magazine, "It was a bad dream."

"Okay." Fair enough, she didn't want to talk about it. He tore the wrapping off the sandwich and started reading the newspaper.

The front page had a picture of a mesh fence erected around the ruins of what used to be the block where he lived. Photos, messages, soft toys and flowers covered the fence from top to bottom. Inserted in one corner of the cover photo was a small mugshot of him. '186 confirmed dead. Nationwide hunt for terrorist magician Chris Asten'. Brilliant.

"I thought you'd gone off with Spyro."

She tutted and continued reading, occasionally stopping to throw a small bone-shaped dog treat in the air for Spyro who jumped up and caught it.

"Have you met many magicians?" Chris said. "Spoken to them, I mean."

"Some. I've stayed in a couple of safe houses since I escaped; barely got out of Brighton in time, thanks to you."

"Hey!"

A weary, mischievous grin crept across her face. She set aside the magazine and put another section of the newspaper in front of her. The inside page had a photograph of the Chinese takeaway where the fight had begun, "How did you know I was in Brighton?"

"My granddad, he knew you were there."

"How?"

"I don't know. Maybe he was in touch with some Cantata people."

Lizzy thought about the magic postcard. "Anyway," she said, without looking up from the paper, "it's a good thing you didn't find me sooner." She shook her head, "What with Alumbrados after you. But still, using magic in front of a gang of witchfinders."

"Yeah, yeah, all right, I get it, I'm a liability, I'll stick a hazard light on my head."

Lizzy giggled. "They think you're a terrorist looking for another target."

"I can handle that."

"What about the shoot-on-sight order on you?"

"You think I'm that wet?"

"I don't know what you're like now, it's been twelve years." Her thoughts drifted off for a second and she quickly brought herself back. "You were a straight until the other day."

"Straight? What, and now you think I'm gay?"

"No, you twit," Lizzy said with a slow shake of her head, "straight as in not a magician."

Twit; Chris smiled, that used to be their most common insult when they were kids.

"Says here he wasn't your real granddad."

"What?" He almost choked on the sandwich.

She tapped the article in the newspaper. "You're not related, not in any way, according to this report. Weston faked the ID, no one knows who he really is."

"No way."

"Yes way," she said, and carried on reading.

"But he knew Mum and Dad, he looked after me."

"So?"

"No," Chris shook his head, "that report's a lie."

"Maybe."

"It's not funny, Alumbrados tried to kill us, killed Granddad, and all those people."

"Straights kill us all the time."

"Those were innocent people, they never hurt anyone."

"Nor do we. Anyway, what's so special about you, or your granddad, that Alumbrados would blow a whole block up, just to kill you?"

"He said something about the fourth book and…" He stopped before mentioning the key he'd been told to give her or the stuff about the tree. Why should he mention it? She wanted to get rid of him. "Do you know what book that is?"

"No. You found anywhere yet?"

"No. Besides, Granddad wouldn't lie to me about who he was."

Lizzy lowered her head, raised her eyebrows and looked up at him, "That forgetting spell?"

"He was my granddad, okay? He was protecting me."

"Okay," she flipped the newspaper towards him. "Anyway, what do you think of this?"

"Yeah, I'm public enemy number one and there's a nationwide hunt on for me." He read beyond the headline, "Thanks." He finished his sandwich and could have eaten another. He started on his drink and stared at the page of houses for sale.

Lizzy looked up. "Is this true? That your best friend was right next to you?" She gave him a wary look. "That was a pretty dumb thing to do; were you arrested?"

"No, and I went with him so he wouldn't be alone, okay? Dawn Patrol found me and threw me in the back of a van with some smelly tramp who'd slept all night while reavers got his friend."

"You sure that wasn't you?"

"Very funny."

"Why didn't they lock you up?"

"Dunno. Got half my skin scrubbed off, then I had a three-hour interview."

"And they never knew about you being a magician?"

"I didn't even know. Granddad told me just before the block blew up. He said I was a sorcerer, not a mage."

"'Mage' is what straights call us. They make it sound like an infection, some kind of disease." Lizzy shook her head. "You, a sorcerer?"

"Yeah, why not?"

"Sorcerers are rare." That same fleeting, sad smile crossed her face. "You never knew? I mean, your parents never told you?"

"No, Mum and Dad were registered as normal. They passed the string filament test somehow. What about your—"

Lizzy cut in before he could ask about her parents. "Never heard that happening before. It's supposed to be a hundred per cent."

Chris shrugged, "They died when I was six. Lycus found out about them."

Lizzy nodded as if she understood, and the sadness hiding behind her eyes rose to fill her face.

"What?" Chris asked.

"Nothing, it's a shame that's all."

"What happened to your parents?"

Lizzy cut him a look that made him wish he'd never asked. They both concentrated on reading the papers.

Lizzy finally broke the silence, "Sorry."

Chris nodded, "That's okay."

"So," Lizzy said. "What about after the explosion, when you folded out, where did you go?"

Chris told her.

"You stole a car and didn't fold to Brighton?"

"That was before I knew how. My Granddad must have tele… I mean, folded us out of the flat just before it blew."

"Oh. Do you want help to find somewhere to go?"

"No."

"Okay. Tell you what, I'll show you a disguise spell. Just don't get into stupid situations and you'll be fine."

"Is that what you do?"

"I don't get into stupid situations."

"Hilarious," Chris said dryly, "so how did you escape? News said you had some kind of mental breakdown and they were taking you to a hospital."

"Huh," Lizzy snorted.

"Well?"

"Some strange smell woke me up."

"Beans for dinner?"

"Oh, ha ha. No, I think my magic was coming back and they wanted to get me as far from the Unit as possible in case they couldn't stop it."

"Why didn't they just kill you?"

"Oh thanks, that's nice. How should I know? Someone said something about turning me into a zombie."

"A zombie? Really?"

Lizzy tutted. "Not a real zombie. They were going to remove parts of my brain."

"You sure they didn't already?"

"Very funny. I got away with some help from Cantata and other magicians who showed me some spells."

"So, do you know a lot... of spells, I mean?"

Lizzy shook her head, "Just a few. It's not like there are books of spells out there, not any more."

Chris changed the subject. "So what happened after?"

"I was drugged up and put in a Lycus security ambulance." She wiped her hands with a paper napkin and dropped it into the plastic bag, along with the sandwich packaging. "The ambulance stopped on the way to the RAT, research and treatment centre, and I escaped."

"They said you murdered three guards, in cold blood."

Lizzy raised her eyebrows at him. "Sure, and you're a mass murderer, right?"

"Okay." Chris thought back to the guy on the beach. "You must be the first person that's ever got away."

"Maybe, I don't know," Lizzy said, a sombre look on her face.

"You should be glad you're out," Chris said.

"I know, but I still think about my friends, all the other girls."

Something in her tone made Chris ask, "What is it?"

"There's a new building, a dome, girls are going in and not coming out. Some nights we hear reavers, lots of them."

"That's horrible."

"A magician told me there were plans for a big rescue, well, until the raids started." She shot him a look.

"What?"

"Nothing."

"You blaming me?"

"No, I know it's not your fault."

"Okay," he said warily, "but a rescue? You'd need the bloody Avengers to get through all that security." Would Thor's hammer work there?

Lizzy's face fell, "if only there was a way magic worked there."

With the treats and food all gone, Spyro settled down and rested her head on Lizzy's knee.

"Getting them out is practically impossible," Chris continued. "I saw a documentary once, about the first prisons and the high security unit."

"I saw some of it," Lizzy murmured with a nod of the head.

"It was unbelievable. Some magicians, the powerful ones, were forced to wear mouth clamps, blindfolds, even strait jackets." Chris paused to shake his head. "There was a whole solitary wing with nothing but totally weird cells; cells showered with water 24/7, thick willow box cells with no windows. It was insane. There was this one cell that had walls lined with the crushed remains of stag beetles to stop the person escaping. They had ten types of lasers around one block where magicians were so dangerous they..." He stopped when he noticed the way she was staring at him.

"What are you saying?" Lizzy glared at him. "You liked the show? Seeing how they treated us? All the freaky, weirdo magicians strapped up?"

Spyro raised her head from Lizzy's knee and looked at her nervously.

"No," Chris protested. "I was talking about after the war when the dangerous—"

"Dangerous? I can't believe you just said that. Is that what you think we are?"

Spyro sat up, turning her head from Lizzy to Chris.

"Hang on, no, course not, but—"

"Yeah, we're the freaking dangerous ones, and they are the ones that torture and murder us."

"Lizzy!"

Her hand tightened around the magazine, the edge of the pages smouldering, and she threw it at his face, "Did you even wonder why no one was over twenty?"

Chris swatted the magazine away and gaped at her. The faint smell of ashen paper hung in the air.

Spyro crossed to the armchair and sat hunched beside it, watching them, little shivers running through her.

"Your head is straight as they come." Lizzy grabbed her jacket and stood up. "I must have been crazy thinking we'd be friends like before." She turned her back to him and shoved her arms into the sleeves of her jacket. "Find a stupid picture and get lost."

"Lizzy, I'm sorry, I didn't know, it was on TV, I—"

"Just shut up," Lizzy said, raising her voice. "Don't talk to me. It's about time I got out of here anyway." She pulled the bike keys from her pocket and the postcard fell out.

Chris knelt down to pick it up and Spyro crept over to him. Chris stroked her head then picked up the postcard. At first the paper was blank then an image of a mound materialised. It stood in a field, a cobbled path led to a large wooden door on the side. "What's this place?"

"Give it back."

Chris held on to it. "What is it, where is it?"

"I don't know," Lizzy held out her hand, palm open. "Hand it over, no one else is meant to see it."

"How come I can see it?"

"I don't know and I don't care, give it here."

"I could fold us there."

"No, I don't need your help." Lizzy snatched the card and shoved it into an inside pocket. "Just leave."

"Lizzy, this is crazy, how—"

The boards across the windows smashed open; fragments of board, broken planks and splinters blasted across the room. Chris instinctively threw his arms out and swung them out sideways, creating a shield that spread out and burst across the room, knocking back the debris. Three Lycus Special Forces soldiers swung in through the window and landed heavily, their assault rifles firing bursts of armour-penetrating rounds that slammed into the shield with loud cracks. Chris punched out with his left hand and the shield rumbled forwards pushing back the armchair and two of the soldiers. The pair stumbled back and fell out of the window to hang off the ropes they'd used to rappel down while the armchair crashed to the street below.

The third saw what was happening. He'd rolled sideways to press against the wall and shifted his assault rifle to fire from the hip. A silver bolt of light shot past Chris and smashed into the soldier's face making him drop the rifle and throw his hand to his face, screaming. The two soldiers outside swung back in through the window as a barrage of jagged white and crimson bolts flew from Lizzy's hands and crackled towards them, driving them back and burning away the ropes. The soldiers cried out as they dropped to the street and a solid wall of crackling electric fire spread across the window. "It'll only last a few minutes," Lizzy cried out over the noise.

"Come on then!" Chris ran to the stairs and, grabbing the handrail, spun round to leap down. He stopped seconds before jumping down onto something scuttling up towards him.

The thing looked like a little kid scrabbling spider-like up the stairs on all fours. Then it...he... she, looked up. It was, used to be, a little girl. She had a horrible face, twisted, trapped and tortured. Ugly bruises grew and faded across her skin, shifting through red, blue, purple, black; with each change releasing dark, blood-red mists that spread across her skin like a churning, crimson-black fur. She, it, the thing, breathed noisily through a thick, sharp throat as its head swayed from side to side.

The girl-thing kicked away from the ground like some weird insect and flew up at his face. Chris grabbed the creature's arms and the dark mist seeped over his hands like scalding water, making him cry out in pain. He stared into the eyes of a small, gaunt, bony girl desperately trying to escape whatever had possessed her.

Grimacing, Chris managed to keep a grip on her arms and hold her away as she thrashed about, screeching and twisting wildly to free herself. Chris slid one foot back, shifted his weight and threw her down the stairs, barely managing to dodge a swipe aimed at his face.

Leaving a trail of crimson-black fumes that hung in the air for a second before swarming back over the kid, she twisted through an ugly distortion, and landed lightly on the bottom steps. Seconds later more girl-things joined her. A soldier dressed head to toe in a black outfit standing at the back of the room barked a command and the half dozen creatures started to crawl up the stairs.

Screams came from the upstairs windows as more spider-kids, their skin peeling white from diving through the magical flames, swarmed in to screech and cower from the onslaught of more heat and light from Lizzy. "I can't do this fast enough," Lizzy said, stumbling back into Chris and they both fell to the ground beside Spyro cowering against the back wall. "Fold us out!"

Chris raised his hands and sharp pains ran up his arms. Then he saw his hands; it was like seeing them through some dark-red-tinted X-rays. "Jesus Christ!" he screamed. "My hands."

"There's nothing wrong with your hands, get us out of here."

The horde of creatures milled around, inching towards them, screaming in pain as they pushed through the burning sparks raining down on them.

"Just burn the bloody things," Chris shouted, staring at his hands.

"I can't," Lizzy said.

Beside him, Lizzy's face was also a dark red skull covered in a ghostly layer of skin; her eyes glowed like red suns.

The skull turned to him and the jaws moved, "Chris, come on, get us out of here."

"Oh, Jeez!" Chris cried. Closing his eyes he lifted a hand and moved his fingers and more waves of scalding pain streamed up his arms. "Agghh!" His face twisted as he forced his burning fingers through the motion and, focussing on the last thing he saw, began the incantation, "Evjarimiq Nggg." He gritted his teeth as a scorching stream shot through the veins in his arm. His chest knotted and he struggled to breathe.

"Chris!" Lizzy cried.

Chris sucked in a deep breath and forced his hand up again and screamed through the searing acid burns that seemed to be dissolving the flesh and bones under his skin. "Evjarimiq Ghelyor Sahami," he cried, forcing every last ounce of breath into the incantation. Then it was late afternoon and he thumped down beside a gravel path in the middle of a field, writhing in agony.

Spyro hit the soft, wet ground and bounced round in confusion, barking. Lizzy jumped up and rushed across to him.

"Chris, what's happening to you?"

Chris stared at Lizzy's ghostly red skull and crimson glowing eyes and pressed his own eyes shut. "It's all gone bloody Ghost Rider," he managed to say through a choking throat, his face knotted in pain.

Lizzy looked around desperately. A barren landscape spread under a grey sky. It was late afternoon and a crisp breeze blew across bare fields. The gravel path led to a wooden door in the side of a large mound. "What is this place?" Lizzy said.

"Your photo," Chris gasped. The mound, fields and houses in

the distance were all a transparent, ghostly red.

Spyro jumped back when the wooden door opened and a woman glided out, her long hooded black-and-green dress not touching the cobbles. A gentle breeze lifted the long feathered cloak slung over her shoulders, sometimes revealing an ornate Celtic necklace. She took one look at Chris and, pointing her wand towards him said, "Aibtaead al'ahmar." She drew the wand back and, as she did, a thick cloud of dark red vapour poured out of Chris's hands and took the form of what looked like an emaciated demon. The thing was the size of a rat, its face looked like a lizard had been smashed flat against a wall and it had a short tail snaking down behind it.

Chris slumped down with relief then leaned up on one arm and wiped a hand down his face. His eyes froze when he saw the reptile demon. The thing had crouched down with its arms raised, hissing at Spyro who had leaned back on her front legs and, baring her teeth, snarled back at the creature. The thing reacted with a high-pitched wail, and spinning round, disappeared.

Chris got to his hands and knees and Lizzy helped him to his feet.

"Welcome to Maeshowe," the woman said in a soft, untroubled voice.

Chapter Ten

"Welcome to where?" Lizzy said.

"This," the woman gestured to the door, "is the passageway to Tír na nÓg, a sanctuary for all who are gifted with the powers of old magic. No ordinary mortal can pass this way. I am Freyja, here to greet you."

A big smile broke across Lizzy's face, "Old magic?" She beamed, "It might work in Salem. Chris, They could help us rescue all the other girls. Their magic would work."

Spyro barked excitedly and ran round in circles, chasing her tail.

Freyja gave Lizzy a quizzical look. "This is our land, I cannot tell the people who live here to leave, to interfere in this realm; but you may join us if you wish."

"Live in a cave?" Chris said, finally able to speak, "I don't think so."

"Not a cave, a doorway to another realm. Beyond the door are fields, villages, enchanted forests, lakes, mountains, even a vast ocean. You are welcome to enter, make it your home." Freyja stepped aside. Beyond the open door, a dusty path stretched through gold and green fields, leading to a village in the distance. A warm yellow sun glowed in a blue sky flecked with wisps of white clouds.

"I can leave any time?" Chris said.

"Of course, if you wish," Freyja said. "But you should know that, for each year in Tír na nÓg, a hundred years pass in your world."

"A hundred years?" Lizzy looked worried.

"Excellent," Chris said. "Give it a year and I could come out in the future. I could get everything I wanted. No one would remember me. They'd think I died a hundred years ago."

Lizzy shook her head. "Do you even care about anyone else, Chris?"

"What?"

"People need us!" Lizzy said, exasperated. "Our people."

"Oh," Chris said, "Oh yeah."

Lizzy glowered at him and turned to Freyja. "You must help, Lycus are torturing us, killing us."

Freyja shook her head. "Conflict is the nature of this world, not ours. Nor is it our concern."

"Course it is," Chris pointed past Freyja to the thick wooden door, still half open, "There's a world of magicians back there, just tell them what's happening out here, they'll want to join, help, once they know."

"No," Freyja said, "we are here because we want no business with the inhumanity and chaos of this mortal realm."

"What are you going on about?" Chris said.

"Oh, like that is is?" Lizzy said. "You think what you're doing is right and the rest of the world is bad and wrong?" Lizzy said. "Just like every other religion."

"We have turned our backs on the chaos, the conflicts of power, greed and desire."

"I've heard that line before," Chris said. "You're right, Liz, they like any other straight religion, stuck up their own arses."

Freyja looked down her nose at them then raised her eyes to the sky. "It is June, you have ample time to find your own solution before the Hunter's Moon."

"Hunter's Moon?" Lizzy said. "What happens then? You know something, don't you?" Lizzy stepped onto the cobbled path and an expression of alarm crossed Freyja's face when her feet touched the stones.

"Stop!" the wand reappeared in Freyja's hand and she pointed it at Lizzy, "Dumruh iy aht."

The spell pulsed through the air and hit Lizzy like a punch in the stomach. She gasped and staggered back into Chris, her knees giving way and almost knocking him over. Chris caught her and helped her to the ground. Spyro jumped up, whining with concern and tried to lick her face.

"Easy, Spyro," Chris pushed her gently off Lizzy and glared at Freyja. "What is wrong with you?"

"She cannot approach, the taking of life resonates within her."

"No!" Lizzy's eyes were fixed on Freyja in shocked disbelief.

"Three men," Freyja stood with her wand raised, ready to cast another spell.

"Them?" Lizzy held onto Chris's arm and got to her feet. "No, that's not right. I couldn't help it."

"Hey, back off!" Chris glared at Freyja and stepped between them. "What's she talking about, Lizzy?"

"The guards... in the transport, they... they tried to..." She shot Chris a look that cut into him.

Chris turned to Freyja, "Chrissake, Freyja, they tried to rape her, it was self-defence, she couldn't control what happened."

Freyja shook her head. "It is not my decision."

"Whose it is then? Get your bloody boss," Chris's raised voice alarmed Spyro.

"Please," Lizzy said, "you have to help. Lycus are hunting us down and killing us."

"There is always conflict and death on this world," Freyja said in a matter-of-fact tone, "it never ends. We do not involve ourselves."

Lizzy was silent for a few seconds as she got her breath back then got to her feet. "Fine." She brushed the soil off her jeans, and zipping up the leather jacket, set off across the field.

Confused, Chris gaped at Freyja then turned and called out to Lizzy, "Hey, Lizzy, wait up."

Lizzy ignored him and continued making her way slowly over and around the criss-cross of long furrows overgrown with weeds and bracken that cut across the field like tangled veins.

"Christopher," Freyja's voice was calm, almost too calm to trust, "you and Spyro are welcome to stay."

"Yeah, well screw you and your stupid fairyland, bitch," Chris snarled and turned away to go after Lizzy, who was already some distance away across the jagged field.

The surrounding silence was eerie. There was no traffic, no cattle, no sheep, not even birds or a single weird creature. The only sound was the feeble, shallow wind breathing across the barren landscape, off the sea in the distance. The closest building was a dilapidated grey stone building and a small car park with several abandoned cars taking up half the space. A farmhouse stood around half a mile beyond that, set back from the tarmac road,.

Chris caught up with her. "Hey."

Lizzy didn't break her stride. Fists clenched, she glanced at Chris, "Don't talk to me." she said and continued towards the farmhouse.

After a few minutes Lizzy said, "Can you believe it? All those magicians, she knows what's going on and she didn't even care."

"Yeah," Chris said, avoiding eye contact with her.

"I just want to get away from here."

"Let's check out that building over there before it gets dark, get off this island tomorrow."

"Island?"

"Yeah," Chris said, "listen, you can hear the sea."

Lizzy shrugged.

After a while, Chris said, "She had a wand, can you believe it? I thought wands were from fairy stories. I bet she's got a broomstick."

"It's not funny."

"Just think," Chris continued, "you'd have to get kitted out too if they let you in. You'd look good in a pointy hat. Good thing you didn't go in there, your nose would start to stretch out like an old bent twig."

"Shut up," Lizzy elbowed him in the ribs and he almost fell over, which made Lizzy smile. "How could she not want to help?"

"Like I said, out of touch with reality, stuck in their own little world."

"She said there's time," Lizzy said, "before the Hunter's Moon. She knows Lycus are planning something."

"That's a full moon at the end of October, months away."

Lizzy relaxed a little, "Since when do you know about the Hunter's Moon?"

"It's an Elegance card; from a board game; there's four decks of season cards."

Lizzy scanned the flat landscape. "Do you think there's something wrong with me?"

"No, no way."

She gave him a sideways glance. "You know what," she said, "you're right, screw her and her wand. We'll find our own magicians, get the girls out."

"Right, I managed to find you didn't I?"

"You say that as if it's a good thing."

Chris elbowed her and she shoved him back.

After a while, Lizzy said, "Back in the bookshop, I... I think I recognised some of those... those girls, from the Unit."

"So that's why you couldn't burn them."

Lizzy nodded, "I think they had those demons inside them."

"It was a Yaji."

"A what?"

"Yaji. A kind of fire demon, that can divide up into smaller versions and possess other living things. Messes up your magic for a while."

"But it's out of you."

"Pain inside; it messes magic when it leaves, lose three turns."

"From the board game?"

"Yes."

Spyro ran ahead, sniffing at the furrows and barking back at them.

Lizzy smiled. "Does she ever stop running around?"

"No, well, she does when she's eating, sleeping or wanting attention."

They crossed the road into the car park and weaved around the abandoned cars to the building where Chris climbed in through a broken window. Lizzy passed Spyro to him then Chris helped her in. Lizzy mumbled a spell that sent thin, glowing threads across the dark room and their eyes adjusted to the dim light. Mouldy leaves and discarded leaflets and books lay scattered everywhere. Crushed and broken postcard stands and broken shelves lay scattered across the floor. Chris picked up a book and shook the leaves and dirt off. "Tormiston Mill Maeshowe Visitor Centre. Orkney."

"Orkney?" Lizzy exclaimed. "The stoor!"

Chris's eyes widened in shocked realisation. "The $%&*£ sea monsters."

Lizzy grabbed a faded brochure and thrust it at him. "Look at a picture, fold us out of here. We can hide out somewhere else, hurry up, it's almost sunset." She pointed at the brochure in Chris's hand.

"It's too soon, I can't fold or do any magic yet." Chris flicked through the brochure, "besides, these pictures are all places here in Orkney."

Something big and heavy rumbled across the gravel outside. Lizzy raised her hands when a deep metallic thump of a car being slammed into was followed by something hitting the shop's wall. They both stepped back when shards of glass cracked and fell from broken windows and a small cloud of dust dropped from the ceiling. Spyro growled and bared her teeth then shot up the stairs, howling as a large, fat snakes head appeared at one of the shattered windows.

Large flat, slate-grey eyes stared at Lizzy and Chris. It slowly opened and closed a wide, bulldog mouth lined with double rows of jagged pointed teeth.

Chris and Lizzy backed away as a grainy, forked tongue extended slowly and flicked left and right. Then, unable to restrain itself, the monster let out a harsh, wheezing cry and forced its way through the window, breaking away the wood and plaster around the frame.

Lizzy grabbed Chris's hand and they raced up the stairs and across the room to huddle on the rubble behind a counter. The chimney had collapsed a long time ago and a hole in the roof exposed a cold, grey sky. Two loud crashes came from downstairs and then the building shook as something hit a wall and they heard the glass panelled doors give way. The stoor slowly made their way up the stairs, stone crumbling away, wood creaking and groaning under their weight as cracks appeared where the steps met the wall. The downstairs shop filled with the gritty crunch of falling concrete. The two enormous worms rounded the top of the stairs and, sensing the magic from Lizzy and Chris, stopped several feel away, curling around and over each other while breathing out dank green fumes. The serpents slithered forward a few feet then shrank back through the fumes pouring from knuckly gills set back from their faces.

"Fold us out!" Lizzy cried through a parched throat.

The stoor were somehow sucking every drop of moisture from the air.

"I can't yet," he choked. Spyro stopped barking and was panting loudly; she crawled onto Chris's lap and curled up. Lizzy struggled to keep her eyes open and fell against him. She tried to raise a hand but it flopped down beside her, "Chris... fold..." she croaked dryly. Then her head lolled back and she all but lost consciousness.

The stoor inched closer, swaying from side to side, shoving each other and breathing with a gravelled rasping while the toxic air became thinner and drier. A sickly retching rose from inside the creatures' guts and, overcome by hunger or rage, they surged forwards. Chris fell back against the wall. Lizzy lay slumped against him. Chris shook her, "Lizzy," he rasped. "Wake up, you have to do something."

The stoor reached the counter and reared up several feet, opening their grotesquely wide jaws. Long forked tongues stabbed out between the double teeth as the monstrous worms leaned back and prepared to strike, knots of muscle tensing along their bodies, black veins pulsing. A wave of fear swept through Chris and, as if in response, Lizzy's body began to spasm violently and her eye became glowing orbs of pure electric-blue.

"oh shit," Chris said and raised an arm over his face seconds before a blinding flash and a sphere of sizzling flames bloomed out across the room, burning everything in its path, The stoor instantly burned and within seconds turned into long, charred and cracked carcasses resembling ashen-grey logs. Scorched floor tiles curled up, exposing cracks that stretched through the floorboards.

Chris, somehow energised by the blast, held Lizzy tight as the wall beside them collapsed outwards with a deafening crash and a cold wind swept in a spray of tiny embers that swirled around them then burst away.

Smouldering chunks of stoor broke off and crunched onto the fragile ground until the floor finally gave way and crashed down into the shop below. A plume of flames and embers burst up and through the hole in the roof, triggering a storm of roars from the gathering stoor outside.

Chris managed to get an arm round Lizzy's waist. "Lizzy," he croaked, his voice barely a whisper, "help me out here."

She opened her eyes and together they crawled slowly over the rubble behind them and fell through the hole in the wall onto the remains of a low, tiled roof. They slid over the debris and down onto a car before rolling off and hitting the ground. Spyro, who had followed them onto the low roof, barked down at them.

Beyond the building and car park, the other monstrous worms had retreated from the flames. With the heat of the fire behind them, Chris and Lizzy staggered across the car park and fell against a wall.

"Spyro," Chris tried to call through a dry throat. "Here girl," Unable to raise his voice, Chris lifted his hand over his head, and touching fingers with his thumb, twisted his wrist around.

"Nerroh horhuk sular," he whispered and clenched his fist, making a pulling motion. Instead of the stream he expected to appear, a shimmering blue gash opened up several feet above him and a shower of water poured over them leaving a wide, crystal-clear puddle on the ground. Chris stopped the downfall with a flick of the wrist and thrust his face into the water. He sucked in several mouthfuls and took in a deep breath then sat up and threw water into Lizzy's face. She spluttered and opened her eyes. Chris pointed to the puddle of water. "Drink," he said and headed back to Spyro. He stopped when a crash from inside the building made Spyro jump off the low roof. Chris caught her and put her down and they headed back to Lizzy.

Lizzy peered at him through a wet face and bleary eyes. "Was that fire me?"

"I'll say. We were in the middle of it, you roasted those two snakes."

Lizzy wiped water from her face, and gave him a quizzical look. "Why am I soaking wet?"

"Sorry, I summoned a stream but the spell maxed out in some weird way."

Chris moved his hands and she stopped him. "I got this. Gulmurin derin," she said, with a barely noticeable twitch of her index and middle finger. The water evaporated off, leaving them both warm and dry.

"I could have made the water disappear," Chris said.

Lizzy shook her head. "Your fumbling would have taken our clothes as well."

"Hey!"

The building collapsed into itself with a long, loud crash sending smoke and flames exploding into the sky. The Stoor fell back; they howled and thrashed into each other, reeling away into the field. Spyro bounced up and down, barking at the burning building.

Lizzy rubbed her eyes and pointed at a farmhouse about half a mile down the long road that curved round the field, "Since your magic is back, can you fold us over to that farmhouse?"

"Hang on." Chris gestured in front of his eyes, "Alguzbak." The farmhouse came into sharp view. He couldn't believe it, it was all in one piece. There was a faint pattern in the wall, formed by bricks of a slightly darker colour arranged in the form of a cross with a loop above the bar, like the Egyptian ankh. Magicians must have lived there. The sight of Alguz revealed a strange glow surrounding the house and garden, keeping Stoor away from it.

Chris blinked a few times and his normal eyesight came back, "No."

"Why not?"

"It's got some kind of magical shield around it. I don't know what'll happen if we try to go through there with magic. We'll drive."

"What? With those things after us?"

The house gave him an idea. "I'll use the Immutable Shield spell. 'No heat or cold nor trace of light betrays your path by day or night'" he said, "one of my favourites, you know, from the game."

"Of course it is. You're going to have to show me some of those spells."

He didn't like the idea of that. "Maybe." Chris pointed to a Honda Accord, "That one."

He used a Swiss army knife to break the lock.

"Old school," Lizzy said.

"Yeah, sometimes magic just doesn't cut it."

"Like your Kung Fu with the gang in Brighton."

"Tai Chi and Kenpo. Didn't have a choice about that. Didn't figure out my magic until after they jumped me."

They clambered into the front seats and after fiddling with the wires, got the car started.

"That was fast."

"I know." Chris shoved the gearstick, looked over his shoulder and reversed out from between the wall and a parked car. He drove out, keeping to the wall and away from the burning building until he brought the car round to face the exit. The stoor had retreated deep into the field across the road and kept their distance from the billowing smoke and flames.

"Is fire and light some kind of default thing with you?"

"Sort of," Lizzy's attention remained fixed on the road. "My dad said something about light or energy."

"How can you remember that far back? I thought you were in prison since you were five?"

"Same way you remember all the spells in that atlas, Sherlock: we're magicians." She glanced in the rear-view mirror. "Get to it with the spell then."

Chris moved a hand through the air, "Evsesdyma." Everything around them tightened into focus with outlines standing sharp against the swarming stoor. "That's it, let's go."

"Really?" Lizzy said. "Are we invisible?"

Chris took a deep breath, "I hope so."

The stoor didn't see them or respond as Chris drove along the cracked tarmac. Steering round the taller, thicker clumps of weeds, they headed towards the farmhouse. The setting sun cast a pale hue across the clouds and pinked the corrugated metal roof of long barns in the distance. Stoor slithered across the fields either side of them, sometimes rising to look around or cry out with hissing snarls.

A loud slow creaking rang through the air followed by the deafening explosion of the oil tank beside the shop. Flames and black smoke towered into the sky while the pressure blasted vehicles across the car park and sent them crashing against each other, some exploding with more loud booms. Nearby stoor scattered, howling and colliding into each other in the rush to avoid the flying debris that crashed down around them.

Chris glanced over at the mound, untouched by the monsters. "No wonder it's a secret place."

Chris drove up onto the driveway then round to the side of the house. He lifted Spyro onto his lap and took Lizzy's hand. She looked at their hands then at him, "Is this necessary?"

"There's magic on this island, who knows what the fold will do."

"You said we couldn't fold here."

"Not through the shield, we're on the other side of it now."

They reappeared in the house and froze in pitch black, paralysed by a deafening storm of howls and screeching coming from outside.

Spyro cowered behind Chris's feet.

Lizzy gasped and moved closer to Chris, her voice barely audible. "It's reavers."

"Windows must be totally blacked out. Do your little sun thing, we're okay."

Lizzy moved her fingers and thin threads of light spun out from the little sun and, carried on invisible waves, glided around them, revealing walls lined with fine, delicate patterns, a narrow shelf under a mirror. Heavy curtains hung over the window at the top of the stairs and Lizzy broadened the streams to illuminate them. The same thick, black curtains covered every window in the house.

"If only that noise and stink wasn't around," Lizzy said.

"Hang on," Chris stretched his arms out, turned his wrists in the air and mumbled, "Evsesdyma, gor." The noise became a muffled whisper.

"It's gone quiet."

"Yeah, I just reshaped the Immutable Shield spell, no sound can get in, or out."

"You did what?" Lizzy said.

"I just thought of it, to keep the noise out."

"No," Lizzy said, a concerned expression on her face, "seriously?"

"What's up, why not?"

"You really are a sorcerer."

Chris gave her a look, "Well duh, I did tell you."

"You don't know?" Lizzy said. "Magicians can't mess about with spells."

"Course we do, we all do, what else is magic?"

"It's not sorcery. You really don't know what being a sorcerer means?"

"Yeah I do," Chris said. "We're from an older family of magicians."

"No, you twit, sorcerers are different. They can mess with magic, transform spells, join them up."

"Isn't that what magicians do?"

"No!" Lizzy said, exasperated. "magicians just do spells, one at a time, not transform them, or join them, only sorcerers can do that."

Chris was still thinking about this when Lizzy added, "Sorcery can seriously mess with reality."

"What do you mean?"

"Magic can't spread and doesn't last that long. Reality pushes it away back to where it came from, sort of fixes itself after a while. Sorcery is different; sorcery stays until you change it, or cancel it out. Magic incantations can't mix up or change each other."

"Really? Wow," Chris said, "I never knew that. Hang on,

you've been changing those lights you summon."

Lizzy nodded, "That's like playing with silly putty, it's all the same thing, and I need to recharge them. Sorcery can change reality permanently."

"You burnt down a whole freaking building, how's that different?"

"The energy faded away; if that had been sorcery those flames would have carried on long after the whole house had burned to ashes."

"Oh," Chris replied thoughtfully, then smiled. "Oh wow. This is more awesome than I thought. I got levels."

Lizzy shook her head in dismay, "Chris, you really have to know what you're doing."

Chris laughed, "I'll be careful, promise."

"You better."

"You know what I don't get?" Chris said. "We only went a couple of feet but lost hours. That's way too long."

"Maybe it's this house," Lizzy said, then a thought occurred to her. "We could see the reavers."

"You what?"

"You did say they can't see or hear us, didn't you?"

"Yeah."

"Great, then I'm going upstairs to have a look; come on." Before Chris could reply, Lizzy headed upstairs, taking the little sun with her. Spyro dashed ahead of her up the carpeted stairs and spun round on the landing, wagging her tail.

Chris followed. The sun above their heads casting a warm light over the framed photographs of cityscapes lining the walls.

"Imagine," Lizzy said, "aeroplanes and ships went round the world, millions of people travelling to different countries every day." She waved the sun further up towards the ceiling and it bounced gently against the edge of the wall before settling in the top corner of the L-shaped landing. At the far end of the hallway, a child's crayon drawing of a colourful dragon was stuck on a door, the words 'Jenny's Room' were scrawled underneath. Two doors nearer the stairs led into the master bedroom and a small study with a desk and table. Chris and Lizzy went into the main bedroom. Like downstairs, thick navy curtains hung over the windows, a large white duvet lay across the bed and a small cable

147

radio stood on a beside cabinet. The dresser against the wall had a hair-dryer and comb resting beside a small jewellery tree. Lizzy picked up the comb, "It's as if they just went out for the day and didn't come back."

"I know, talk about weird."

The windows of the master bedroom faced the fields. Chris inched the curtain open and pale moonlight cut into the room. The dense constellation of the Milky Way stretched across a sky saturated with more stars than he'd ever seen.

A rage of reavers bounded across the fields, diving onto worms and tearing into them with long howls, thrusting claws into fatty flesh, gouging out thick, dark clumps while the stoor writhed and let out shrill, agonising screams.

"They're horrible," Lizzy whispered. "What are those lights on them?"

"Armour, I think they're part of some kind of army."

A rumbling rolled across the fields as older stoor arrived, monstrous sea serpents covered in scars and several times larger than the other stoor. They stopped some distance from the battle and rose up to balance on their rear halves. The monsters scanned the slaughter, and with a roar, swept into the fight. The gargantuan Stoor crushed whatever was in front of them, both reaver and smaller stoor in their path. Then their long forked tongues scooped up unrecognisable mushy lumps of flesh and bone, throwing them back into their throats.

The field become a muddy expanse of mangled reaver and stoor entrails. On the fringes of the carnage, more reavers arrived and dived into the battle, tearing and gouging the sides of the giant stoor. Clustering into groups, the reavers ripped through thick skin and flesh, tunnelling into the giant beasts. The serpents thrashed about then dropped dead as more reavers dived through the gashes to devour the monsters from the inside out.

"That is gross," Chris grimaced. Lizzy had turned away and Chris nudged her and pointed to the sky where a thick black stain grew and spread as it came closer, blotting out the stars. The dark, oily mass swarmed and gathered over the battle. Screeches filled the sky and the mass shattered into hundreds of sky reavers, their gaunt, slate skin swallowing what little light there was. Dense black-scaled wings flapped like leathery sails as they swooped across the fields, forming groups that grabbed and lifted smaller stoor off the ground, tearing them apart to feed mid-air.

Stoor scattered in all directions and within minutes only reavers were left feasting noisily in small packs. Then the sky reavers dropped to the ground and clumsily foraged around the field to feed or carry the remains of stoor carcasses off into the night.

"I've seen enough." Lizzy went and sat on the bed. She kicked her trainers off and swinging her legs off the ground, leaned back and yawned.

Chris swept a hand through the air, "Sesstace," he whispered and the noises outside faded away. Spyro trotted across the room and jumped up beside her and Lizzy stroked her head a couple of times then picked up the book lying on the small beside cabinet: *The Years of Rice and Salt*. Leaning back and guiding a tiny sun over her head, she began to read.

"The protective shield you said was around the house, it must have been put here by a sorcerer." She slid her hand over the bed, "Everything is still clean and fresh."

"I wonder what happened to them, where they went."

"It feels safe here; reminds me of home." A sad, distant look filled her eyes. Chris couldn't help but wish he could take away whatever memories were haunting her.

She caught him looking at her. "What's up?"

"You must have lived in some weird part of town."

She gave him a sad smile. She put the book down and yawned then rubbed her eyes, "I'm going to get some sleep. You can use one of the other rooms."

"You want to stay and sleep here?"

"With monsters all over the island and the shield round the house, this is probably the safest place in the country." She lifted a finger, moved it around, and the little sun faded to a dim glow.

"That's true," Chris said. She was smart, tough, and...

"Oh, and those looks you've been giving me? Don't even think about trying it on."

"Jeez," Chris responded with a tired shake of the head and wandered out. Lizzy closed the door and, removing her clothes, climbed in under the duvet. Still too warm, she pushed away the duvet and settled down under the sheet. In the next room, Chris collapsed on the bed and was out in seconds.

***

The next morning, Lizzy slipped on her knickers and T-shirt then drew back the curtains. She inched open the window and a cool breeze drifted into the room. Dawn spread slowly across the still landscape. In the distance, behind thin lines of cloud, a slender dome of sun stained the horizon blue-grey. Sunlight cracked through the dense, skeletal hedges and cast a mosaic of shadows that stretched over the scarred and butchered fields. Sunlight dissolved Stoor and reavers' remains into wispy plumes of smoke that rose and disappeared, leaving nothing to show they'd even existed.

Lizzy yawned and stretched, then got dressed. The strange, comforting aura of the house seemed to be stronger today. The door to the next bedroom was open; Chris was still asleep, curled up under the sheet, his clothes thrown onto a chair by the bed. She smiled. He slept naked, like all magicians. She left him snoring and checked the room at the far end, opening the curtains to let some light in.

The child's room had a platform bed over a small desk, and an old wooden toy box against the wall beside the window. The box was empty except for a large sketchpad and an old biscuit tin full of broken crayons. She carefully took out them out and climbed onto the bed and sat down to draw, losing all track of time.

"Hullo," Chris yawned and wiped a hand across a sleepy face.

"Oh," Lizzy looked up. "What time is it?"

"Noon sometime." Chris wandered in and fell onto the large beanbag against the wall. "Last night was totally insane, wasn't it? What you up to?"

"Nothing, just drawing. Can you do that water thing again?"

"What, and get us soaked?"

Lizzy responded with a short laugh, "Maybe not then."

"I'm going down to the kitchen to magic, I mean sorcerise, something up."

"Sorcerise, that's not even a word." Lizzy put the sketchbook and crayons down and followed him downstairs.

In the kitchen, she went over to the sink and tried the taps. A clunking gurgle echoed from somewhere then rusty brown water poured slowly out into the sink. As the water slowly cleared, Lizzy gazed out of the window facing the garden where a child's bike leaned against a tree.

""Subahkana Ekemei" Chris moved his hand in a graceful arc across the table and it filled with plates full of food. Cold meats, bread, cheeses, bowls of fruit, wooden mugs of milk. "Man, I am so killing this sorcery."

Lizzy sighed.

"Hey, look at this, breakfast is ready." He passed her a mug of sweet, hot milk.

Lizzy took the mug and responded with a barely visible nod, and continued looking out across the wreck of a garden. "I had a bike like that," she said in a sad, distant voice.

***

Little Lizzy steered the little bike along the narrow path around the small lawn. Singing to herself, she went up towards the greenhouse, round the pond, through the shadows of the apple tree, and back down past the tomato plants. Growing in confidence, she reached out to touch the bushes over to the right of the path. The phone rang as she approached the house and Lizzy stopped by the bird table at the end of the path, listening for her mother's call. That could be Julie's parents on the phone. Julie had promised to come over that day. Fear swept through her when her mother came running out of the house, a look of terror on her face.

"Lizzy!" her mother dashed up to Lizzy and swept her off the bike, knocking her knees against the handlebars. "We have to leave, now."

Lizzy clung to her mother's neck as she rushed into the house and through the hallway. Her mother stopped at the front door when the rumble of cars, big cars, came from the street beyond and screeched to a stop outside their house.

"No!" her mother screamed and ran back towards the garden and the small gate at the end that led into the derelict site beyond the wall. A crash made Lizzy look back to see several men in heavy, dark uniforms stomping through the house. Lizzy's mother put her down and pushed her forwards. "The back gate, Lizzy, run, hide."

Lizzy almost fell as she stumbled towards the gate. When she realised her mother wasn't following, she stopped. "Mum?"

"Go!" her mother screamed, then raising her hands, she turned to face the house. "Now."

Her mother raised her hands and moved them like a conductor in front of an orchestra. Long silver ribbons shot out and exploded into flecks of flame that struck the oncoming police. Lizzy turned and ran.

"Banks, stop that kid!" someone shouted as Lizzy reached the gate and fumbled at the bolt. Seconds later the agonised cries of men filled the air and Lizzy fell to cower against the gate. Beyond her mum, several men stumbled about while others writhed on the grass, their clothes on fire, liquid flames dropping onto the grass and disappearing with no trace.

The side door smashed open and her father fell through, his hands bound by some kind of hard, grey foam, his mouth sealed by strips of thick black tape. A loud snap rang through the air and her mother cried out and fell to the ground, blood pouring from her leg.

More uniformed men rushed up the side of the house, dragging her father with them. The two men holding her father threw him down beside Lizzy's mother and stepped aside. A tall burly man marched up to Lizzy, and grabbing her arm, lifted her into the air, holding her so tight she screamed as the man carried her over to her parents on the ground.

"Jack and Rosa Francis, you are charged with the crimes of making false statements that jeopardise the stability of the British Government and its people; not registering a female birth; conspiring to conceal a magician child and resisting arrest. How do you plead?" He spat on the ground. "Who cares," he said and with his free hand, took out a pistol and shot her parents dead while she watched. The man was laughing as she lost consciousness.

***

Lizzy seemed to be unaware she was rubbing her arm. "His name was Cameron Palant, it was on his shoulder." Her face dropped. "Sorry," she whispered.

Lizzy didn't look up when Chris raised his arm slowly and put it over her shoulder. "You're the first person I've told." She put her hand over his, "We used to talk so much, Chris, didn't we?"

"Yeah."

"It's this house," she sniffed, "the magic of the family that lived here. It feels so safe."

"I know," Chris could feel it too; warm, familiar, a security where the world couldn't get to you, where it was safe to remember, to miss people.

"Sometimes I wish I could forget." She put the mug down and fixed her eyes on the fruit bowl. "For months I told myself it was a dream. I believed that for a long time. They didn't even get a funeral. Sandy taught me how to push feelings back, something she did when she saw horrible things."

Her words reminded Chris of his grandfather's gestures, and out of sight of Lizzy, turned his free hand in the air. The emotion he drained from Lizzy bled into him; grief and pain.

"Anyway, let's see what's for breakfast," Lizzy said. Leaving Chris with all her sadness, she sat down. "Wow, Chris," her eyes widened, "not bad, let's eat." She smiled at the spread. "What world did this food come from?"

Chris shrugged and took a seat beside her, wondering how his granddad had managed to deal with all the painful emotion he'd taken from Chris through the years.

"Are you all right?" Lizzy said.

"Yeah, I'm fine."

"No you're not."

Her grief awakened his own. "I didn't go to my parents' funeral."

"Really?" She picked up a hard-boiled egg and turned it in her hand. "Didn't your... your grandfather take you?" She sniffed the egg and took a bite out of it.

"No," Chris replied flatly.

"What happened?" Lizzy said in between mouthfuls of food.

"Lycus went after them. Granddad escaped with me." Chris started eating and hoped the conversation would go somewhere else.

"Oh," Lizzy tore a piece off a thick slice of bread.

"Before he died, Granddad said they gave me to him because Lycus were getting close to finding out who they were. That was the last time." Chris drank some milk, it tasted sweet and he stared into the liquid, wishing she'd stop asking questions, wishing he could make himself forget.

"So before then you didn't even ask? About your own parents?"

"No." A tide of sadness, and anger at himself, his grandad stirred inside him and he wished he didn't feel Lizzy's pain so much. Taking her pain was a stupid idea. Who did he think he was?

Lizzy was staring at him.

"What?" Chris snapped.

"Maybe they... maybe he wasn't telling you the truth, maybe—"

"What? They ran away and left me with a stranger?"

Lizzy shrugged, and a fleeting, familiar, cheeky smile crossed her face. She was trying to cheer him up and it wasn't working.

"Just shut up."

"Sorry."

They ate in silence for a while then Lizzy asked. "Didn't you ask what happened, even when you were older?"

"No!" He threw the bread onto the table. "I said I never thought about them, right? So stop bloody interrogating me, okay?"

"All right," Lizzy said. "Fake Granddad must have put one heavy-duty forgetting spell on you."

"You think I don't know that?" Chris pushed the chair back and it crashed to the floor as he stood up and glared at her.

"But Chris, it doesn't make sense. Your granddad casts a spell that makes you forget about them for years. Then, when he takes away the spell, the Alumbrados blows your block up just to try to kill you. And you don't know why?"

"No, but yeah, you nailed it," Chris raised his voice. "I'm in the middle of a massive conspiracy, okay?" He threw the mug across the room and it smashed against the wall. Magic – messed up his whole stupid life. Chris moved his hand and the shards of broken crockery gathered up and flew towards a fist-sized black hole that sucked up the food and everything else on the table. Then the rest of the food he'd magicked up took off from the table and crashed into each other. Big, ugly clumps of broken mugs, plates and mashed-up food shot through the air towards the small void.

Lizzy jumped up and moved away from the table. "Chris," she cried out, "stop it!"

Chris sliced a hand through the air and the black hole blinked out of existence. The mess of food, bowls and plates swirling through the air crashed back onto the table in a globby, crunched-up pool that spread and leaked to the floor in heavy, loud squelches.

Breathless, Lizzy leaned against the kitchen unit with a hand to her chest, gaping at Chris while he stared down at the mess on the table and floor. There was a scrabbling in the hallway then Spyro ran into the room and jumped up at him for attention but he pushed her away.

"You scared me."

"And you're giving me a bloody headache."

"We were just talking, I didn't expect you to freak out because you don't know stuff. It's not my fault."

"Forget it, just leave me alone." Chris stormed down the short hallway into a large living room and slammed the door shut. He stood for a few seconds then swore at the walls before falling onto a sofa. Spyro pawed at him for affection and, feeling guilty, he reached down and stroked her head. "It's all right, Spyro." If only he could get rid of these crappy feelings in his head.

"You don't have to worry about this kind of shit do you?" he said, stroking Spyro. After a while she went and lay on the bare wooden floor in front of the large fireplace and looked up at him. Chris looked around the room.

A couple of books, a small stack of comics and some coasters were scattered across a square coffee table between him and another sofa opposite. To one side of the fireplace, a cable TV box rested on a low cabinet under the TV on the wall.

Chris got up and pulled the curtains open, letting bright afternoon sunlight stream in through the patio doors. Stains of absent photographs covered the walls. A few old colouring books lay on the floor beside an empty bookshelf. Taking the atlas and key from his pocket he put them on the coffee table then picked the key up and turned it in his hands. He should give it to Lizzy, like Granddad asked.

Lizzy came in and sat beside him, "You okay?"

"Yeah, sorry about that. Twelve years, Lizzy, I never even thought to ask about my mum and dad, not even once; thanks to my granddad's spell." Spyro sat up and leaned against his leg. Chris spoke as he stroked her head. "I did stupid things sometimes; got really mad because I couldn't remember stuff. I've been the wrong person for years because of him. I wish I knew who he was, what he really wanted."

"You miss him?"

"Yeah," Chris sighed, "crazy, innit?" he blinked rapidly and swallowed. "He cared a lot. I guess... I guess he was just protecting me."

Chapter Eleven

"This was everything in my granddad's pockets," Chris pointed at the key on the coffee table. "He told me to give that to you, I don't know what it's for."

"A rusty old key?"

"He gave me this too," Chris lifted the crystal from under his T-shirt.

"A crystal," Lizzy said, wistfully. "I had one like that," she paused then added, "Mum and Dad too."

"Granddad says it hides me from other magicians."

"Not me though, then again, I already knew you were a magician."

"Sorcerer."

"Yes, a sorcerer who doesn't know about crystals."

"Yes I do, it hides me from other magicians."

"You don't know it can open portals for instant travel, do you?"

"Oh, no, I didn't know that. Wait, you're not joking again are you?"

"No. What about your atlas?"

"That was probably on the bookshelf for years. I think. Alumbrados could have nicked that any time." He stopped and thought for a second. "If they knew about it. Besides, blowing up my flat would have ruined it."

Lizzy picked up the key. Thin streams of golden light flowed through the tiny scratches that were along one side. Lizzy gasped as letters 'ST JEABAD' appeared below the glowing lines. Lizzy threw the key down and it bounced and slid across the coffee table. The cracks and light on the key faded away.

Chris caught the key, "What's going on? What just happened?"

Lizzy had crossed to the other side of the room, "What the hell are you doing with that key?"

"I just told you," Chris said, also raising his voice, "don't just stare at me like that, what is it?"

"That was a tree."

"What tree?"

"Those scratches on the key."

"Okay. So?"

She raised her eyes slowly to his and stared at him with a look of trepidation. "Did your granddad say anything else about it?"

"Jeez, now you're creeping me out. He said bring it to you, find the fourth book."

"The key," Lizzy said. "Your granddad didn't say 'fourth', he said 'Thoth'."

"Meaning?"

"That key, ST JEABAD, it's a clue to where the Book of Thoth is hidden."

"The book of what?"

"Not what, who. Thoth, an ancient Egyptian. The god of magic and writing."

"So?"

"Your family must be the custodians of the key," Lizzy said. "I thought it was just a story. Only the custodians can open the resting place of the book."

"I got no idea what you're talking about."

"Okay. One family through history, related to Thoth, is the custodian of the key."

"I'm related to a god now, yeah, right. And we look after this key?"

"Yes," Lizzy pointed, "that key, going right back to ancient Egypt."

"Just to protect one book?"

"The most powerful book of spells ever written; talking to animals, bringing the dead to life, controlling the weather. Talking to gods. The kind of magic that could change the world."

The realisation dawned on them at the same time and Chris said, "No wonder Alumbrados killed hundreds of people just to get at me. Hang on, they tried to kill me, how does that help them?"

"That magic blast threatened your life so it probably kicked off your innate magic, like what happened to me in the ambulance."

"Granddad, all those people were killed because of me, this book?"

"And they'll keep on doing whatever they need to until they get it. All those raids are just to flush you out."

"How do you know all this stuff? I thought you were locked up for twelve years."

"I've been staying with magicians since I got out. We do this thing called talking, and reading, you should try it sometime." Lizzy stopped talking abruptly.

"What is it?" Chris said.

"I'm here, with you."

"And?"

"Don't you see? They wanted me to escape. They knew my innate magic could help you find the book." Lizzy looked over to the mound and Tir Na nÓg, where hundreds of magicians across time were doing nothing to help. "We could use the magic from the book to rescue everyone."

"We... no." Chris shook his head. "Forget it."

"What?"

"No way, if we've been set up, I'm not going to play along. I should use some kind of magic, sorcery or whatever, to destroy the key, make sure Alumbrados don't even try to get their hands on the book. Then they'll back off from me."

"Chris, with that kind of magic we could..."

"No, no no no," Chris jumped up and walked across to the window. "It's bloody obvious Alumbrados are psychos. I'm not getting myself killed, oh and the hundreds of other people they might kill along the way to getting to me again."

"All you think about is yourself."

"It's worked fine for me so far."

"Newsflash, Brainiac, the key can't be destroyed, nor can the book."

Chris threw a hand in the air. "Well that's just brilliant, so now I'm bloody cursed with it."

"You're not cursed, I am."

"Oh yeah?" Chris snapped. "How'd you figure that out?"

"That tree. It's how I'm going to die."

"What?"

***

Sandy's story

The storm took hours to arrive. Blinding bursts of light splashed through a sky weighed down with dark clouds. Thunder rolled towards the Secure Unit like giant, crashing boulders. Flashes of lightning illuminated the grey cell, squeezing thin shadows out of the few pictures glued to the walls.

"Lizzy," Sandy's shivering voice was barely audible against the shattering downpour outside. "Can I come into your bunk?"

Lizzy had been waiting for her to ask. Four years younger than Lizzy, Sandy was the newest arrival at Salem and had quickly attached herself to Lizzy so the wardens put them together.

"Come on then," Lizzy said.

Sandy climbed in beside Lizzy. "It's so loud."

"Thor must be angry tonight," Lizzy said.

"Maybe he'll come and rescue us," Sandy said.

"Maybe."

Sometimes the sound like that of a great beast howling and crying out in a distant cave pushed through the storm and Sandy would hug Lizzy even tighter. They lay and listened to the storm and strange howls. When it was over, Sandy quickly fell asleep. Lizzy listened to Sandy's breathing settle and deepen, then she, too, drifted off.

The hollow murmuring of Sandy's visionary voice whispering in that eerie tone that sounded like it was carried on her fading breath, woke Lizzy. "Lizzy, the little room, so dark under the tree, all alone in your tomb. So still, so cold. No book, no spell to call you back. No borrowed breath, no spell, no breath, no spell, no more birthdays..." Her words merged into her breathing and Sandy fell silent.

Lizzy stared at the slats under Sandy's bunk, her heart pounding so hard she feared it would wake Sandy curled up beside her. Haunted by the thought of dying after her eighteenth birthday, she drifted in and out of restless sleep until the morning alarm rang through the prison.

***

"She predicted how you were going to die?"

Lizzy sat on the sofa opposite Chris, shrugged. "We have to get the book, Chris. If we don't, Lycus will keep hunting girls, locking us up, experimenting on us, killing..."

"Wait, you want to get the book and use the magic to rescue all the girls in Salem?"

"And liberate all the magicians everywhere."

"Fight Lycus, the army, police, the whole country, start another bloody war?"

"Magicians never kill people."

Chris gave her a look.

"Okay not intentionally."

Chris's thoughts went back to being surrounded by the decimated building, the remains of all those people around him; hundreds dead because of him, and now Lizzy wanted him to start a war. Well that wasn't going to happen, ever, not the way things were now. He got up and headed for the door.

"Where are you going?"

"Outside. This whole thing is doing my head in. I need to get out of this space." Chris marched out of the living room and swung the door shut behind him.

Chris went through the kitchen into the garden. A hazy, cool sun hung behind a pale grey sky and a light breeze drifted through the eerie silence. Head down, he stomped around the garden, kicking stones and swearing at himself.

Magicians; bloody idiots, why didn't they just keep quiet and hide away, mind their own business? He spotted Lizzy at the window, watching him. She was ready to give her life for magicians. He turned away and wandered over to sit on a swing.

He felt a push on his back and almost cried out. Lizzy was standing behind him.

She sat on the swing next to him. "I scared you didn't I?"

"No."

"You almost screamed."

"No I didn't."

"Like a little girl."

"Shut up. How come you're not scared?"

"About what?"

"Dying, under that tree?"

"I was, at first." Lizzy shrugged and began to swing. "I wondered how I'd get out of the Unit for it to happen. After a few weeks, or maybe it was months, I stopped thinking about it."

"Until now," Chris swung slowly beside her. "And you still want to do it?"

"I know, but it's different now, it's not for nothing. I think about all my friends being free, what we could do together; stand up to Lycus and Alumbrados and those other things."

"What other things?"

"Vampires and Fae."

"Yeah and werewolves and Frankenstein."

161

"Chris, they're real."

"Sick, and whose side are they on?"

"It depends on whose side you're on."

She was right, doing nothing is to side with the enemy; just taking care of himself, forgetting about everyone else, wasn't an option.

"So," Chris said, "who is this ST JEABAD? Have you heard of him?"

"No. We'll have to find out. Wait, are you saying you'll help?"

"Yeah," Chris said, "I suppose."

A broad smile spread across her face. "Show me some of your spells, I'll need them if we are going to do this."

Chris sighed, "Fine." he said and slipped off the swing.

Back in the living room he flicked through the atlas. "Some spells are stops on the board where something can happen. Other spells and abilities are on cards or written along the lines that are a path from one stop to another; which means you can join spells up." He looked at her. "If you're a sorcerer."

"You don't know I'm not."

"Yeah, right."

"I want a useful spell, a good one to start with."

"I suppose we could do with a waypoint. Draw a circle, with water."

"You're giving me orders?"

"You wanted me to teach you a spell."

"Teach? You mean show, show me how to do a spell."

"All right, show; draw a circle and I'll show you."

Lizzy went around the low square coffee table and knelt in front of the fireplace. Using the water bottle, she wetted her finger and drew a circle on the wood floor with her finger. "A secure house in the middle of an abandoned island crawling with monsters? It's perfect. We can come here if we need to get away."

"The *Atlas of Elegance* calls it 'A Singular Refuge'."

"There." Lizzy completed the circle.

"Okay," Chris said, "we need to make a real, I mean a personal, connection with the symbolic, so only we can use it."

"Right." Lizzy pulled out a small Swiss army knife. She pricked her finger and let a few drops of blood fall into the ring. "There, come on, your go."

"A strand of hair would have done."

"Probably for the game version. This is real; blood is stronger, what keeps us alive."

"Since when did you become an expert?"

"Since there was such a thing as the patently obvious. Come on, your blood."

Chris crossed over to her and before he could stop her, Lizzy jabbed the end of the penknife into his thumb.

"Ouch." He winced and let a few drops fall to the ground then sucked the end of his thumb.

"Aw, did it hurt? Do you want me to kiss it better?"

He sucked his finger and gave her a look.

Lizzy shoved him, "You're disgusting."

Chris laughed.

"Shut up," Lizzy said. "What's the hand movement and spell for folding?"

"I still want a strand of hair."

"No."

"That's what it says in the atlas."

"Blood's from inside the body, part of what keeps us alive so it's more personal. Besides, you can't have my hair."

"I just need one strand."

"No," she glared at him. "Forget it. That was for the game anyway. This is real."

"Why are you getting so uptight? It's not as if I want all of it."

Lizzy turned away from him.

"Well I'm doing it anyway, just in case." Chris pulled a hair from his head and dropped it in the circle. "Come on, be fair, give me a strand of your hair. A deal's a deal."

"No!"

"Jeez, what is it with you? getting all upset over one little strand of hair. You OCD about your hair or something?"

"Fine. You really want to know?" Lizzy swiped a hand over her spiky short blonde hair and it disappeared. "There, happy now?" She crossed the room and fell onto the sofa. Chris went and sat beside her.

"Sorry," he nudged her shoulder with his. "I think it looks cool."

"You would."

"No, really."

"I look like a criminal."

"You are."

She shoved him so he tilted over.

"It's like Spyro's hair." He stroked her head.

"Get off," Lizzy pushed him away and managed a smile.

"Those three guys," Chris said. "They got what they deserved."

"I'm wanted for murder."

"They kicked it off, not you. You didn't make it happen, they did, those guards got themselves killed. It was self-protection."

"I didn't mean to. It just happened."

"Like the stoor back at that shop," Chris said.

Lizzy nodded, "I got out of the ambulance and ran."

"They must have known about your defence."

"No one in the Unit knows who's got what magic; and they'd pumped so many drugs into me they probably thought I was helpless."

"What happened then?"

"The road went through a forest. I just kept running until I came out on another road. Someone picked me up and then I made my way to Bristol." She crossed the room and sat beside Chris. "Then it all went wrong."

"Really? What happened?"

"You turned up."

"Hilarious," Chris said, dryly, "please stop, oh my ribs."

Lizzy smiled. "We should use your crystal and go before sunset."

"Go where?"

"London, get some real food, not this medieval stuff. I'm not staying here another night." Lizzy crossed the room and closed the curtains. "Hold it out, I'll show you."

Chris grinned. "Really?"

"Shut up. Just hold the crystal out."

Chris held the crystal at arm's length and Lizzy moved his arm so the crystal was between her and the thick curtain. "Sahami Noruk, Dilius mroalim," she said and cast a thin beam of light into the crystal. As she moved the light gently around the surface, broadening and narrowing the stream, images flashed on the curtain; stone circles, pyramids, cave mouths, waterfalls, ancient mounds, rock formations, churches, temples, houses.

"Wow," Chris said. "That is some awesome spell. I wish I could—"

"Chris, I'm trying to concentrate."

"Sorry."

Lizzy steadied her hand and images flickered on the curtain.

"I recognise some of those places," Chris said.

"Places linked to magic," Lizzy replied, her eyes focussed firmly on the crystal. "It's a livestream from around the world."

"Slow down a bit."

"I'm working on it." The images blinked between gigantic stone carvings and rocks leading into the sea. Lizzy managed to steady the refraction on a waterfall.

"That's no good," Chris said. "We need to be inside."

"Duh."

An old church surrounded by high walls and 'Keep Out' signs appeared. "That's a London street sign," Chris said. "That'll do. Here, Spyro."

"Wait," Lizzy said and her face tightened in concentration and the fuzzy interior of the church steadied into a sharp image. "Okay."

Spyro trotted up to them and Lizzy took Chris's hand and they stepped forward. The image expanded and spread around them until they were standing in a musty church hall. Dust particles floated in the light coming in through three tall arched windows that illuminated the white walls and blue floor tiles.

"This is so much cooler than folding." Chris walked around and knelt down to pick up an old hymn book. "Saint Silas Church," he said and continued to wander about the hall, stopping at a large collage put together by the families. "Says Merlin lived near here. There're caves between here and Kings Cross."

Lizzy found an old photograph of some kind of party with people sitting at a long dining table. "I could do with some proper food."

Chris tapped the photograph. "Who do you want to be?"

"You know the camouflage spell? What's it called in your little book?"

"Guise and Guile. A special talent is learned in a strange land. You are a stranger no more." Chris smiled to himself. "Granddad used to have a hat and fake beard."

Lizzy pointed at a young woman. "I'll be her." She uttered the incantation and transformed into a young woman with short blonde hair and round glasses.

Chris took the form of an older white man in his thirties dressed in a slate-grey suit; he could be her father.

Lizzy smiled at him, "Not bad."

"You prefer older men?"

Lizzy thumped his arm, "The spell, you twit."

"Why don't we use your crystal magic to find the tree?" Chris said. "After all, how many trees have magic in their history?"

Lizzy shook her head at him. "Hundreds, maybe more. Druids? Trees at crossroads? Why do you think so many old churches have even older trees in the graveyards?"

Chris shrugged.

"Because," Lizzy said, "the early Christians built churches over the old pagan and Druid sacred sites or near them."

"How do you know all this stuff?"

"Didn't you have books at home?"

"Yeah, okay, fine, I wasn't interested. I get it. Hey, how about that professor woman?"

"What professor woman?"

"She was on TV, supports lighter laws for magicians. Isabelle something."

"Isabelle Cross, she visited Salem a few times, I met her. What about her?"

"You met her? Great, maybe she'll help. After all, she's on our side isn't she?"

"She talked to a lot of people, besides, how would she know what tree it is?"

"Not her. I bet her computer's got access to all those university libraries, even the restricted ones with books about magic."

"She wouldn't risk helping us."

"Call her, it's the only way to find out."

"No, she won't remember me."

"Go on, tell her what happened, she'll believe you. After all, she even bothers to visit magicians in prisons."

"I don't know."

"Oh come on, Lizzy, she'll either say yes or no, we might as well give it a go."

"You call her if you like. I don't want to get anyone into trouble."

***

They stepped out into the early evening air and Chris took in a deep breath, "I never thought standing in a street would feel so good."

They both froze when a convoy of Lycus vehicles rumbled past. A long prison bus, a truckload of soldiers and two armoured Jeeps.

An old lady with an even older brown-haired scraggy dog on the end of a bright red lead, stopped beside them on the corner of the street. "They get round to sorting those reevers out." She crossed the road and headed towards the high street where another convoy had ignored the red lights and rumbled down towards Kings Cross.

Lizzy pointed across the road to a sign on a chalk 'A' board standing on the pavement outside the pub. "They do food. How much money do you have?"

"What's that look for?" Chris said, reaching into his pocket. "What the... Hey."

"How do you think I bought the food and papers the other day?"

"So where's the rest?"

"I gave it to some monks."

"You're being serious aren't you?"

"They protect magicians."

"For that money they could run a bloody hotel."

"Well, if you've got no money we could eat medieval again."

"Tch, I got more," Chris grumbled.

They ordered their food, then took their drinks to a table outside. Chris examined the key while they waited, turning it in front of his face. "Maybe there's some other signs on it."

When the food arrived, he put the key down on the table. Spyro had a minute steak for herself. Chris cut it up and dropped pieces down to her. She seemed indifferent to their change in appearance and more interested in the pieces of meat. The last of the stallholders from the Chapel Street market locked up and smiled at Spyro as he passed them to go into the pub.

"Well, what's the incantation to get us back to the farmhouse?" Lizzy said.

Chris leaned over and whispered, "Evsular banabak." He waited a moment and moved his hands between them, "And you move your left hand like this."

"Cool, next I want you to show me the Immutable Shield."

They had just finished eating when Lizzy tapped his foot with hers, "Chris, don't look now, but that guy across the road has been watching us for a while, he's coming over."

Chris turned just as the teenager broke into a sprint. Running past them, he grabbed the key and shot off down Chapel Street. Chris rose to go after him when a man jumped up from a table at a café down the road and grabbed the teenager. They tussled and the teenager twisted out of the man's grip and ran off.

Lizzy leaned over to Chris and whispered, "It's a scam, they're in it together."

"What?"

"It's a trick we play on new nurses, a way of getting them to trust us. That guy's after something. They're both in on it."

Aside from his wide-brimmed fedora and handlebar moustache, the man seemed ordinary enough. Dressed in dark grey jacket and trousers, he approached them holding the key up.

"You're sure you're not paranoid?" Chris said.

"You should learn to trust your gut feeling," Lizzy replied. "That's half of getting the magic right."

"What would he want?" Chris said.

"Who else knows about the key?"

"Oh crap."

The man smiled and handed the key over, "I believe this is yours?"

"Thanks," Chris took the key.

"You are most welcome. That's a very old key. It must be of great value to you."

"It's been in the family a while," Chris said. "Let me buy you a drink."

"Thank you," the man nodded and took the remaining chair at their small table. "I'll just have a lemonade, I understand it's locally made."

Chris went into the bar and came out with the drink; a few cubes of ice and a slice of lemon floated on the top and condensation had already formed around the glass. He sat down and passed the glass to the man who was talking with Lizzy about the midnight robberies.

"… They knock on doors a few minutes before midnight asking if they can stay because of the reavers. They then rob the house, holding the residents, usually elderly people, hostage. Police are warning people to watch out for vans parked nearby. It's where the criminals go if they can't gain entrance in time."

A flash of suspicion crossed the man's face when he reached for the glass, and instead of lifting it to drink, he moved it closer to him along the table, "Thanks, Chris." A look of surprise crossed his face, "Well, that is quite unlike me, to falter in my deception." He put the glass down and rubbed his thumb and forefinger together, "Clever, you put the spell on the condensation around the outside of the glass and not the drink."

"Yep," Chris said with a smile and nod. "I guessed if you were good enough to see through the disguise spell, you'd notice others. I just put it where you weren't expecting it."

"A drop to loosen the tongue," the man nodded. "Well played, sir. You have the advantage of me." He dried his fingers on a paper napkin then wiped his thumb and forefinger along his moustache.

"Who are you and what do you want?" Chris said.

"I am Fernando Méndez, humble servant of the Alumbrados."

Chris shot Lizzy a glance but Lizzy was looking up and down the street.

"Yes, as for the second part of your question, I seek access to the custodian of the Book, namely you." Fernando leaned forward. "The Book of Thoth," he said, barely able to hide his excitement, "written by a god himself, hidden for millennia; so long believed to be a myth. Just think, to control the weather, animals, bring the dead—"

"Yeah, yeah. What was your plan?" Chris said.

"My masters have been looking for you ever since your parents disappeared."

"You mean they're not dead?"

Fernando shrugged, "All I know is you are the last in the blood line, so I presume they are." Fernando paused to lick his thin, pale lips, then continued. "As custodian, only you have the ability to use the key and are immune to the protective, and very deadly, enchantments surrounding the Book. I was to gain your trust and help you find the Book's location. After you handed it to me, I was to have you killed and deliver the Book to my masters."

"Why did it take so long to find me?"

"Lycus learned of your parents twelve years ago but did not know they had a child. We learned about Weston and his central role in the rescue attempt and came across you. That led us to look closer at the DNA sample taken at the police station and discover who you really were. The explosion was to awaken your innate powers. Blaming you for it triggered a nationwide hunt and put pressure on you, making the job of finding you easier."

"Was it you?" Chris said, his face grim. "Did you blow the block up?"

"Me? No, that kind of work is left for the shadow fae."

"The who?"

"Fae. How can I explain? Imagine fairies but as large as you and me and with magical powers greater than any magician or sorcerer you know."

"And they're evil?"

Fernando shook his head, "Evil, such a human term. What does that even mean? No, the fae clans effortlessly traverse between our realm and theirs. Their realms are bountiful and ideally suited to each species. They have no need to invade other lands, abuse, exploit, persecute the vulnerable or fight wars."

"But your shadow fae mates are okay about killing humans."

"Shadow fae? Yes, their land is uniquely barren, they are outcasts and mercenaries."

Chris was about to ask another question when Lizzy leaned over and nudged him. "This is weird," she whispered, "can we go?"

"No, he knows stuff, I want to ask him some more questions."

"Try talking to regular magicians."

"What's that supposed to mean?"

Fernando sat back, sipped his drink and watched them bicker, a smile on his face.

"Magicians, people who are not crooks."

"I'm no crook," Fernando said.

"Okay, people who work for Alumbrados or Lycus."

"I don't work for…" Fernando began and both Chris and Lizzy glared at him. Fernando raised his eyebrows, shrugged and took another sip of his drink and continued to watch Chris and Lizzy bicker.

"Oh right," Chris said, still angry with Lizzy. "You mean meet up and chat with decent people like you did."

"Yes," Lizzy replied.

"Well I'm sorry I didn't have time to make social calls. I was too busy trying to stay out of sight while the country hunts me down."

"Fine job you did of that." Lizzy said, glancing at Fernando who pursed his lips and with a shake of the head raised his hands as if to say, 'keep me out of this'.

"What, you blaming me for this too?" Chris said, then turned to Fernando. "How did you find us?"

"A shadow fae hound. After you folded from the bookshop, Lycus gave it the essence of your folding. It has been waiting here in London for you to return. When your folding essence reappeared, it tracked you here."

"So now you can track me anywhere in London?"

"Not anywhere, the essence of a folding cannot be tracked over water: rivers, streams, lakes. Similarly the Fae hounds cannot cross water."

Lizzy glanced at Chris and murmured, "You should have showered back at the house."

Chris kicked her under the table and Fernando smiled.

"Come on, Chris let's go; and make him forget he ever met us."

Chris nodded and said to Fernando, "Who is your... I mean the Alumbrados' leader?"

"I have no idea. I receive a phone call with instructions and I carry them out." Fernando sniffed and brushed nothing off the knee of his trousers and took another sip of his drink. "In return for my services I am not bothered by the authorities, and given sufficient blood to survive."

"Blood?" Chris and Lizzy said in unison.

"Of course, how else are Alumbrados expected to survive? We are vampires after all."

Chris gaped at him then turned to Lizzy who gave him a brief 'told you so' smile. Chris went to ask another question when Lizzy kicked his shin. Chris nodded, leaned towards Fernando and whispered something. Fernando stood up and walked away.

"Where's he going?" Lizzy said.

"Back to start. He's going home to think he just got the phone call to come find us here." Chris got up and unhooked Spyro's lead from the table leg. "I bet they've been looking for that book for hundreds of years."

Lizzy shuddered, "Who knows what else they'll do to force you to get the book?"

"They can forget it," Chris said as they headed to the phone box. "They're not getting it, I am." He swung open the red door and picked up the receiver. "Better not waste any more time then."

***

Chris had a grim look on his face as he came out of the phone box.

"So did you speak with her?" Lizzy said.

Chris responded with a glum nod.

"See? I told you," Lizzy said. "I knew she wouldn't help."

"Gotcha," Chris beamed. "She wants to meet us, she remembers you."

"Really?" Lizzy arched her eyebrows. "Even though we're wanted for terrorism and murder?"

"She believes we were set up. She knows no magician has ever killed a straight, ever."

"Still, Chris, it could be a trap."

"I know, we'll be careful." Chris hailed a taxi, a three-seater thing pulled by a pair of bicycles ridden by two women in their twenties.

Chapter Twelve

The cab dropped Lizzy and Chris off a couple of streets away and, still in their disguises, they walked the last few hundred yards to the street where Isabelle lived. Chris felt out with the eyes of Gorzhep to detect the force of any magical traps or concealments. There were none.

"Just ordinary people," He said as they turned into the street.

Professor Isabelle Cross lived in a tall square house on the corner of two tree-lined streets in Tufnell Park. A path from the driveway led up one side of the house. On the other side of the house, the garden wall ran down the side of the street. Easy place to break into, Chris thought, along the path or over the garden wall, high enough for no one to see.

They went up the steps to the door. Lizzy hesitated and rang the bell. They waited a minute but no one answered. "It only took us half an hour to get here, where could she be?"

"Give the door a knock, maybe the bell isn't working." Chris had his back to the door and was looking up and down the street. A couple of houses had scaffolding across the front with workmen repairing a roof and fixing windows. In the drive of another house, a woman was leaned over the open bonnet of a car, repairing something. A raven appeared over the rooftops opposite and flew straight over the professor's house. A minute later they heard movement and a tall woman with long black hair neatly tied back opened the door. "Yes?" she had a slight accent Chris couldn't place.

"Hi," Chris said. "I'm Chris, I called earlier."

"Chris, you look so different. This is astonishing. Come in, come in," Isabelle said, "and Lizzy, it's good to see you again."

She led them down the hallway and Lizzy nudged Chris. She gave him a confused, worried look and mouthed something Chris didn't understand. She. Spyro snuffled along the floor as they walked. "He can probably smell my cat."

"Spyro is a she," Chris said.

"Oh, I'm sorry," Isabelle smiled. "Well, this is all rather exciting isn't it?" She pushed open a door and led them into a large room with a kitchen at one end and a dining table at the other.

Beyond the table, the far wall was a series of wide glass doors with a strange, non-reflective tint to them. Isabelle pointed to a sofa and a couple of armchairs beside a small bookcase. "Please, sit down. I'll make us some tea."

Isabelle returned to the kitchen area and Lizzy gave Chris another worried look as he sat down on the sofa. Isabelle was being strangely casual about having two wanted criminals in her house, "Are you okay about this?" Chris said.

"Yes, you are not the first clandestine magicians who have visited. Speaking to them is invaluable to my research. Plus you bear no resemblance to your true selves."

"You've met other magicians here?" Lizzy said, examining the books on the bookshelf. She took out an atlas with a bookmark in it. Sitting down she began to flick through the pages.

"Yes," Isabelle said, eyeing Lizzy, "I've learned much from my discussions with them. There is only so much you can learn from observation and literary research." She filled the teapot with real, brown tea and opened a small packet of biscuits. "I see you are interested in the atlas, Lizzy?"

"Oh, just wondering where the Unit was."

Chris couldn't help noticing the scarcity of food in her cupboards. "What?" he mouthed to Lizzy, who had replaced the atlas and gave him another worried look.

Isabelle put the cups and small bowl onto a tray.

Spyro lay down beside Lizzy and rested his chin on her foot.

"Can I use the laptop, please?" Lizzy said.

"Unfortunately the network is down, a car struck the cable junction box at the top of the street." Isabelle placed some biscuits in the small white bowl. "Chris," she said, glancing over her shoulder, "I'm sorry to hear about your grandfather's death. I understand he took you in and cared for you after you lost your parents."

"Did you know him?"

She glanced over her shoulder, there was something predatory about the look she gave him "No, why do you ask?"

"Oh, uh, he taught part-time at the academy. I just thought, well, what with you being a professor."

"I see," Isabelle seemed to relax. "No, we never met, different circles and all that."

"Okay," Chris replied. Now he started to sense something wasn't right.

Isabelle brought the tray over and sat in the armchair beside Chris. "So, what brings you here, are you looking for somewhere to stay?"

"No," Lizzy and Chris replied in unison, then Lizzy said, "It's a good thing you trust us, after everything they're saying we did. A lot of people wouldn't."

Isabelle paused with the teapot in her hand then began pouring. "I consult with senior police and Lycus investigators. Their accounts of the incidents attributed to you both had too many inconsistencies and errors; and I am familiar in the methods they use to censor and reframe news of events to suit their own purposes. That is why I am strongly inclined to believe you are both innocent. So, how can I help?"

When Chris finished the story of their encounter with Fernando, Isabelle sat back, "My God."

"What?" Chris said.

"You have the key?"

Lizzy shot Chris a look.

"Not on me." Chris said. It was true, Lizzy had it.

An expression of shock slapped across Isabelle's features.

"It's in a safe place," Chris said.

"I see," Isabelle's tone fell. "The spells in the Book are extremely dangerous, they could damage the very fabric of reality and lead to the destruction of our world."

"Are you saying no one should find it?" Chris said.

"No," Isabelle quickly replied.

"But if it's so dangerous then why—"

Isabelle raised a hand, "It is imperative we find the Book, together. I will make sure it goes to a secure place and doesn't fall into the wrong hands. You do agree that's the right thing to do?" she said, nodding, trying to get him to nod in agreement. Chris knew this trick and didn't fall for it.

"What do you know about the Book, Professor?" Lizzy asked.

"The Book of Thoth is an ancient Egyptian book said to be written by Thoth, the god of writing and knowledge. Personally, I believe Thoth was a being from another realm. The Book contain incantations for five primal spells: control over nature; understanding of animals; ability to see anywhere, even the deepest oceans and the farthest reaches of space; bringing someone or yourself back from death."

"Death?" Chris exclaimed. "Seriously?"

Isabelle responded with a sombre nod, "And the ability to communicate with powerful beings in other realms; or as the Egyptians said, understand the minds of gods. According to legends, the book was buried in the tomb of Neferkaptah in Egypt. There are rumours the CERN incident affected the Book in some way and that was what brought magic back."

"Never heard that before," Chris said.

"The book was brought to England soon after. No one knows where it is hidden."

"How can incantations like that be possible?" Lizzy said. "I've never heard of anyone doing any of those things."

"Nor I, such abilities involve interdimensional energies far greater than any magician or sorcerer can attune to." Isabelle hesitated and made an effort not to look at Chris before continuing. "Those powers could bring a country to its knees. Imagine dominion over an army of every living creature that walks, flies, slithers or crawls, all working together. Raising the dead? One could summon an army of undead. The Book of Thoth could make the wielder of its spells the most powerful and dangerous person on the planet."

Chris smiled down at Spyro who looked up and wagged her tail. He gently fed her half a biscuit. "Talking to animals would be cool though."

Lizzy still looked worried. "I never heard anyone in Salem say anything about other realms and creatures."

Chris shared another biscuit with Spyro, "I bet the book's just a story."

"That's what most Egyptologists thought," Isabelle said. "However not long after the CERN incident, a flood and landslide revealed the upper remains of a temple just outside the city of Khmun in Egypt. Inscriptions inside indicated it was built over the tomb of Neferkaptah, the legendary hiding place of the Book of Thoth. The first to enter was a young man who trekked there every day. It is believed he somehow knew of the Book and was waiting for an opportunity to steal it. The archaeologists who arrived later to secure and catalogue the tomb's contents found no trace of the Book, just an empty chest."

He must have been the custodian, Chris thought. "They never found who stole it?" he said.

Isabelle shook her head, "No."

"Coming back from the dead?" Chris shot a glance at Lizzy. "Really?"

"The resurgence of magic as physiological links to quantum probability and infinite universes means anything is possible."

"No," Chris said. "That sounds like some tuned-out quantum physics."

Lizzy gave him a small, nervous smile.

"Regardless," Isabelle said, taking a sip of her tea and looking into the almost empty cup, "if that book exists, it may well allow communication with beings who have unimaginable powers, powers that made them the gods of legends."

"Do you think these stories are real, professor?" Lizzy said.

Isabelle poured herself another tea, "It is not beyond possibility. I've witnessed devastation that convinced me such powerful beings exist."

"What?" Chris and Lizzy said in unison.

Isabelle though for a moment then said, "What I'm about to tell you is only to emphasise the importance of bringing the Book to me if you find it; the kind of powers that threaten this world." She looked from Chris to Lizzy, and with a glint of pride in her eyes, began. "As part of my research I witnessed an interview with a magician in a purpose-built, top-security prison at a special ops preparation facility. This magician had a unique skill not found in anyone else; he could go into a trance and be possessed by an entity that called itself Urizen. I had to sign the Official Secrets Act to get in. That was where reavers first appeared."

Isabelle stroked Spyro's head and slid her hand along the studded leather collar before she composed herself and continued. "The magician agreed to work with the army in return for a few liberties; a cable TV and radio, some magazines, to work in a garden. As I said, he was the only magician with the ability to speak with the Entity."

***

The Reavers

The lecture hall filled with senior government politicians and over four hundred generals from all military forces. Silence fell as

177

two men walked onto the stage where two yellow padded chairs with narrow armrests had been set facing each other diagonally. A small table stood in between. Professor Brian Howard, easily recognised by his long white hair, faded jeans and a leather biker jacket, sat on one of the chairs. The magician, a guy in his twenties, short cropped hair, dressed in a prisoner's orange jumpsuit, sat in the other chair.

Behind them, a large screen displayed the two men sitting, comfortable and relaxed.

"How do you feel, Roy?" the professor asked.

"Okay, thanks, Brian. Should I start?"

"If you would, please."

Roy leaned back, closed his eyes and took a few deep breaths. His body fell limp and he slumped back into the chair. Five minutes passed and a few people in the auditorium became restless and shuffled about.

"Silence." The deep voice coming from Roy resonated through the lecture hall and filled it with a fearful hush. Roy's motionless body now emanated the presence of a being of unimaginable power sitting on a throne. The voice one that had seen aeons of civilizations come and go, seen countless deaths and slaughter, commanded armies that had conquered galaxies. The awe and fear in the hall was tangible. He continued to speak, as if tired of explaining things to imbeciles not worthy of his time or attention.

"Above all, your soldiers must know that firstly victory will be theirs; but they must also be driven by the fear, nay, the dread, of defeat, that death in defeat would lead to timeless, agonised suffering. These two senses are required; the arrogant presumption of conquest, the pleasures and rewards this brings, and second, the utter fear of death in defeat. How can they both be carried into battle at the same time? Know that the crafting of this is what has made me, Urizen, a god in my domain. You wish to learn the secrets of establishing dominion on this petty mote in a mere spit of a realm? Very well."

Roy spoke of military strategy, preparing soldiers for war, victory, and the use of weapons. He spoke of psychological warfare, the weather, the use of drugs and magic, poetry, art, hunger, food, desire and fear. "The true leader is a master strategist, a composer, a conductor. Turning all societies ambitions into military conquest, turn all culture has to offer into instruments of war, he must create a symphony that brings to the enemy the sound of complete and utter destruction; to his own army, the fanfare of total, absolute victory. That is all."

An elderly man with a hearing aid, dressed in a grey, ill-fitting suit, stood up and someone handed him a microphone. "I understand you won the war, but was there a battle you ever lost?"

Roy's strange smile, magnified on the screen behind him, sent a ripple of foreboding through the hall. Men who had seen countless gruesome injuries, horrific deaths and hours of suspects being tortured; all shuddered at the sight of that smile. Urizen, still speaking through Roy, said, "My enemy summoned reavers, creatures from Diman-Ar, a dark, remote, chaotic realm, at the time unknown to me. These creatures exist only to slaughter and devour their victims. They are born for the violence of war and fight to the death. A death that only decapitation can bring. With almost all my forces destroyed, my army was weak, but my strategy was superior. With the last of my energy, I combined two simple spells and took control of the reavers' most basic desire. My enemy's final, desperate attempt to defeat me thus failed. He surrendered and I let the reavers, now my reaver army, feast until nothing was left of him, his army or his race. Then I let them loose to feed on his homeworld. Thus was it known that for just one to stand against me will lead to the destruction of millions. Only one other planet of those in my realm has ever made that same mistake."

An ageing general broke the rule of speaking while Roy was possessed. "Only decapitation?" the old man said. "We could do with these reavers in our army."

A cruel smile crossed Roy's face and the lecture hall filled with guttural howls and the deafening sound of a wild, rushing wind. The hall filled with loud snaps as cracks spread across the stage. The cracks widened and chunks of stage fell into darkness that grew into a great chasm. The void sucked in the rear wall, the partitions on the side of the stage and first half dozen rows of the auditorium. Pandemonium broke out and people fell over each other in an attempt to reach the exits. Before a single person reached a door, something sucked every sound from the hall, leaving it in total silence; then, everything that had been sucked through the chasm into that other dimension blasted back out. Smashed up pieces of stage, seating, auditorium and body parts showered over the terrified rabble that was once the audience.

At the back of the hall, Isabelle fell to the ground, cowering face down with her hands over her head. Then the reavers emerged and began their savage feeding.

**

"I thought it went on for hours but I was told it only lasted several minutes. I didn't move until the noise died down and I heard someone crying for help."

"So those entities, those gods, are real?" Lizzy said.

"I'm very much afraid so. I suspect the Book of Thoth has the means to allow anybody with the right spell to contact them without having the innate ability Roy was born with. Fortunately there is no other person with that skill, well, not that we know of."

A cat wandered in through the patio door and froze when it saw Lizzy and Chris. Chris shuddered as a wave of dread swept through the room. The feeling was like the one he had when sitting beside his grandfather's cold, unresponsive, body, heavy with death. This was more intense, as if a mangled ton of corpses had been dumped in the room, sucking the warmth and life out of the air. Beside him, Lizzy's face had gone white with fear.

"Pedro!" Isabelle said, surprised by the cat's appearance.

The cat looked at her then at Chris and Lizzy, then turned and shot out of the garden where it disappeared over the fence. Isabelle's face twisted in a momentary flash of rage, then she composed herself.

Lizzy grabbed Chris's forearm, "Chris, we should go."

"Ignore it," Isabelle said, "he's just the neighbour's cat, it's nothing to—"

"Sorry, prof," Chris stood up, quickly followed by Lizzy and began to head for the front door when Lizzy stopped him. She led him past Isabelle, who stared at them with a strange expression, and went out the back and round to the path that led down the side of the house and fell against the wall, Spyro trotting excitedly beside them.

"Fold," Lizzy said, "just get us out of here, now."

**

180

Back in the Orkney house, they both paced around the room, still charged with adrenalin. "That was close," Lizzy said, "way too close."

"You're not kidding. What was that cat?" Chris paced up and down by two long windows, the landscape outside sharpened by the Immutable Shield protecting the house. "I've never been so scared in my life. Jeez, that was the creepiest feeling ever" Chris raised his hand,"Look, it's still shaking."

Spyro went from Lizzy to Chris, confused by their pacing. She tilted her head from side to side and Chris called her over, "Here Spyro." Spyro trotted over to him, and he knelt down and looked in and behind her ears, "What's up, Spyro, there's nothing there." He scratched the top of her head and stood up. "Good thing it's early morning, last thing I need are the stoor and reavers tearing lumps out of each other again."

"It's Isabelle," Lizzy said.

"What about her?"

"She didn't have an aura, nothing. I thought it was me still getting the hang of it. She's a vampire. I think she's one of the Alumbrados, the leader."

"What, wait, hang on, you said you met her in the unit."

"I know, that's the strange thing, she looked exactly the same after 12 years, not one thing different about her face, nothing."

"There was an Isabelle De La Cruz back in the fifteen hundreds. In English that would be Isabelle Cross. Two of her followers were Pedro Ruíz de Alcaraz and Fernando Méndez, the guy we met earlier Just seeing her connected it all together for me. Isabelle, Fernando, Pedro."

"But the vibe came from the cat. How does that work?"

"Pedro, he must be the one who does all the killing, Pedro Ruíz de Alcaraz. He was the bookkeeper. He must know the spell of transmutation. Did you see Isabelle's face when the cat came back unexpectedly? She was furious."

"But they didn't kill us. They could have finished us off with some dark magic."

"You twit, they need us alive to get the book."

"This is unbelievable. Vampires, really?"

"Didn't you notice there were no mirrors or glass picture frames or cabinets anywhere?"

"What a bitch," Chris hesitated, then asked, "What about the tree, did you find anything?"

Lizzy bit her lip and her voice lowered. "It's a yew, I know where it is, where I'll die."

Chapter Thirteen

"I promise, Lizzy, you won't go near the tree, I'll go get the book myself."

"Okay, and if anything goes wrong, don't expect me to come get you."

"Harsh."

"I mean it, Chris."

"All right, I get it," Chris said. "A yew tree; that must have been what my granddad was saying."

"You knew?"

"No, I thought he was saying 'you' as in 'me and you'."

Lizzy had taken the key from her pocket and was examining it.

"Well, Liz," Chris said, "where is it, who's the saint?"

"There is no Saint Jeabad. It was the map grid references that gave me the answer. ST JEABAD is code for a map location. ST is the letters, and JEABAD is 051214. One of the oldest trees in the country is at grid reference ST051214."

"How did you even think of that?"

"We used codes in prison, to send messages the guards couldn't read."

"Lizzy, you're a genius," Chris went to hug her and she leaned away, a worried look on her face.

"I saw it, Chris, the place where I'll die."

"You won't die. You won't go near the tree. Wait, you saw it?"

"A photograph."

Chris took the crystal from his pocket and held it out, "Let's go. We'll bring the book here. No one will know."

"No."

"I can't fold there, Lizzy, I haven't seen the picture. Look, just bring it up on the wall for a second so I can see it then switch off. You stay here and I'll fold there, get the book, job done."

"It could take me ages to find the tree."

"Try concentrating on the picture in your mind."

Lizzy gave him a wary look, "Just make sure you pull the crystal away soon as you see the tree."

"I promise."

Chris held up the crystal and almost fell when Spyro scratched at her neck and toppled onto his leg. He pushed her away gently and lifted the crystal again. "Ready?"

Lizzy responded with a nervous nod. She raised a hand palm down and sent threads of soft, golden light through the darkness. The threads stretched towards the crystal, bent through and cast a blurry image over the wall.

She pursed her lips and concentrated on the image of the tree in her mind. Her fingers delicately moved the glowing threads that merged into a single weave of light and slid through crystal.

"Spyro," Chris said, "stop scratching, you're getting a flea collar soon as I get back." He turned to Lizzy. "Are you thinking of the tree?"

"The one with the room where I might die? What do you think?"

"Shut up, you're not going to die. You're staying here, you won't go anywhere near the tree."

The wall filled with the image of Ashbrittle. A few streets of grey stone houses stood in the bright afternoon. The stream of light curled past a red phone box beside an old school building and wound its way through the streets to a churchyard. A broad tree in the corner of a cemetery appeared, glowing in the sunlight.

"You did it, Lizzy, that must be the tree." The image blurred and Chris turned to Lizzy, "What are you doing?"

"I can't stop my hand shaking."

"You're staying here, remember? Just find the room where the Book is then switch off."

"No."

"Lizzy, please, we're trying to save the world here."

Lizzy laughed nervously and furrowed her brow in concentration. On the wall, a hazy image sharpened to form a small, dark room, illuminated only by Lizzy's threads of light drifting through it. Roots of the tree had broken through cracks and spread along the walls, clinging to them like vines. It was as if something was preventing them from reaching beyond the wall. Behind the dried and broken roots, faded hieroglyphs and images of Egyptian gods covered the walls.

"Wow. Okay, Lizzy, switch off. I'll fold there, grab the book and—"

Lizzy gasped in horror when her light touched a glass case at the far end of the room. "It's pulling me," she screamed, "Chris!"

"Shit!" Chris blurted and grabbed the crystal. It burned his palm and blinding white light cut through the gaps between his fingers making him cry out in pain and let go. The crystal shot out to hover into its original position.

Lizzy stood paralysed, her arm outstretched, hand open. A swirling beam of white light shone from her eyes and merged into the floating crystal then her body started shaking uncontrollably. The image on the wall turned blood-red and the deep, dark stain flooded out around them.

Then everything around the two sorcerers went dark and the air filled with an earthy, stale odour. Spyro tugged at the lead, whimpering. Chris let go and reached his arm out and moved it around in the dark. To his left he felt hard, moist soil and thick gnarled roots covering the wall.

Searching through his memory,. Chris found, 'Grootslang's eye', a spell card to help him see in the dark. "Vula amehlo am," he touched each eye with a thumb and the room lit up, illuminated by a ghostly light. Lizzy lay motionless on a smooth, paved floor, the crystal by her head.

"Lizzy!" Chris fell to his knees beside her and touched her hand; it was cold and lifeless, she'd been dead for hours. Chris fell back against the gnarled wall and groaned, a sickening feeling in his gut. "I screwed up, Lizzy." He moved forward to sit beside her and, afraid to touch the hand again, buried his face in his hands and shook his head,

Spyro settled down at his feet, whimpering. At the far end of the room, inside a glass case secured with an old brass lock, the Book of Thoth rested on a tall narrow lectern.

He pocketed the crystal and taking the key from his pocket, slowly got to his feet and approached the case. The Book was a small thing, just six or seven sheets of yellowed papyrus bound in a soft, dark leather cover. He'd been expecting some large volume with arcane text and patterns carved into a thick leather cover. Crap. This whole thing was a joke.

Chris inserted the key into the lock and murmured, "Fath alkitab almuqaddas." He expected some resistance, but the key turned effortlessly and the lock opened with a rusty clunk. He had his hand on the edge of the door when a loud crash made him spin round.

A cone of torchlight swept across the chamber. A tall, burly man, slightly hunched in the low ceilinged chamber, stood silhouetted against a pale rise of narrow steps. He stepped into the room and pointed a gun at Chris. Spyro stood snarling between Chris and Lizzy.

"Hands like you're praying where I can see them and don't move," the man growled, "anything funny and I'll put a bullet in you and your dog."

Chris did as he was told and the guy threw a handful of fluorescent sticks into the room. The glowing sticks scattered across the floor and lit up the space in a sickly yellow-green light.

The man walked slowly towards Chris who stood with his arms stretched out in front, palms pressed against each other.

"Easy now, kid, I'm watching you, don't move those fingers." The man pulled a can from a coat pocket and sprayed a grey foam over Chris's hands. The substance quickly expanded and solidified.

"There you go." The man dropped the can and it clanged on the stone ground, rolling to stop against Lizzy's body. Another man appeared at the door. "Dan, Isabelle said kill the girl, I—" Seeing Lizzy, he took a step back. "You already shot her?"

"No, Josh," Dan said, not taking his eyes off Chris. "Check her."

Josh knelt beside Lizzy and put his hand to her neck, "She's dead."

"Good," Dan said. "Grab the book and let's go."

Josh nervously approached the glass case, "She said only he could touch the case and take the book out."

Dan waved the gun at Chris, "Grab the book and hand it to Josh."

Chris looked down at the lump around his hands then up at Dan. Dan swore under his breath.

"Josh, get over here and break off this foam." Cutting a strip of thick tape, he pressed it across Chris's mouth and cheeks then gave him a gentle slap before jabbing the muzzle of the pistol against his neck.

Taking out a small aerosol can, Josh sprayed a pungent, watery liquid over the foam, and it dissolved away. Chris winced in pain and slowly stretched out his bruised fingers and inched open the door to the book. As he did so, a powdery cloud burst from the pages of the book and covered the inner layer of the glass case.

Chris instinctively took an intake of breath and leaned back.

"Gloves on, Josh," Dan said. "Isabelle spent a whole night casting protective spells on the bloody things."

Josh put on a pair of cotton gloves and took a large muslin bag covered in runes and bony symbols from a small backpack. He held the top of the backpack open, "Put it straight in, I ain't gonna take no chances with any curse."

Chris slipped the book into the cotton bag.

Josh sealed the bag and placed it gingerly into the backpack, "What about him?"

"Isabelle said leave him, something about a curse." Dan tapped the barrel of the gun against Chris's head. "I lied about killing you. Come on Josh, let's get this back to the temple." Dan searched Chris and found the atlas, the flicked through its pages then tossed it aside, "Board game, c'mon, lets get out of here."

Chris wasn't expecting the whack on the side of his head with the pistol and he dropped heavily.

The two men left, Josh closing the door behind him.

In the dim light, the dust drifted off the inside of the case and gathered into flat, swirling spiral in the centre of the case. Bright spots appeared inside the cloud, increasing in number while the could spun faster and faster. The cloud soon resembled a tiny, glittering galaxy. The atlas lifted off the ground and drifted upwards. Long, curling tendrils reached out from the galaxy and, in response, the atlas shot across the chamber to thump onto the lectern where the ancient book had rested. The galaxy poured into the atlas leaving the case crystal-clear and the atlas motionless.

Chris woke to Spyro licking his face and a throbbing ache pulsing on the side of his head. He pulled the tape from across his mouth and rubbed his reddened cheeks and lips. The fluorescent sticks were running low and their flickering light illuminated a short flight of narrow stairs. Chris sat dazed for several seconds then staggered to his feet and fell against the wall before sliding to the ground. Spyro settled beside him and scratched at her neck. She'd been at it ever since they left Isabelle's house. His head felt heavy as he lifted it and in a tired voice he said, "Stop it, Spyro."

Might as well go back to that house in Scotland then head for Toblerone, Toby Nog, that place; when it was safe, tell those numpties what Isabelle and her gang were about to do. Let the world get what it deserved for treating magicians like criminals and lab rats. At least Lizzy wouldn't be around to see all her friends, all those magicians, slaughtered and the world run by a bunch of vampires. He'd take Lizzy with him. Maybe, just maybe, Freyja's people had some way of bringing her back since he didn't have the Book.

Spyro suddenly went to scratch her neck and fell against Chris's leg. "Spyro!"

Spyro shook herself and settled down beside Lizzy, her muzzle on Lizzy's chest. Chris swallowed down the lump in his throat, and was about to incant the spell to get them back to the farmhouse when he saw the atlas on the lectern.

"Yeah, very funny," he murmured. Well, at least those goons didn't know what the atlas really was. He pocketed the little book. "Guess I'm stuck with just this."

Spyro shook her head, sat down and started another round of scratching at her neck, "Spyro!" Chris leaned over and took the collar off. Spyro immediately relaxed. Holding the collar, Chris sensed the enchantment inside it. Isabelle had run her finger along it. That's how she'd tracked them down. He tossed the collar across the room then folded himself, Lizzy and Spyro back to the farmhouse in Orkney.

It was early morning; sunlight streamed in through the narrow windows above the thick curtains over the patio doors and illuminated the living room. Lizzy's body lay in the centre of the waypoint circle she had created. She was dead and Alumbrados had the Thoth Book, along with his only chance of bringing her back. He fell onto the sofa and gazed up at the narrow beam of sunlight. How many people had died because of him? Magic; no wonder it was illegal; no wonder people crowded into churches, synagogues, temples and mosques every weekend. Maybe he should just burn the damned atlas.

He took the book out and began to flick through the pages then stopped. There were more pages with new islands. Deserts, salt plains, lava pits, icebound regions where vast blue ice cliffs towered into a bare, white sky; churning seas, mountainous landscapes and wild terrains. Dark pyramids, ominous castles and towering walled cities. Hieroglyphs surrounded these new pages, beautiful illustrations of gruesome animals and strange creatures. The seas were wild with storming waves that crashed against jagged cliffs and high castle walls. On two pages, strange constellations and flying ships battled gigantic beasts across a crowded night sky. Like the rest of the atlas, more routes and paths had appeared; along with the spells that should have been in the Book of Thoth. As he looked at each page and new section the new spells pulsed into his memory, leaving him with a dull headache.

"Bloody hell!" he said, "Bloody hell." There it was, the spell to bring back the dead, bring Lizzy back. Would she come back the same or would she be a mindless zombie? Would he have to kill her if she was just a zombie? He shuddered, could he even do that? He'd have to. He fell back against the sofa and Spyro nudged his arm. "What do I do, Spyro?" he said, stroking the dog.

"Oh what the hell, we're screwed anyway." He went into the kitchen and came back with a large steak knife and rolling pin, just in case.

***

Lizzy stood on the shore facing a black sea, the oily waters rippling gently into the distance under a cloudless, slate-grey sky. To her left and right stretched a beach of pale, colourless sand, sparsely flecked with grains of gold.

A small rowing boat, empty but for a small chest, like those found in pirate stories told to children, bobbed and drifted away on the waves. She knew what was in the chest; all her attachments. It kind of made sense; being dead, things that used to matter, like the need for stuff, or being attached to things or feelings – all seemed pretty pointless. Let it go, let it all drift away. The thought gave her a profound serenity and she calmly turned away to see a tall figure dressed in loose-fitting saffron trousers, T-shirt and baseball cap. The man smiled at her, "It seems you are ready."

Lizzy simply nodded.

"Good, come, follow me, I'll take you to the Bardo."

"Who are you?"

"Sid, and you are Elizabeth Francis."

"Yes. Bardo, that's the place in between lives isn't it?"

"Correct, another life awaits you."

"Chris said he'd come for me."

"I know."

"How?"

"Everything is connected, therefore there are threads of probability in destiny, countless possibilities. And in all of those possibilities, a connection, a thin one but a connection nonetheless. Existence, life, would not be so interesting if everything was totally random or completely predictable; don't you think?"

"I suppose. So he will bring me back?"

"Perhaps, do you want to go back?"

"Will it make any difference?"

"Perhaps, perhaps not. No one knows for sure; as I said, it's possible. So, do you want to go back?"

"I don't mind."

"Good."

"Why is that good?"

"Those who do mind and wish to go back usually find themselves in a life similar to the one they just left; so they fail to progress."

"But I don't mind, what does that mean?"

"It means your next life will be a little more exciting, more difficult, more challenging. You will begin with less, or perhaps more; more to lose that is. Either way you will have far more to gain."

"And if Chris does bring me back?"

"Same difference. You will be stronger, happier, endure more, serve better."

"I don't understand."

"You will."

"I think I felt something."

"Fascinating."

***

Chris took a deep breath, and with the knife in one hand, placed his other palm against Lizzy's chest and recited the resurrect incantation, then sat up and waited. Colour returned to her cheeks but she didn't move. He leaned forward and examined her face. She still wasn't breathing. Something wasn't right. He checked the spell; he'd remembered and read it perfectly. Maybe it was all a lie. He touched her chest, pressing a little harder, "Oops," he murmured when the tips of his fingers touched a breast.

He lowered the knife and took a few breaths to clear his head then spoke the spell again. This time a strange hum resonated through him. It was kind of slow and instant at the same time; starting from the centre of his chest and rippling slowly outwards through his body, like millions of tiny gaps popping open all over him, inside and out. The weirdest thing was that his eyes felt like they were expanding to fill his face.

The room and the world outside the window became a ghostly grey haze. The misty pale landscape stretched into the distance beyond the gossamer patio doors. A tall, slender figure stood in the field across the road; it disappeared and reappeared on the road, then snapped again to appear in the front garden.

The green-skinned man, dressed in a black suit and thin red belt, stared straight at him. Chris recognised Osiris from the Elegance characters. Chris heard the god's voice even though his lips weren't moving, "Her consciousness is untangling, Christopher, seeking release from the mid-world. Time is of the essence."

At first, Chris didn't move, then jumped when the voice commanded, "Now!"

Chris got to his feet and walked through the coffee table, sofa, curtains and patio door, and went out into the garden. All colour and warmth had been sucked out of the world. Even the sun was a pale grey orb in a dull, lifeless sky. Osiris raised a hand and beckoned, "You wish to bring her back?"

Chris nodded. "You're Osiris, right?"

"Only through the filters of your perceptions and understanding; I have no form. Let us begin. Remember this, once we leave this realm, whatever you see or hear, say nothing, speak to nothing or no one, only me, touch nothing; not until you see Elizabeth the Seshat. You will have questions. I will hear your thoughts." He touched Chris's temple and Chris winced as a momentary, piercing pain shot through his head. A darkness inside a howling wind rose up around him, filled with anguished cries and wailing, then they were flying across the surface of a dark ocean.

"Who are these people?" Chris asked.

"The newly dead, those who still cling to memories."

"What's so horrible, what's happening to them?"

"Grief and fear, their refusal to let go of all the things in life they held so dear, the dependencies that defined them. Their fear to lose is tearing them back to rebirth. Their suffering begins here, again."

"Reincarnation?"

"Yes."

"Is Lizzy there?"

"No, she is one of the rare few who welcomed leaving that yearning and grief behind."

"She wants to die?"

"She wants no more, she is transcending. We must go on."

"Wait, I'm confused, maybe I shouldn't—"

"Everything is connected, but destiny is a fragile thing; if you wish to shape it we must hurry."

"Hurry? So time is the same here?"

"Only because you make it so."

They flew at a phenomenal speed, and their surroundings changed, diving through vast cosmic webs where galaxies undulated in invisible waves. They slowed and stopped by a monstrous moon that loomed up over Chris to his right. Off down to his left, the Earth hung in a starless black. The shock knocked his mind back and Chris gaped in awe, unable to take in what he was seeing.

"Has it never occurred to you how large the Moon really is, and Earth, your home-world?"

Chris managed to murmur, "Huh?"

"Your attention draws us to irrelevances, focus on Lizzy, we have little time."

Lizzy, yes. A question somehow coalesced in his mind. "Why are we going through space?"

"The path of transcending consciousness is not one we can take, Child of Asten. We must find other ways to reach Elizabeth, and restore her before her little knot of Being reaches the Bardo."

"The what?

"Remember to lend her your breath."

"Lend her my breath?"

"We have arrived. It is time for me to leave."

"Wait," Chris said, "are my parents here, are they reincarnated?"

"They did not pass this way, not yet." Osiris knew his thoughts, "Do not seek to find them thus. Thoth spells draw upon the dark energy of entities spawned in another realm at the dawn of time.

Spells infected with the will of these entities resonate an energy that infects and feeds on desire and greed, making you a pawn in their plans. The vampires are a testament to a mere glimpse of that diseased will. Never use the power of the spells for your own gain and you will be safe."

"Then how do I find my parents?"

"You have the talisman, use it. First, and above all else, you must stop Isabelle sacrificing the children. She has already sacrificed many and infected others beyond redemption. Thus will she gather unto herself and gain mastery over the reaver hordes. The fate of the world is at stake."

"But you're Osiris. Why don't the other entities like you, the good ones – gods – do something?"

"Gods," Osiris said with a sad nod. "Long ago, our battles came close to destroying not only mankind but your entire universe, the very realm we fought over. We established a truce and agreed to allow the humans and other sentient beings of the realm to live freely. Thus, we arranged for humans to learn a different mastery of the energies that flow in your realm: science. In this way, magic and the supernatural were allowed to naturally subside and all but disappear. Isabelle and her small group of vampires managed to evade us, buried in their tombs. Now they rise and plan to use magic to rule again, and in doing so risk reigniting the cosmic battle. Take care you do not do the same."

Osiris nudged Chris into a thoughtless daze and disappeared.

***

Lizzy and Sid left the beach and now walked through a grove of peach trees; a vast palace towered on the horizon. They were about to approach a small narrow bridge when a flash of golden light stopped them. The flash became a large, glowing gold ring and a man walked through. Sid turned to Lizzy and with a nod sent her into a trance then turned and smiled at the newcomer.

"O, my man," Sid said, "how goes it?"

Osiris returned the smile, "Hi, Sid." The two men shook hands, "Damn kid's only gone and done it, hasn't he? Kicked it all off just to get his girlfriend back."

"Is that what he's calling her?"

"No, but you can tell a mile off he's soft on her, in a big way too. He doesn't know it though."

"I shouldn't be surprised, considering who they both used to be."

Osiris nodded, "It would be nice if the right people could remember occasionally."

Sid ignored his friend's musing, "Did you break your act with him?"

Osiris gave him a look and Sid said, "I knew you'd back out again."

"I just can't do it, Sid, we're legends, gods. Screwing with people's archetypes," he shook his head, "fallout would set off all kinds of cosmic weirdness."

"Jones, that American Guru, saw right through us all," Sid said. "He could handle it too. What happened to him?"

"Sahaj samadhi."

"Wow!"

"Anyway," Sid said, "where did you leave Chris?" He glanced over at Lizzy who seemed unaware of the two men and was about to bite into a peach she'd plucked.

"On the beach." Osiris gestured and the peach lifted into the air, leaving Lizzy to gaze dreamily at her empty hand.

"Thanks," Sid said, "that was close. I'd better get Lizzy over to him. Catch you later, O."

"Later, Sid."

***

Chris was alone and Lizzy was walking towards him. Her eyes were closed and her footsteps left no marks in the sand. His heart skipped a beat. She was definitely coming back with him. Lizzy didn't resist when Chris grabbed her arms. What was it Osiris said, lend her his breath? Didn't Sandy say something like that?

He leaned forwards, took a breath and placed his mouth gently over her lips. They were warm and soft. He breathed out, whispering the spell into her mouth and her chest lifted. The sun crept up over the horizon and rose into the sky, infusing the sky, sea and sand in a radiant, golden glow. The light intensified, shining brighter and whiter until he had to close his eyes. Then the sounds of the sea faded; the ground under his feet became hard and the warmth dissolved into a cool, dry stillness. He opened his eyes. Lizzy lay on the floor in the centre of the circle and he was kneeling beside her, exhausted and light-headed. It was early morning and a golden dawn rose in the sky, beautiful but a pale reflection of the realm they'd just left.

Some primitive instinct in her led her lips to respond to his, search out the warm affection in the kiss and their tongues exchanged a moment's gentle caress. Lizzy took in his out-breath and the colour returned to her cheeks and she opened her eyes. "What the... Get off me, what the hell are you doing?" With a shove, she sent him falling back against the sofa.

Chris climbed up onto the sofa and dropped his head back. Lizzy got to her feet unsteadily and, unable to stop herself, fell onto the sofa beside him, "What is wrong with you?" she said, shifting away from him.

"You... just give me a minute."

"God, you're such a creep."

"You died, I had to bring you back."

"Really? By kissing me. Well of course you did. Why else would you want to kiss me?"

"It's true, you know we can't lie to each other," Chris said. "Your light touched the book and it took you to the secret room where the book was."

"And you said you'd stop that happening."

"I couldn't stop it, bloody crystal almost burnt a hole in my hand. The room kind of came out of the wall and swallowed us in."

"And I died?"

"Yeah, dead in the room under the tree, like Sandy said. Then Isabelle's goons arrived and took the book. Isabelle knew where we were."

"Isabelle has the book?"

"Yes."

"Wait a minute, if she has the book, then how did you know the spell to bring me back?"

"The spells left the Thoth book and went into the atlas. The spell summoned Osiris and he took me to you."

"Okay," Lizzy said, and stared at him, thinking. Then she punched his arm, hard.

"Ow! I'm not lying, that's what happened."

"Sure, and I'm Snow White," she went to punch him again and he raised his arms.

"Yeah," Chris snapped back. "The seven dwarves are in the

195

kitchen right now."

"Very funny, since when was kissing part of the resurrection spell?"

"Fine, don't believe me," Chris shrugged. "It's true whether you believe it or not. I don't care."

"I should punch your lights out right now, and don't try any of your Kung Fu crap, you deserve this. You were kissing me, full on."

"I had to give you my breath, like what Sandy said. Anyway, if you must know, you were the one that started kissing me, full on when we came back here."

"I's never – Sandy, that's right," Lizzy lowered her fist and looked away sheepishly. "Okay."

"Jeez, about time," Chris took a breath and closed his eyes.

"Are you okay?"

"Just tired." Chris tilted over to lie down and rest his head on the cushion that was leaning against the arm of the sofa. "I think going to that other place, bringing you back, really took it out of me."

"Okay," Lizzy's expression softened. "Get some sleep, I'll take Spyro out for a run around."

"Mm, okay," Chris said, closing his eyes and stretching his legs out on the sofa. "Oh, and your hair is back too."

Lizzy looked in the mirror and a broad smile spread across her face. She ran a hand through her short spiky black hair. Then going over to him, bent down and kissed his cheek, "Thanks for saving me."

"That's another one you owe me."

"We'll see."

Chris drifted off to sleep thinking about his parents, wondering if the talisman was gone with everything else in the flat, or if it was somewhere in the rubble and wreckage. Maybe he could use an incantation to find it.

***

Chris woke up in an empty house and wandered into the kitchen, hungry for some hot food. A simple spell conjured up toasted bread, hot soup, slices of cured meats, and scrambled eggs. The smell brought Spyro rushing in from the garden. Lizzy followed.

"Great," she said. "I could do with some food."

They sat down to eat and Chris put some slices of meat into a bowl on the floor for Spyro.

"We got the Book of Thoth," Chris said. "Awesome or what?"

"Now we need to work out how to use it to rescue everyone at Salem."

Chris nodded, "Before the Hunter's Moon."

"I wonder why Freyja mentioned the Hunter's Moon."

"Full moons I guess. Alumbrados and Lycus are sacrificing the girls to control the reavers. The big one is going to be on the night of the Hunter's Moon. That's when Isabelle will be able to get control of the reaver army."

"What?" Lizzy spluttered and wiped her mouth. "How do you know this?"

"Osiris told me."

Lizzy gaped at him, "We can't waste any more time, Chris."

"I know."

Chapter Fourteen
S.A.L.E.M

A raven landed on the very centre of the dome's roof and pecked at a round button. It jumped back as a small panel slid open, then it dropped through and flew down to the concrete floor. Above it, the panel slid shut with a faint hiss. The bird fluffed its wings, indifferent to the pools and thin streams of blood, broken skulls and bones, scattered around the hall. Satisfied the hall was empty, the raven transformed into Isabelle.

With a single shake of her head, she ran her fingers through her long black hair then slid her hands down the sky-blue gown that flowed around her, straightening creases that weren't there. Isabelle crossed to a circular dais about ten feet in diameter that stood in the centre of the round hall. Arcane, jagged runes carved from gold lay embedded between two thick band of gold that ran round the perimeter of the dais. Isabelle went to the centre of the dais and stepped on one of three levers in a recess. A tube of steel glass ringed with gold bands rose up around her to the ceiling.

A door at the far end opened and two tall, slender Lycus Elite Guards in blood-red uniforms dragged in a burly, barefoot man with a cloth bag over his head. Patches of blood covered the bag and his heels left a broken trail of blood on the floor behind him. He dropped heavily when the two soldiers let go of him and walked out. The man, dressed only in thin pale grey trousers and a T-shirt, groaned and stiffly removed the cloth bag from over his head. Blinking in the light, he looked around.

"Dan Hague," Isabelle's soft voice was a haunting whisper in the man's mind.

Dan shook his head slowly and squinted at Isabelle. Pressing a hand to his thigh, tried to stand, but stumbled and fell to the floor, letting out another cry. His face twisted in agony, no longer the burly, six-foot-four, arrogant thug. Seeing the blood and human remains surrounding him, he dragged himself back to lean against the wall. He took several deep breaths and peered at Isabelle inside the tube, "Why are you doing this?" He coughed and spat blood.

"You bring me a binding of blank parchments and expect to keep the payment?"

"Bring you…?" Hague said, confused, "No, I… I didn't look in the bag, I did what you asked, exactly. I—" Seeing the remains of a bright yellow spotted dress, clean from blood, a look of horror froze on his face.

"Yes," Isabelle smiled, "the dress your wife bought, with the money I gave you. She'd become quite a nuisance this past week, looking for you, calling the police, Lycus, pestering her MP. Such a plain woman, even her blood was tasteless." Her smile twisted into an ugly scorn.

"Her..." Hague's eyes widened and he stared at Isabelle. "No," he groaned from the pit of his stomach. "You... can't be." He buried his face in his hands, "Oh my God, oh God."

He slumped back and coughed blood again, letting it dribble down his chin. Isabelle's eyes widened and she licked her lips.

Hague began sobbing and didn't look up, "But I brought you the book."

"No, you failed," Isabelle stepped on the second lever, cutting off all sound from outside the tube.

A deep hum resonated through the hall and, several feet from Isabelle, a slender metal pillar, around ten feet tall, rose from the ground and, with a blinding flash, snapped open into two tall rods. Dull, oily colours rippled across the surface of the rods and jagged bolts of black lightning crackled from their tops as the rods slid away from each other, leaving a broadening black gash between realities.

The gash between the rods continued to stretch and open out, flashes of lightning rippling along the jagged white edges as they moved further apart.

"Did you know," Isabelle said, examining her fingernails, "that emotions, like terror, anger," she glanced at the widening gash, "compassion, love," she snorted, "have a resonance, are a form of energy?"

The gash yawned open and a blast of pure terror swept out into the hall. Hague froze as the wave washed through him, then he started to shake uncontrollably. Forgetting his pain, he dragged himself, still shaking, along the cold, concrete floor towards the door and pulled at the handle. After just a few yards the pain cam flooding back and he collapsed to the ground amongst a pile of bones.

Hollow howls resonated out behind him and the ground began to shake. Hague slowly turned round. The bones on the ground around him shuddered and the pools of blood rippled and cracked out out thin, shivering streams that made shaky red lines along the grey floor. Hague fell on his back and pushed the palms of his hands against his ears to shut out the awful howls.

He continued screaming when the sound stopped and a rage of reavers leaped out of the portal, their feet clattering onto the concrete.

Some rushed towards Isabelle while the others bounded across the hall towards Hague, a few stopping to lick and suck at the small pools of blood.

The first reaver to reach Hague killed him when it thrust its claw under his rib cage. With an upward thrust, and using both hands, the creature tore out Hague's heart and most of one lung. While other reavers crowded round to tear at his entrails and limbs, a younger reaver squeezed in between the feeding reavers and the wall. It grabbed the man's arm with one hand while the long claws of his other hand stabbed deep into his shoulder. It ripped off the Hague's arm and threw it aside. The creature gripped Hague's head and forced it back as it pressed its mouth into the gaping wound. The monster began to rhythmically thrust its long, hard, muscular tongue into the bloody hole, gorging itself, widening the wound and probing with bony fingers, wantonly searching out the soft, tender flesh, sucking out blood and veins.

Isabelle ignored the reavers howling and circling the protective gold-lined tube. Licking her lips and stroking her arm gently, she watched the reavers feed. She took in a long, slow breath whenever a reaver turned to her, its mouth full of meat dripping with blood, and she would almost mimic the creature's raising of its head to chew and swallow, opening her own mouth.

"Yes," she whispered under her breath, "feed, feed." Smiling with her mouth open, she ran her fingers through her hair and caressed her neck. "Soon we shall speak and you will be mine to command."

The feasting over, Isabelle tapped the third lever and panels opened slowly in the roof of the dome. Thin shafts of sunlight streamed in and the reavers panicked. They hurled themselves back through the tear and the metal rods clunked together, closing the tear between realms then withdrew back into the ground.

The steel glass tube retracted and Isabelle stepped off the dais and crossed the room, ignoring Hague's butchered remains.

Back her office she settled into the wide leather chair and pressed a button. "Palant, tell someone to find that Josh White boy."

"Right away, ma'am," Palant's gruff voice responded over the intercom.

"But first, get in here, I want you, now."

"Yes ma'am."

Two hours later, Josh arrived at Isabelle's office. Isabelle sat at her desk. Palant stood with a drink in his hand looking out of the window. A large black cat lay on a sofa beside an old, ornate cabinet.

Josh looked fearfully at Palant, whom he recognised from more executions than he'd like to remember.

"Don't look so scared Mr White," Isabelle smiled. "I simply want to ask you a few questions about the most recent job you did with Mr Hague. Please, take a seat."

Josh sat down nervously on the edge of the chair and looked from Palant.

Isabelle flicked through the now empty pages of the Book of Thoth, put it down and smiled, "I want you to tell me in as much detail as possible what you can remember from your recent work with Mr Hague."

"Mr Hague picked me up from the—"

"Start from when you entered the chamber under the tree."

Josh recounted the events and repeated what the case looked like when the book was in there and what happened after.

"Dust around the inside of the case?" Isabelle said.

"Yes, ma'am."

"Was there anything about the dust or case that looked unusual?"

Josh shook his head, "It was just a layer of dust, it was dark though, not grey."

"Anything else?"

"Mr Hague searched Asten and found a book. He looked through the pages and dropped it. He told me later it was some kind of fantasy atlas."

The barest hint of surprise flashed across Isabelle's features. "Thank you, Mr White, you have been most helpful."

Relieved, Josh smiled, went to stand up then checked himself. "Is that all?"

"Yes, you may go."

Josh left and Isabelle turned to Palant. "Well?"

"There was no dust when I went there to check. The girl's body was gone too."

"Interesting. White said she was already dead when they arrived." Isabelle laced her fingers together sand rested them on Book of Thoth on the desk.

Isabelle crossed the room and opened the door to a small refrigerator. Taking out a bottle, poured herself a glass of blood and sipped at it slowly as she thought. She was about to fill the glass again and stopped. "No!" she exclaimed. "It's not possible."

"What?"

"No!" she screamed and threw the glass across the room where it struck a painting on the wall. The cat jumped up, alarmed, and in doing so transformed into a man.

Dressed in an expensive looking black suit, the man was tall and muscular with a head of thick black hair.

"I wish you wouldn't do that, dear." The man glanced at Palant and they exchanged knowing smiles. "Cameron," he said.

"Peter," Cameron Palant replied, "good to see you up and about again."

"I rest better as a cat."

They both turned to Isabelle who was pacing up and down. "He can't have it, it's impossible," Isabelle said and sat on the sofa. "That fool has Zoroaster's atlas," Isabelle said, shaking with rage. "Charting his journey and conversations with the god Amesha Spenta. I thought it was a myth."

"Who?" Cameron looked at Palant

"Zoroaster, an Ancient One." Peter said. "The atlas is a magical book of spells. It has the ability to absorb spells from any magic books nearby."

Cameron gave Peter an admiring look, "Is there anything you don't know?"

"The answer to that question."

"You think he has the atlas?" Cameron said.

"He must have," Isabelle snapped, "it's the only explanation."

Peter crossed to the window. "Then we have a problem, the

imbecile could use the resurrection spell to bring the girl back to life."

"Palant," Isabelle snarled, "I want you to use every man you can spare to find that atlas."

Chapter Fifteen

Chris knocked and inched the door open. "Lizzy, I've brought you a cup of tea."

Lizzy smiled up at him and continued drawing on a large sheet of paper.

Chris crossed the room and sat next to her on the sofa and put two mugs on the coffee table beside the drawing she was working on. "Is that Salem?"

Lizzy had almost completed a colourful drawing of Salem. The pentagon-shaped prison stood in the centre of the disused airfield. The entrance to the single narrow road to the prison was a fortified checkpoint at the twenty-foot tall wall made of a strange combination of wood, stone and metal. Past the checkpoint the road went through a fifty-yard deep ring of tangled razor wire then hundred yard wide circle of open space dotted with mines. Another wall, same as the first circled the prison building.

"Yes," Lizzy dropped the green pencil and picked up the mug of hot tea.

"What are those other buildings?"

Lizzy pointed at different buildings in turn. "Where the wardens and other workers live; the armoury; that's the medical centre, where they experiment on us." She pointed to a big domed building. "That's the newest. Girls don't comes out of there once they go in."

"Jeez," Chris said. "You think that's where she's doing the nasty?"

Lizzy nodded. "Only soldiers come out."

"Maybe there's an exit on the other side."

"No, I saw them building it, there's only one door."

"What's that place there?"

"That building in the middle?" Lizzy tapped on the smaller, solid pentagon building she'd drawn in green in the centre space of the prison. "I think it's the recycling centre."

"Was the door really that big? Didn't it have windows or anything?"

"Every month they empty food waste bins through a chute." Lizzy thought for a moment then drew thirteen tiny domes spread around the roof and what looked like vents along one edge of the roof.

"Are those burst footballs?" Chris said.

"Don't know."

"Are they organised like that?"

"Yes."

Chris flicked through the pages of the atlas. He pointed to a swampland. "I thought I recognised it. That is where the Sufario live."

"What's that got to do with the recycling?"

"Look," Chris turned to the section where each page was a copy of a particular card. He showed her the 'Sufario and the Cursing Cry' card. Above the image of a tall, six-legged lizard spread a net with thirteen orbs, each containing a crystal. "If your path takes you into the Sufario swamp and you throw a double, you have to deal with the Sufario."

"So why would they be keeping a Sufario?" Lizzy asked.

"The Sufario is why magic doesn't work. You need regular weapons to defeat it unless you have the eggs of thirteen Firegold birds."

***

Sufario and the Cursing Cry

Appearance: The Sufario is a tall six-legged mammalian reptile that grows to a height of thirty to thirty-five feet. Being deaf and having an intolerance of light, it does not stray from its shadowy habitat.

Diet: The Sufario feeds on carcasses of dead creatures, rotting roots and decaying vegetation.

Habitat: Sufario live in Necheb Tan-ghur, the dense boggy marshland at the heart of the vast Hukmet Jungle covering most of central Zugara.

Threat: None – the Sufario is a docile creature and has a deep baritone song, used by males for courting, and females when they are fertile and wish to mate. It is non-migratory and lives in herds consisting of several family units, leaving only to mate. Parents share the care of their young who leave at adolescence to form their own family unit.

Defences: When attacked or in distress, Sufario eject chigura, a tar-like substance, from pores along its back, either side of the spine. Upon contact with air, chigura shoots away from the body.

Chigura is an extremely volatile substance that is readily combustible, reaching volcanic temperatures.

In addition to the spray of fiery liquid, the Sufario is immune to almost all magic. When distressed it emits a barely audible wailing sound that renders powerless any magical properties a plant, object or person may have and displaces any magical phenomena directed at it.

Weakness: The Sufario can only be contained by a Net of Thirteen Orbs, crafted from the eggs of Firegolds, and fuelled by the stars.

***

"Thirteen star-charged orbs," Chris said, tapping on Lizzy's picture.

Lizzy handed the atlas back. "So, that's what's on the roof. They've got one, they've been torturing it all these years, just to keep our magic down. That's awful."

"They could even be using the energy from it to power all the buildings."

"The poor thing. Can you fold it out or something?"

"Nope, it displaces any magic or magician that gets near it. That is why magic doesn't work. We're screwed."

"So there's nothing we can do?"

Chris shook his head. "Any magic we throw at it will just fizzle out as soon as it gets near the prison, we'll need an army to get in or get people out of there."

"No," Lizzy stood up and paced across the room to the window. "No, there has to be a way."

"Not while those Crystals are there. He glanced out of the window. The sun was setting. "The stoor will be back soon. The shield's up though so we're all right."

"Chris, we have to do something."

"Like what? Magic is totally useless against the Sufario."

"I don't know. What about those thirteen orbs? They must be magic."

"They're dried eggs from Firegolds, some kind of bird. They stop the Sufario from folding out."

"So it can't go back?" Lizzy said. "What?" she added when Chris's attention drifted off.

"My granddad said that; he said go back."

"Did he?"

"When we were in the flat, he said we had to go back."

"Go back? Where to?"

"The way he said it, I think there's only one place I could go back to: home."

"Home? That doesn't make sense," Lizzy shook her head.

Chris reached into his sweatshirt and took out the crystal. "We could have a look."

"Where, at what?"

"My mum's house, where she lived before meeting my dad. Whenever we were going to visit, they would say 'go back'. If my parents were from a long line of ancient sorcerers, then my grandparents' place must have some seriously old magic in it. Loads of magicians used to come and go from there. Look, I'll hold the crystal and concentrate on the house and you can do your thing."

Lizzy shrugged. "Might as well." She drew the curtains and the room fell into darkness until she threw a small glowing orb into the air. Chris held the crystal out to one side between his thumb and forefinger. Lizzy raised her hand, moving her fingers gently up and down, a fraction of an inch at a time, guiding a thin thread of light out towards the crystal. As the thread neared the crystal it flicked and caught the edge, as if it sensed Chris's memory, and the image of his house spread over the wall.

Lizzy's face tensed in concentration as she focussed more light along the thread. The view of the house began outside and glided in through the window into the living room where two women in their twenties sat on a sofa. The woman with the black hair sat with a laptop computer on her lap, the long network cable stretching over the side of the sofa to a router link on the wall. The woman beside her, a towel wrapped round her head, a strand of blonde hair down over one cheek, watched TV, sometimes glancing across at the laptop screen.

"Do you know them?" Lizzy said.

"I think that's Sparrow, she babysat for me a few times. She lived down the street with Aunty Jen."

"Aunty Jen?"

"Not my real aunt, I just called her that."

"Do you think they knew about you and your family?"

"Maybe, she did play Elegance with us sometimes."

"Okay," Lizzy said, "we should go there, maybe your granddad was working with them to plan the rescue."

"Really?"

"Yeah, your granddad wanted you to find me didn't he?" The thread disappeared, as did the image on the wall, and Lizzy pulled open the curtains.

"We can't just turn up there," Chris said, "it could be the middle of the night by the time we do."

"That's true, but what choice do we have? It's not as if we can phone or email. Come on, gimme your hand. I'll do the fold spell this time."

"What?"

"Let's go. Spyro, here girl."

Spyro raised her head from where she was curled up at the foot of the bed and yawned at him. Chris found her lead and clipped it on. Spyro got to her feet and shook herself, almost falling off the bed as she did, which got a laugh out of Chris and Lizzy.

"Wait!" Lizzy said and grabbed the drawing and pencils.

It was daylight outside when Chris and Lizzy folded into the living room of his mum's parents' home, the same room where Sparrow and her friend had been sitting. Spyro yanked the lead and shot across the room to the sofa where a cat had jumped up from a sleep. Spyro skidded to a stop on the mat several inches from the sofa. The cat sat and eyed Spyro who leaned forward sniffing and the cat swiped her nose. Spyro jerked her head back and, looking sideways at the cat, wandered out down a hallway, her nose to the ground; the cat jumped off the sofa and went after her.

A scream followed by a shattering came from the kitchen then Spyro rushed back into the living room, her nails skidding on the polished floor. Chris and Lizzy looked at each other just as Sparrow's friend came into the room. Seeing Chris and Lizzy, she gasped and took a step back.

"Uh, hi, I'm Chris, an old friend of Sparrow's?"

The woman nodded, "You're pictures have been on TV every day. How did you get in here?"

"Magic."

"Oh, of course. Just give me a minute," She stared from Lizzy to Chris, blinked and shook her head. "Jen said there was a chance you'd turn up here, just not like this. I'm not used to magic."

"Sorry," Lizzy said, "I didn't want to take chances, we think Alumbrados can see through our disguises."

"Oh," the woman said, "you know about Alumbrados."

Lizzy and Chris nodded.

"I suppose you should sit down," the woman said, "Sparrow and her mother should be back in a couple of hours. Hey!" She stamped on the end of Spyro's lead, stopping her from dashing back into the kitchen. "There's broken glass in there."

"Here, Spyro," Chris called.

"She's probably after the cat food," The woman said, still a little confused. "I should clean up the floor," she turned to go back into the kitchen then stopped. "Oh, I'm Julie, Julie Wong."

"Hi, Julie," Lizzy said. "I'll give you a hand cleaning up."

"Thanks."

Julie and Lizzy headed out to the kitchen leaving Chris standing in the middle of the room. Memories flooded back. The walls were a different colour, and pictures he didn't recognise hung on the walls, but there was still something homely about it. He wandered over to a bookcase where the top three shelves had mostly framed photographs, trophies and small statues. One of the photos was of Sparrow and Aunty Jen in a field, both holding long rifles. In another photo, a teenager stood next to a woman in combat gear. Chris stared at it for a while, then realised it was granddad and Aunty Jen, both a lot younger. There were photos of Sparrow standing in between two older women and one of his grandfather as a young man, his arms round a red-haired girl. Sparrow holding a rifle, several photos of Julie and Sparrow doing various activities: abseiling, running alongside a country stream and an old railway track, swimming in a river. Other pictures had the two of them together, holding different kinds of pistols and rifles. At the back of the top shelf was a solid glass cube with what looked like a phial of shining liquid in the centre.

He was about to reach for it when Julie and Lizzy came back in. Lizzy carried a tray with three mugs of tea and some sandwiches, which she put on the coffee table. Chris sat down and took a mug. "Thanks, do you live here too?"

"Yes," Julie glanced at Lizzy. "I'm a friend of Sparrow's."

Chris got the feeling they were more than friends. "Oh, okay,"

Chris paused then added. "I was looking at the photos. You do a lot of army kind of stuff, shooting, climbing, exploring."

"Mm," Julie swallowed down a bite of sandwich. "Sparrow got me into it, her mum thinks it's important, we enjoy it."

"Cool. Do you keep the rifles here?"

"A few. In fact, I've got something of yours." Julie went upstairs and came down with a large box.

"You've got Elegance!" Chris exclaimed.

Julie nodded. "I tried playing it with Sparrow and her mum a couple of times, but couldn't get the hang of it. It's all a bit too weird, fantasy was never my thing."

"Nah, it's easy," Chris said.

"No it isn't, all those winding paths and waypoints and cards."

"It's easier if you decide from the beginning what special skills you want to work on and focus on them. That will help you decide which paths to follow and places to go to."

Chris took the board out, unfolded the atlas on the coffee table, and for the next two hours they all talked about the game and the spells. Lizzy kept interrupting and asking questions about some of the more complex spells.

The front door opening interrupted them. Julie jumped up and rushed to the hallway. After a brief exchange of muffled voices, the door swung open and Sparrow stood in the doorway. "Chris!" she cried, and dashed across the room with a big smile on her face. Chris stood up just in time for Sparrow to wrap her arms around him in a big hug. "It's so good to see you, we were really worried. Look at you, you were a skinny little kid last time I saw you." They exchanged broad smiles.

Julie and Jen followed into the room.

"It's Chris," Sparrow said, the smile still on her face.

Jen smiled. "Hello, Chris." She still had her New York accent.

"Hi, Aunty Jen," they hugged briefly. "I didn't know you bought the house."

"I think you're old enough to drop the 'aunty'," Jen said. "I was wondering when you two would show up." She turned to Lizzy. "Lizzy, welcome."

"Hello, thanks," Lizzy said.

Chris glanced at Lizzy. "We think Granddad wanted us both to come back here."

"He did," Jen said, putting down the bags in her hands and taking her coat off. "How about a coffee, Julie?"

Julie nodded and, followed by Sparrow, went off in the direction of the kitchen.

Jen sat down and took her shoes off. "Time was I could jog twenty miles with full gear," she said, rubbing her feet. "Seems you two have been moving around quite a bit too."

"Non-stop since Granddad died. Did you know he wasn't really my granddad?"

"Yes," Jen nodded. "I've known Al – Lawrence – since he was a teenager. We were there, in CERN; Lawrence, Suzie and myself, when the incident happened, when magic came back."

"Suzie Emerson?" Lizzy said, "in No Man's Land."

"That's her."

Chris gaped at them, speechless.

"His granddad coming back here?" Lizzy said. "Did it have anything to do with, what was it, the Hunter's moon?"

"That and other things, we were working on a rescue."

"Why didn't any of the safe houses know?" Lizzy said, "Nobody I met even knew about you or this house."

"Cantata doesn't know about us, nor any magicians. It's safer that way. Lawrence and I made sure no one knew or suspected me or the girls here of having anything to do with sympathisers or magicians. We've successfully managed to stay below the radar of an organisation with superior numbers, weapons and technology."

"By living in my mum's parents' house?" Chris said.

"Alumbrados never knew your parents' true identities. They only knew that two sorcerers were out there somewhere. Lawrence wiped all records of your family and this house from the Lycus system. It became just another plain house whose owners went missing during the war. Me and the girls have spotless records. No files on us anywhere. We bought the house with no problems."

"But if you've known Granddad so long, how come Alumbrados didn't find out?"

"We're better at keeping secrets. Alumbrados might have advisers and handlers in the top levels of government and vampires on the street working for them, but we have our own tricks and can hack any network."

"Why haven't you done anything yet?" Lizzy said.

"We knew magic didn't work in or around the prison and there's a small army guarding it. It looked like an impossible task."

"Lycus are killing us every day," Lizzy said.

"I know, Lizzy," Jen said. "But rushing things isn't the way to go." Jen turned to Chris. "Lawrence went to Bristol to speak with someone about a plan he had. Now he's gone we won't know what it was. Chris, do you have any idea who he'd gone to meet?"

"I don't know what he was doing in Bristol. Why didn't he tell you?"

"The less each of us know, the safer it is. Nobody spills the secrets because nobody knows them all. Coming here with you was going to be the start of sharing what we knew, then put the plan into action."

"I was in Bristol for a while when I first escaped," Lizzy said, "with some guy called Ozzy."

"Ozzy? What do you know about him?" Jen asked.

"Not much really, he was a tech guy. In the summer he worked as a chaser for a skateboard firm that owned a hot-air balloon." Lizzy smiled. "He had an old dog, Ben."

"Ben?" Chris said. "Was it a black dog, little, long hair, tooth missing?"

"Yes," Lizzy said, "an old dog."

"Never mind that," Jen said. "Is that all?"

"No, just that on the day I left, he'd been up early, which was really strange for him; said he'd met with someone from London. The man who'd given him the dog."

"I think it was Granddad," Chris said to Jen. "What if Ben was Benjy? Granddad said he'd gone to a good home. But why would he visit a tech guy out in the middle of nowhere?"

"He was working on the collars, ones that we made in the prison."

Jen shook her head, "That was going smoothly." She leaned back. "So now you know what we're up against, magic won't work and there's a hundred or so heavily armed Lycus soldiers."

"There's a way," Chris said, "Show them your drawings, Lizzy."

Lizzy laid her drawings on the table. Jen's eyes lit up and she sat forward. "This is pretty detailed," she said.

Both Chris and Lizzy looked at her.

"Don't look so surprised, only once did Lawrence and I get close enough to see the prison perimeter and even then we barely managed to evade the dogs. This diagram is the best representation we have."

Julie and Sparrow came in. Jen gestured to them and they put the tray of coffee and biscuits on the table and joined them. Jen continued. "It's a map of Salem," Jen said to the women. "We didn't know Salem was a hollow pentagon shape." She pointed at the pentagon-shaped building in the centre of the prison. "Or this."

"That building in the middle is why magic doesn't work anywhere in or near the prison," Chris said.

"How so?" Jen said.

"There's a Sufario in there, it sends out a vibe that kills off all magic."

"And you know this how?"

"Those thirteen orbs, I recognise them from Elegance."

"The board game?" Jen gave him a quizzical look. "What about the power supply? That really confused us, where's the power generator?"

"The creature in there is the power supply."

"The Sufario creature can do that?"

"It throws out burning goo."

"Okay, and those orbs are what keeps the Sufario from escaping?"

"Yes."

"Huh!" Jen sat up and took the coffee handed to her by Sparrow. "Thanks, and that's the new domed building where kids go in and don't come out?"

"Yes," replied Lizzy.

"Two buildings to get kids out of," Jen said. "This is going to be real tough."

"I think they kill people in there," Lizzy said. "We hear reaver noises, even during the daytime."

"Okay," Jen said with a sombre nod. "Ozzy had access to a hot-air balloon, you say?"

"One shaped like a skateboard wheel," Lizzy said.

Jen took a sip of coffee, "We need to find him."

Chapter Sixteen

An alarm buzzed, and using his heel, Chris nudged Sparrow, asleep in her sleeping bag on the thin camper mattress.

"I heard it," Sparrow grumbled. "I'm awake." She sat up slowly and focussed her eyes on the mug of tea in Chris's hand. "Thanks." She wrapped her hands round it and looked over to the other sleeping bag. "Julie, Julie, wake up."

Julie, curled up in the sleeping bag beside Sparrow and turned away to face the inside wall of the truck. Sparrow leaned over and shook her gently by the shoulder, "Julie."

Julie wiggled her arm out of the sleeping bag and swung it round, missing Sparrow's hand completely, "All right." She turned onto her back and rubbed her eyes, "What time is it?"

"Ten to five," Sparrow said.

Julie sat up and wiped the hair from over her face then took her drink, "Thanks."

They drank in silence, listening to the growing dawn chorus outside. Julie broke the silence. "This is it, girls."

Chris smiled nervously.

"Chris," Sparrow gave him a gentle nudge, "you ready for this?"

"Definitely. Let's hope the guy inside got the message to all the girls."

Sparrow and Julie, already dressed in their grey combat gear, finished drinking and began preparing their rifles. "I always wanted one of these," Sparrow said. "Warping, I mean folding, invisibly into the Lycus base in broad daylight and just picking the guns was so easy. How come other magicians haven't done it before?"

"I'm a sorcerer," Chris replied, "I can bundle and morph spells. Magicians can only do one at a time and their spells don't last; easy for Lycus to detect and stop."

Julie clunked something on her rifle, "Right, I'm ready."

Invisible behind the Immutable Shield, they edged round the small Jeep that took up half the inside of the truck and used a small ladder to clambered onto the truck's roof.

Julie lay down and set up her sniper rifle, an Accuracy International L115A3. "I never realised how big that place is." She adjusted the bi-pod and took a look through the scope. "It's bigger

215

than Wembley stadium."

"Three times the size," Chris said, looking at his watch. "Jen should be coming in from the west in about ten, fifteen minutes."

Lying beside Julie, Sparrow looked down the spotting scope and after several seconds said, "I have the distance at 1855 metres."

"1855, copy that," Julie said and smiled across at Sparrow, "that's some bullet drop though."

"Mm. Once we have the wind direction we should be good to go," Sparrow said. "Hey Chris, what happens if the Sufario doesn't fold straight home?"

"I guess the soldiers will kill her. Poor thing. Either way the kids get their magic back and make it easier for us to deal with the guards. I'll send the spell to protect the girls from gunfire, then me and Lizzy can start to fold them out to Toblerone, Toby Nod – that place where all the magicians live."

"Lizzy and I," Julie murmured.

"Her?" Sparrow glanced up at him then put her eye back on the optical scope. "How do you know the Sufario is a she?"

"I'm guessing, females are bigger, stronger and live three times longer than male ones."

"What if it doesn't leave and they don't kill her?"

"Then we're up shit creek." Julie said.

A small cylinder dropped out of the sky where the balloon was hidden behind an Immutable Shield. It landed on the Sufario's building where it released a thin stream of smoke that rose into the air and drifted to the right.

"There's the smoke trace," Chris said, "I'll do the cables." Going to the tall telegraph pole beside the truck, he put his palm against the cold, damp metal. "Husasol venura Melakesh," he said, then stepped back. A sizzling band of golden light ran up the pole and gathered into a glowing, white-hot ball at the tip, then disappeared. The shoebox-sized junction box, where the prison cables rising from their underground pipes joined the local telephone network, began to ripple. "Okay, that's a good few hours delay," Chris called down. "Any warning they send out will arrive some time this afternoon."

Peering through the binoculars, Chris watched the thin trail of smoke rise from the pentagon roof. Julie and Sparrow concentrated on the thin wispy line rising into the air, showing the furthest wind direction. Seconds later the sound of sirens reached them.

Sparrow fired first and Julie after; two of the orbs exploded and a line of sparks shot into the sky.

"Oh crap," Chris said. "If that hits the balloon…"

"Should we stop?" Sparrow said. Julie had already fired another shot and destroyed two more orbs when the bullet ricocheted off the roof and hit another orb as it angled away, sending two more lines of sparks up into the air.

"No," Chris said. "Lizzy's Immutable Shield round the balloon should keep them out."

A patch of sky just below the clouds shimmered and the hot-air balloon blinked in and out of sight. "Damn," Chris said. "Keep shooting, we have to get the Sufario free and out of there in time for Lizzy to—"

The pentagon block holding the Sufario exploded and sent a shock wave through the air. A ring of flaming rubble and twisted metal blasted out and crashed down onto the surrounding yard. Smaller pieces flew out and smashed into the inner wall of the prison.

The Sufario lumbered out of the smoke and rubble, shaking itself like a wet dog. It arched its back and stretched its six elephantine legs. Stamping them on the ground, it grunted and snorted as plumes of dust rose up around it. The creature, twice the size of a bull elephant, squinted and shook its head then tensed the thick, sinewy muscles along its neck and back. Its deep, long, roar sent ripples through the air and it stumbled over the rubble, sending up clouds of dust. Sensing the magicians in the cells that filled the building around it, the creature crashed into the prison walls, exposing the walkways and cells inside. Then, with a final loud roar, and a blinding green flash of light, the Sufario was gone.

Cell doors and walls started to disappear or dissolve in clouds of dust and bursts of light; others melted to the ground or turned into shimmering confetti. Armed guards were magically hurled through the air to fall heavily onto the concrete yard below. Chris held his arms out, palms towards the prison and said, "Kurajolin idami selbesig."

Gleaming octahedrons burst from his palms and swarmed towards the prison, spreading out to a glittering mist, then dissipated. In the distance, girls of all ages emerged from the debris, glowing like angels.

Sparrow gaped wide-eyed then slowly turned to Chris. "They're bulletproof?" she barely managed to get the words out.

Chris nodded, a big grin on his face, "The grace of Drafik."

Beyond the outer perimeter fence to the West side of the prison, portals appeared; shimmering liquid circles out of which poured more magicians. Spreading out left and right as they emerged, the magicians began to move their hands around and call out their spells. The first to emerge cast magical shield that joined to form a long wall between them and the prison. The first girl prisoners to emerge from their cells lifted into the air and flew over the prison to be plucked from the air by firegolds summoned by another group of magicians The enormous gold-red birds swooped down and plucked the girls from the air and, gliding through a hail of bullets, brought them down to beside the magicians who guided them away through the portals.

Bullets and missiles exploded harmlessly in the sky around the birds and magicians creating a spectacular, colourful firework display.

"Now that's what I call magic," Julie said.

Sparrow lowered her binoculars, "I can see fireworks over on the east side too. Time for us to hit the front door, girls." Sparrow said.

"Copy that," Chris jumped down onto the bonnet of the truck then down to the ground and ran round to the back, punching the ramp button as he did. He climbed into the Jeep and starting it up, slammed the gearstick, and crashed out and down to the ground just as the ramps touched down.

Sparrow and Julie clambered in and grabbed the assault rifles

"Buckle up," Chris said and steered off the road and into the field, heading straight for the prison.

"We'd better be invisible," Julie said, bouncing around the back as she struggled to put her safety belt tightly on.

Gripping the steering wheel, Chris concentrated on the gate directly ahead of them. "Hold on to something." He said as the Jeep smashed through the farm gate and Sparrow whooped as chunks of wood crashed over the Jeep and flew past them.

Hands tight to the front seat, Julie looked back over her

shoulder. "That farmer's gonna be really pissed," she said over the noise of the Jeep crunching along a dusty road towards the prison. Minutes later they drove onto the tarmac road leading to the prison and into a howling wind.

Sparrow tapped Chris on the shoulder, "Pull over."

Chris pulled over and Sparrow lifted her binoculars. "Gunfire; can you see the balloon?"

"No, it must have landed on the far side of the prison."

Sparrow jumped behind the steering wheel, "Let's go," she shouted over the gale swirling around them.

Fifty yards from the prison entrance they stopped as small groups of children staggered or ran towards them along the road, running away from gunfire.

"Dush El Yanur." Chris shouted and the air formed into two giant hands that gripped the checkpoint and ripped it from the concrete then threw it into the field of razor wire.

Chris jumped out into a wind that blasted round the prison in short bursts. "The Sufario has left a wind storm behind. It shuts down magic as it comes round." He leaned into the wind and, pushing forward, reached the first group of children crawling on their knees away from the prison. He waited for a gap in the wind and called out. "Hold hands, I'll fold you to a safe place."

Terrified by the sudden gusts, and many of them still dazed, the children stared at him in confusion. "Okay," Chris said and concentrated. The first lull in the wind came and Chris said, "Holael Mirakush." Immediately the children reached for each other's hands and were joined by others nearby until over thirty children held hands or clung to each other's clothes as they were buffeted by the storm. Before he could utter the incantation spell to fold the children, the wind surged again, nullifying the magic, and several children, unprotected by the grace of Drafik, were hit by bullets.

"This better work," Chris growled and waited for another pause, and when it came, raised his hands. "Noru Shima Kaup Yra sha." The children disappeared and a second later the wooden doorway to Tir Na nÓg appeared a few yards from the Jeep. "Looks like Freyja's made this personal," Chris murmured, surprised by its appearance.

Sparrow and Julie climbed out of the Jeep and raised their

assault rifles, their grey combat outfits and masks over their faces shifting the light so they were barely visible. They seemed not to notice the door and rushed past Chris, "Stay back, we'll clear a path for you."

Behind Chris, the wooden door opened and Freyja strode out, "How dare you?" she bellowed, "how dare you transgress the—"

"Shut it, Freyja. Kids are being shot," Chris snarled back. "You just try to stop them coming in. I dare you."

Enraged, Freyja raised her hand, her wand appearing as she did so. Chris quickly raised his hand, turning his palm upwards as he did, slightly curling his fingers. Freyja recognised the gesture and stopped. "You wouldn't dare."

"Oh yeah? Try me." he said, and with a nod, gestured over his shoulder. "You'd let innocent kids die because of your ancient rules?"

The wind picked up again; more loud snapping came from the prison and small groups of children rushed forwards, some falling over while others dashed past Freyja and in through the door.

One child stopped and grabbed Freyja's hand, and raising her head, looked up and smiled at her. Through the wind that blasted around them, both Chris and Freyja heard the child's voice like a clear whisper to their ears, "I saw you in my dreams, you came to rescue us."

Freyja's expression changed immediately, she smiled down at the frail girl in her tattered pyjamas, "Come, Jill, let's find you some nice clothes." Freyja flicked her wand and all the children turned their heads to her. Freyja mumbled something and the girls began to filter through the door. Freyja stood to one side and ushered the children and young teenagers through with comforting and reassuring words.

"Thanks," Chris said.

"You have a good heart, Chris, but your anger beats stronger."

"I'm working on it," Chris said. "Can you stop this wind?"

Freyja peered into the wind. "We can reach into the unseen spaces between the winds, it may offer some brief protection."

Chris nodded. Why didn't he think of that? He took the stance of the weaver and moved his hand through the air. As he did so the air rippled and expanded into a foaming wave that crashed through the wind. Almost all the bullets fired from the outer windows slowed and dissolved.

"Well done," Freyja said. "The Sufario's departure has left a rift. Even as we speak, the spirits of the wind fight to heal it and restore order to this realm." She raised her wand to stand like a statue and after what seemed like minutes, the wind died down. "The calm will not last, Chris, you and your friends must hurry."

"Thank you, Freyja." Chris rushed towards the prison entrance, stopping when he reached around twenty children lying on the ground bleeding. "Milamu Isimiana," he said with a sweep and twist of his hand, then added, "Khonshu Borushima Pilaroumo." The air filled with ghostly figures of the children who had been shot when the wind dissolved their protection. Their spirits lifted their physical selves and carried them towards Freyja and through the door.

As the last of the children rose into the air, Chris ran over to Julie, crouched behind a tall mound of rubble on the opposite side of the road from Sparrow. He pressed against the rubble when a burst of wind blasted past them.

"Were those ghosts?" Julie said over the noise.

"No, Ka, astral spirits. I gave them a bit of being solid so they could carry themselves in."

"Hey," Sparrow called. "Can you do something about those guys shooting at us?"

"Oh," Chris said, "yeah, sorry." He waited for a lull in the wind and gestured in the air. A swarm of golden, winged spiders appeared over his head and swarmed towards the windows from where guards were firing.. Landing on the walls and soldiers, the spiders sprayed webbing covering the windows and the soldiers inside. The men screamed as the webbing burned through their clothes.

"That was a bit harsh, Chris," Sparrow said.

"Hey, it was the first thing I thought of. Besides, they were shooting at the kids, and us."

The squall started up again and swept around the prison. "Let's go," Sparrow cried out. "Stick to the plan."

Julie ran to stand beside her and they dropped narrow goggles over their eyes. Chris ran up behind them and placed a hand on each of their shoulders. Buffeted by sudden gusts of wind, they pushed forwards, phasing in and out of visibility. Ahead of them the prison doors had been ripped open by some magical force. With rifles raised, the girls fired into the building, occasionally jolting back when their outfits took gunfire. Chris, glowing with the grace of Drafik, stuck close behind them, bringing up the Immutable Shield whenever the wind died down.

Ahead of them, the tall metal doors hung twisted and buckled against the wall; the heavy, riveted panels letting out loud creaks. Thick slabs of concrete fell to the ground as Chris, Sparrow and Julie approached. The bursts of wind finally died away for good and they stumbled into the long service tunnel leading through the prison to the vast open space in the centre.

Behind them, one of the doors finally gave way and crashed heavily to the ground sending up a swirling cloud of dust. The edge of one panel lifted off and a swarm of shadowy ghosts, all girls, flew out of the hollow door and the air filled with their mournful cries. Drifting away, the ghosts filled with a golden glow and they flew upwards to disappear into the clouds.

Sparrow cried out and threw a hand to her mouth.

"My god!" Julie gasped, "what was that?"

"Julie, come on," Sparrow said, "let's keep going."

At the other end of the tunnel, another pair of enormous doors blocked the entrance to the central arena. Chris stood and placed a hand on each of the doors, "Svargke Lieseedhee." Long, glowing cracks appeared in the doors then widened to release a radiant, ghostly crowd of girls who filled the tunnel with a golden light as they flew past and out into the daylight, curving up towards the sky.

Julie touched Sparrows hand, "They're ghosts, the poor girls."

"Not ghosts, worse," Chris said, grimly, "I think Lycus did something to the girls."

"Elegance?" Julie said.

Chris nodded, "There's an aetheracivism spell. Alumbrados must know it. The bastards."

The towering doors crumbled to dust. A long, wide ramp that led down to the vast space surrounded by the pentagon prison. Chris, Sparrow and Julie looked down at lines of soldiers, hundreds of them, dancing round the crater, all that was left of the Sufario's prison. In perfectly formed lines, the soldiers danced and leapt gracefully through the rubble.

Chris, Sparrow and Julie stared speechless as the line of soldiers, ten deep, danced past, some waving their coats or weapons. Over on the far right of the pentagon prison building, more soldiers rushed in, only to find themselves helplessly joining the dance.

"Oh my God," Chris said, laughing, "It's the dance of the Seekers!"

Something moved in the centre of the rubble, "There!" Sparrow said and pointed to a young teenager waving her arms like the conductor of an orchestra. She laughed as she made the soldiers dance fast and slow, moving in and out so the lines of soldiers curved and snaked around the arena.

"Looks like some weren't so lucky," Julie pointed to soldiers who lay against the walls, holding wounds or broken limbs.

On the building itself, cell doors that hadn't been transformed hung open; others looked like they had been ripped away along with part of the wall. Burst pipes jutted out of gaps in the ceiling or stuck out of rubble around the walls drenched with gushing water. Children dressed in loose-fitting trousers and long-sleeved T-shirts stood amongst the debris or in doorways while younger children gathered in small groups around older girls. Flashes of light exploded from upper levels where girls used magic to defend themselves and each other from soldiers and guards. The building resonated with the hollow cries men screaming in pain, calling for help or pleading for mercy.

***

The hot-air balloon phased in and out of sight as it dropped slowly towards the prison and began taking fire as the Immutable Shield created by Lizzy fizzled in and out of existence.

"Forget the shield," Jen shouted as the balloon ripped apart and the basket began to drop.

Lizzy swore and reached over the side of the basket to move her hands and curl her fingers while speaking an incantation. A dense cloud of bushes burst out across the roof below them.

Jen barely had time to gape at Lizzy and shout,"What the hell…?" before the basket sunk into the deep swathe of growth. The bushes acted like a sponge and soaked up the impact. The basket tilted over onto its side and both women rolled out as gunfire peppered the base.

"Stay behind me!" Jen cried, returning fire in short bursts. A strong wind swept out of nowhere and the bushes faded away, lowering Jen and Lizzy onto the roof of the prison. "This way," Jen said and the two women scampered sideways to fall behind a crate-sized ventilation fan.

"What happened up there?" Jen shouted over the wind. "Your damn shield thing kept shutting down."

"It must be the wind, it wiped away the bushes too."

"Great," Jen said, pressed against the fan while a hail of gunfire sprayed around them. "Watch out!" Jen pulled Lizzy away as the wind swept the deflated balloon along the side of the building, dragging the basket towards them. The basket slid past, hooking the ropes around the fan casing while the balloon dropped over the side of the building. Then the wind died down. Seconds later, the screaming of men replaced the sound of gunfire and Lizzy peered round the side to look over the centre of the pentagon and the smoking crater where the Sufario had been imprisoned.

Sparrow, Julie and Chris were approaching from the distance. The two women glowed on and off like Christmas lights, and children were running towards Freyja, who was standing beside a portal; Lizzy smiled. A couple of soldiers, arms and legs flailing, flew across the courtyard and made a gruesome noise when they crashed into the opposite wall. Lizzy turned away grimacing and saw the dome-shaped building. Soldiers were roughly herding a group of around twenty children along the path towards it, pushing into the wind that had swirled up further away.

"This way, we have to save them," Lizzy said, pointing.

"Not if you can't make us fly," Jen said.

"The balloon," Lizzy said and running towards the edge of the roof, stopped, looked down, and jumped.

"Son of a bitch," Jen said and followed just as the wind rose up again and, ripping the balloon and basket away from the roof, dragged it downwards.

Lizzy barely made it to the ground, dropped the last couple of feet and took several steps back when a guard stumbled out of the rubble towards the dome. Pushing against the wind, the guard fell sideways, his rifle crunching onto a rock.

The man scrabbled to his feet and picked up his rifle then raised an arm against the howling gale. "Elizabeth Francis?" he shouted, his words fractured by the wind. The gunfire from inside the prison became sporadic. "I should have known you'd have something to do with this." He raised his rifle to fire and it jammed. Without hesitating, Lizzy hurled herself at the man, slamming her shoulder into his chest.

They tumbled down over rubble and the guard got to his feet first and kicked at her. Lizzy rolled and blocked with her arm as she tried to get up. Spotting a fire extinguisher, she grabbed the short hose, swung it round and up at the guard, now approaching her with a long baton. The man stepped back and the extinguisher scraped down his trailing ankle and smashed into his foot, making him cry out in pain and crumble to the ground. Lizzy stood up and swung the extinguisher again, landing it on the side of the guard's head, toppling him over unconscious.

The sound of gunfire rang through the building as Jen made her way down, jumping through holes in the walls and floors. She emerged from a gaping hole at the top of a pile of rubble overlooking Lizzy. "Sorry I'm late. Had to zigzag my way down through this wreck." She gestured over her shoulder with her thumb, "How's your arm?"

"Still working," Lizzy said, rolling her shoulder. "Why didn't you help?"

Jen responded with a slight shrug, "Did you need it?"

Lizzy turned to the motionless guard. "I guess not." She picked up the baton and swung it round through several perfectly executed moves.

"Where'd you learn to do that?"

"*The Raid: Redemption*, one of the films we watched back at yours."

"Hm. C'mon" Jen swung the assault rifle over her shoulder. "Any idea what the layout might be like inside there?" Jen said as they jogged along the windswept road.

"Only from when they were building it. Rooms round the outside and a corridor that goes all the way round, then a big round hall in the middle. It looked like they were building a stage at one end."

They reached the doors to the domed building and Jen put a hand on Lizzy's arm. "You should wait here, that body armour can't stop bigger shots."

"Wind's gone." Lizzy said, "I'll be all right."

"Okay, stay beside me at all times and do your invisible shield thing for us. If it does fade, get behind me."

"Copy that," Lizzy said.

Jen gave her a sideways look, "And don't get cocky." She replaced the clip on the assault rifle. "Okay, let's go."

Lizzy uttered the incantation while moving her hand around and they disappeared behind the Immutable Shield. She nodded to Jen who pushed open the door. An entrance hallway ran between two glass walls behind which six heavily armed soldiers stood, three on each side. Beyond these rooms stretched surgical laboratories, some with young girls in cages. The doors slammed shut behind them. "Can they hear us?"

"No."

"Remember the pla…" Jen looked down at the pressure pad tiles on the floor and swore under her breath. On one side of them half the glass wall slid away and the soldiers opened fire into the entrance hallway. Bullets ricocheted off the shield and smashed into the door and far wall of the corridor. A klaxon alarm echoed through the corridor and soldiers emerged from rooms further down the hallway, then stopped to look around, wandering what the danger was.

"Oh hell," Jen said, "I'm going dark. Keep the shield and wait here." She pulled on a short string on her belt and disappeared. A few seconds later the soldiers in the room on the right quickly dropped, one after another, blood splats hitting the walls and glass.

The soldiers in the room opposite rushed out, shouting at the new arrivals, who ran to the fallen soldiers groaning and bleeding on the floor.

Lizzy jumped when Jen's voice said, "I'm back, I'll go left, wait…" The door behind them swung open letting in a rush of wind and for an instant, the Immutable Shield went down. With Jen still invisible, several soldiers stared in shock at Lizzy before they dropped under the fire of Jen's assault rifle. Lizzy spun round behind Jen and sent a spray of blinding white lights in a narrow arc.

Soldiers raised their arms to guard their faces from the burning lights and Lizzy dived at the window. Hooking the handle of the baton on the edge of the window, she swung her legs in and kicked the nearest soldier back onto the two soldiers behind him. Landing in the room, she swung the baton and slammed it into the temple of one soldier then another. Dazed, the two soldiers struggled to get up but another couple of blows knocked them out cold. Lizzy ducked and grabbed a circular riot shield off a soldier when gunshots cracked up and down the corridor. Pressed against the wall, Lizzy conjured up the Immutable Shield and jumped to her feet, casting blinding flashes out in all directions. The gunfire stopped within seconds and Jen appeared beside her.

"You idiot," Jen said, "if I hadn't had my back to you I'd be Swiss cheese."

"What's Swiss cheese?"

Jen shook her head, "Never mind, come on, let's get the girls out."

***

"There's the basket," Sparrow pointed up at the roof of the building beyond the central yard and crater where the Sufario had been imprisoned. Chris spotted Freyja gliding along an exposed upper corridor, beckoning and guiding children through a portal that hovered along behind her trailing a silvery, glowing mist.

"Let's go," Sparrow said.

They waited for a gap in the line of dancers and ran across to an entrance to the prison over on their left. Chris and Julie followed Sparrow towards the upper level where the two women began to herd children into small groups. "Okay, hold hands everyone," Chris said and repeated what Sparrow and Julie told them, "You're going to a safe place where all the magicians live." As one group disappeared, Chris would go to the next group along the corridor.

"This is going to take hours," Julie said and Sparrow nodded in agreement.

"We got no choice, just keep going," Chris said. Finishing one level, they clambered up to the next. Ahead of them, children and teenagers headed towards Freyja who was using a spell to call them all to her.

"Up there," Sparrow pointed to where a large swarm was descending from the sky.

"It's the ghosts from the doors," Chris said.

Sparrow lowered her binoculars, "What are they doing?"

Chris shook his head, "I don't know."

Guided by winged creatures like the ones Chris had seen on the rooftop in Manchester, the golden ghosts spread out and flew into the prison.

"Wow, they are beautiful," Julie said, transfixed by the semi-naked young men and women. "Are those angels?"

"Angels, half naked wearing nothing but shorts?" Sparrow managed to say.

"Light fae," Chris murmured. The Thoth book had included them in the atlas. They live in Alfheim, the realm from where Lizzy's innate power came.

The fae formed a wide circle in the sky above the crater and moved their hands, casting spells that gave the ghosts mass and density. Seconds later the ghosts flew back out, carrying girls towards Freyja, sweeping through the air. Placing the girls gently on the ground, the ghosts would again fly off to collect more children who were now coming to the edge of the walkways to be collected.

"Might as well help," Sparrow called. "This way, we'll go round and take kids to the woman with the magic door."

"Good idea," Chris said. "I'll go this way and fold the kids straight through."

Chris set off but Sparrow called him back.

Sparrow held the hand of a small girl, whose mouth moved as if she was speaking but made so sound. "This kid seems really worried about something but I can't hear what. Can you?"

Chris turned to the girl.

The girl looked worried. "The soldiers, in black," she said, "they came with a lady, they took some of us."

"Soldiers?" Chris said.

"Yes," the little girl nodded and pointed to a double doorway at the far end of the pentagon directly below where the balloon with Lizzy and Jen had crash-landed.

Then three other girls, two teenagers and a thin child that could have been anywhere between six and ten, materialised out of nowhere and took the girl's hand. The tallest one pointed across the yard to Freyja and, holding hands, the four lifted in the air and floated towards the glowing entrance to Tir na nÓg.

One of the older girls pointed to the same doors at the far end, "Some of us have been taken to the dome, your friends have followed."

"Hang on," Chris lowered his head and closed his eyes. "Guzush Arima," he said and his vision shifted to a point in the sky over the prison complex. "The soldiers have just gone inside the dome, they've got hostages. What the hell? That's Jen and Lizzy, they're heading in without us."

Sparrow flicked her assault rifle to burst. "Let's get going, lead the way, Chris."

"What about the rest of the kids here?"

"You two go," Julie said. "I'm going to make contact with Harold, our inside man, make sure he's okay." Julie pressed a button on her belt and disappeared.

Chris stepped back and almost fell and Sparrow grabbed his arm, "She's a magician."

"No," Sparrow said, "that's nanotech camo gear, Jen had a few uniforms from when she was a soldier before the CERN incident. Let's go." Sparrow hooked her arm through the assault rifle strap, took a step then stopped and pointed to the doors a hundred yards away "Get over here," Sparrow flexed her fingers and unclipped two short, thick tubes attached to her belt and squeezed them. Straps whipped out of the tubes and clamped round her forearms. "Hold on."

Chris put his arms round her neck, "You smell nice and sweaty."

Sparrow used a thumb to slide open a panel on the side of each tube to reveal a button underneath. "You're not a bed of roses yourself, Fungus." She pointed one tube up at the wooden cap on the top of the nearest pillar and pressed the button. A three-pronged hook attached to a cable shot out and buried itself in the thick oak and Sparrow jumped, the cable retracting as they swung towards the pillar. As they neared it, Sparrow fired at the next pillar fifty yards away with the tube in her other hand. The girl conducting the soldiers waved as they flew over, then continued guiding the soldiers around the yard and pillars.

Sparrow quickly swung across the wreckage and smouldering ruins of the Sufario cell to land on the opposite roof, just a few yards from the door and stairs. Sparrow twisted the tube, retracting the hooks and the cable that shot back into the container.

"You okay?" Sparrow said.

"Yeah, I'm fine," Chris said, rubbing his arm. "You're strong."

"We work out."

Over to their left, the balloon flapped wildly in the breeze. Below them, a narrow road stretched a hundred yards to a large grey dome covered in jagged runes.

Sparrow kicked open the door that led down a dark stairwell. Chris grabbed Sparrow's arm. "Wait, something's not right. Isphog Izvikan," he whispered and rubbed his eyes. Grootslang vision lit up the stairwell.

Sparrow peered into the shadows, "I don't see anything."

"I do." a crude lattice of Blood-red slashes criss-crossed from stairs to ceiling and one wall to the other, all the way down to the bottom. "Achaya web, wraps and sticks around you, drains the life from you."

"So what now?"

"I get rid of it," Chris said and thrust both palms out. "Belamishimma!" An ice-blue wave burst out from his hands and swept through the darkness, filling it with translucent streaks that exploded into steam then dissolved away.

"Wow," Sparrow said, "what just happened?"

"It's gone, we're good."

They took each flight of stairs with a couple of strides and reached the ground level in under a minute and jogged the rest of the way to the dome. As they neared, the rumble of metal sliding along rollers made them look up. Long, curved metal shutters covered in more runes closed over thick glass panels.

"Any idea what those runes are, Chris?"

"Keeping something magical from getting out; we should hurry."

At the dome, Sparrow pushed straight through the double doors. Chris followed behind and they found themselves in an outer ring of small laboratories, cells and offices. Soldiers lay motionless on the ground.

"Looks like we missed the action," Sparrow said,

"I'll say," Chris made his way over and around soldiers in black combat gear lying amongst shotguns, bullet casings, heavy handguns and riot shields. Either side of him the walls were peppered with bullet holes and blood.

"How did Jen and Lizzy get past all these guys?" Sparrow said.

"I guess Lizzy binge-watching fight movies on Netflix and your combat training paid off," Chris replied.

Sparrow smiled. "That would do it."

A flash of light burst out from somewhere ahead of them. "There," Chris pointed to a door that had inched open.

They edged forwards just as the door swung open. A group of children rushed out into the hallway and stopped when they saw Chris and Sparrow. About twenty girls in flimsy grey pyjama bottoms and pale green T-shirts hanging on frail, thin bodies, huddled together. All were barefoot and had shaved heads covered in small cuts and scratches; some had barely enough strength to stand; others looked pale and drained of blood.

"It's okay," Chris held his hands out, "we're here to help."

The children stared from him to Sparrow, wary expressions on weary faces. Then the group shuffled and parted; a tall girl came to the front, "I'm Melanie," she said and the other girls nodded.

Chris shot Sparrow a look, then said, "Hi Melanie, get all the girls to hold hands, I'm sending you all to a safe place."

"Is that what's happening?" Melanie said and, reaching out her hand, stepped forwards and touched Chris's chest, "you breathed them in, there are spells inside you."

"I what?" Chris said perplexed. Then his heart skipped a beat and he quickly stepped back from Melanie's touch. "Oh crap," Chris let out a groan from the pit of his stomach and collapsed to the ground, a sharp, agonising wave coursing over his entire body.

"Get back!" Sparrow screamed and Melanie stepped back, shocked and afraid. "I, I'm sorry. He needed to finish."

Chris sat up, taking in slow, deep breaths through a tight throat. The waves of pain quickly subsided and his breathing started to come easier. He winced at the occasional ache that ran across his flesh.

Sparrow helped him to his feet and looked him up and down, "What happened?"

Chris shook his head, "It felt like fire burning across my whole body."

"You okay now?"

"Yeah."

Behind them the door swung open and a group of glowing ghosts drifted in. They hovered several inches off the air, beckoning the children who rushed forward without waiting. Some girls began crying and calling out names as they ran, arms outstretched towards the ghosts of their friends.

Chris and Sparrow stood aside and watched in silence as ghosts and girls embraced in tears to disappear out through the door.

Sparrow swallowed and took a breath, "Poor kids."

Chris simply nodded and cleared his throat, "Let's go."

Sparrow stopped beside the door to the central dome and, pressed against the wall, tilted her head to listen, her hand outstretched to keep Chris back and silent. "Jen and Lizzy are still in there." She listened for several seconds then raised her assault rifle and clicked it to burst. "It's gone quiet in there, come on."

Sparrow reached out and pushed the door open. Nothing happened and she peered round into the domed hall then gestured to Chris to follow. They walked into the aftermath of a vicious gunfight. Bodies of soldiers lay in pools of blood, some clearly dead, others moaning in broken whispers. The bulk of the dead and injured soldiers lay round a towering transparent tube inside which Isabelle stood with her arms crossed.

Another group of soldiers, their body armour covered in scorch marks, lay against a wall stained with black burns. Jen crouched over Lizzy, trying to stop blood oozing from a wound on her shoulder. Seeing Sparrow, she gestured her over, "Bring your kit."

Overhead, the shutters on the ceiling closed with a foreboding, metallic clank. A foot-wide band of light circling the wall blinked several times before staying on to emit a steady, pale, grey-blue glow. The domed hall looked like it was bathed in moonlight.

Sparrow dropped down beside Lizzy and swung the small backpack from her back. Pulling at the Velcro seals she took out a bandage and thrust it into Chris's hand. "Put this over the wound soon as you see it," she said, "there's gonna be blood and you have to stop it."

Chris nodded.

Using a knife, Sparrow ripped away the fabric over the wound, Chris laid the pad over it as gently and quickly as he could and Lizzy's face twisted in pain.

"Easy kid," Jen said, "the pain will numb in a second." She nodded to Sparrow who ripped out strips of surgical tape and secured the bandage in place.

"Cruella over there said something about feeding time," Jen said and pointed to a scar stretching and widening between two poles moving slowly away from each other along a narrow metal track. An ominous low, heavy bass thump resonated through the hall and Chris felt it pulse through his chest. Lightning flashed around the scar which had bow grown to a gaping jagged gash surrounded by flashes of lightning.

"I got a bad feeling about this," Sparrow said.

A metal shutter dropped across the door they came through and Isabelle's cackling laugh boomed from the speakers. They all turned to the widening void and the hollow howls coming from beyond. Chris swore under his breath.

"What is that?" Sparrow said, lifting the pad from Lizzy's injury and squeezing a clear gel over the wound. A little blood soaked into the gel then the bleeding stopped. Lizzy's face relaxed as the pain subsided.

"Reavers," Chris said, "stay close, I'll fold us out."

"No," Lizzy groaned and gestured for Jen and Chris to move aside so she could get a good view of the widening portal, "help me up." Grabbing Chris's arm, she struggled to her feet and pointed at Isabelle. "She can't get away."

"Hold still for Chrissake," Sparrow pressed a clean pad over the wound and it stuck. Lizzy began moving her hand and mumbled an incantation.

"Are you nuts?" Jen said and looked at Chris, "Get us out of here asap."

"Lizzy?" Chris said.

The screeches and howls from the void became louder and Jen's eyes widened, "Holy Mike Foxtrot, Chris, what the hell? Forget the crapracadabra and warp us out."

"No," Lizzy said with a pained grimace, "Isabelle has to pay. That portal, only my light can damage it."

The savage noise ripped through the air and a rage of reavers stumbled out of the dark portal scrabbling over themselves, frenzied by the smell of fresh blood. They quickly spread out across the concrete floor and dived onto the dead and wounded soldiers.

Jen and Sparrow started firing single shots and one by one reaver heads began to jolt back and explode like balloons being popped. "You better make this quick, girl," Jen said in between shots.

Feeding reavers looked up from corpses to see what was going on and raised armoured elbows to shield their faces, bullets clanging sharply against the studded metal bands covering their forearms.

Lizzy grabbed Chris's arm to stay on her feet but her head lolled back and her eyes rolled in their sockets. Chris caught her before she fell, "Lizzy!"

Lizzy opened her eyes, "I'm okay." Raising her hand, she muttered an incantation and streams of light burst from her palm and swirled into a solar ball. Reavers' skin smoked and turned to ash. The creatures howled and dropped to the ground while others close enough to the portal ran back to dive through.

Lizzy focussed on the portal and the muscles on her face tightened. She raised a clenched fist, whispered another incantation and punched out towards the portal. Opening her palm, she threw out out jagged shards of gold lightning; then, exhausted, slumped into Chris's arms and murmured, "Did it work?"

The streaks flew through the air, growing and stretching into thick ribbons several feet long that melted across the surface of the gash between realms then spread out towards the rods either side.

More lightning sizzled up and down the rods and increased in ferocity until the rods could no longer contain them. The pooled lightning slowed and merged into heavy, oozing, blood-red veins that pulled and tilted at the rods until one of them snapped off the rail.

The loose rod swung towards the tube, sweeping up the remains of half-devoured soldiers and burning reavers as it went. The rod wrapped the void portal around the lower part of the tube with Isabelle inside. A shrill, terrified scream boomed through the speakers followed by a frenzied flapping. Then a large black raven flapped wildly up the tube, fighting against the force sucking it down.

Gold ring, runes and bolts came into contact with the void and exploded into shimmering shards. With the protective gold overwhelmed by the deluge of the void portal, cracks spread along the tube. The top of the tube broke away from the ceiling and snapped from the dais, fragments snapped away and fell into the void and around the hall.

Caught in the debris the raven fell, transforming into Isabelle before she disappeared into the void. Then the two poles crashed into each other and silence fell across the hall.

"Chris," Lizzy said, her voice barely a whisper. Chris lowered his ear to her face. "If we don't make it.." She said.

"Don't worry, we'll make it."

"If we don't, don't try to bring me back."

"What are you talking about?"

"You're an awful kisser."

"Shut up."

Lizzy smiled, her eyes still closed.

Jen went over to the platform Isabelle had been standing on and stepped on the middle of three pedals. A grinding came from above and the roof panels slid open. Sunlight streamed in, lighting up the bodies of dead reavers in the centre of the hall. Layer by Layer, reaver bodies disintegrated into ashen flakes that dissolved and disappeared. First their ragged clothes, then their thick, leathery skin and finally their armour. Then the sunlight reached the reavers lying or slumped against the wall. Their horrific screams filled the air as flesh, tendons then bones flaked off and floated up in the warm, sunlit air and disappeared. Only the butchered remains of the soldiers scattered across the floor remained.

Chris grimaced at the stench of slaughter, "Let's get out of here."

"Not yet," Jen said and used her knife to peel away the thick foils of gold covering the wooden base of the round platform, stuffing the sheets into her small backpack.

***

Sparrow and Chris helped Lizzy to her feet, and with Jen leading, the group headed out of the dome. Julie sat on the rubble around the exit of the prison, a bandage around her right hand and knuckles.

"Well," Julie said, wincing as she stood and rubbed her side. "We did it."

"All the girls out?" Jen said.

Julie nodded.

"Did you speak to Harold?"

"Yes," Julie said, "he got out with the rest of the cleaners,

235

kitchen workers and chefs," She pointed to a thick, twenty-foot high wall of churning ice, "before that happened."

"What is that?" Jen said.

"One of the girls said the workers and soldiers live in long houses behind there."

Jen looked at Chris for an explanation.

"Frost giant's fortress."

The girls exchanged bemused looks and Julie continued.

"Another door, portal-thing opened up and a bunch of people came out; guy with a beard, couple of goth girls and a woman in a wheelchair."

"A wheelchair?" Jen said. "That must have been Suzie."

"They took a lot of the girls away. Freyja was happy to see them arrive."

"Suzie?" Lizzy raised her head. "I know them." Holding onto Chris's arm she steadied herself.

"Hey," Chris smiled at her.

"Hey," Lizzy replied.

"They remember you," Julie said, "Baz, the bearded guy, mentioned your name."

"Okay, Chris, get us home," Jen said.

"Right, we ready?" Chris said.

"No," Lizzy interrupted. "I'll do it. We don't have time. In there," Lizzy pointed to the tunnel leading through the prison to the central space.

Jen scratched her cheek, "Lizzy's right, we could lose a day before we get home. Okay Lizzy, let's move."

Inside the tunnel, Chris took the crystal from under his sweatshirt and held it out. Lizzy raised her hand and curled her fingers in a gentle curve, sending out a glimmering thread of light that drew itself to the crystal and wove through it.

Sparrow leaned to Julie and whispered, "She is so cool." Julie nodded and smiled. The image of their living room took form on the wall and spread out to surround them and a second later they were back in the house. Spyro dashed in from the kitchen, barking loudly, and almost knocked Chris over. The cat, who had been asleep on the sofa, jumped up and over the back of the sofa to thump on the floor.

Jen shifted the rifle from her shoulder and removed the clip. "Is that dog okay?"

"She's fine," Chris said, "she does that when she's happy." He knelt down to stroke her.

Jen gave Spyro a wary look and walked round them to a large metal box. She put the rifle and clip carefully inside then removed other items from her belt and put those in the box too. Then she dropped onto a chair and began to untie her boot laces, "Sparrow, Julie, go sort your gear out then come down for a debrief."

"Okay, Mum," Sparrow said, "I could do with a shower." She tapped Julie on the arm. Both girls took their boots off and headed upstairs.

Lizzy flopped onto the sofa, a sad and exhausted expression on her face.

"You're welcome to stay here, Lizzy," Jen said, "you too Chris."

"Thanks," Chris fell onto the sofa to sit beside Lizzy. "It's not all bad, Lizzy, least you got me."

Lizzy gave him a sideways look and her lips curved into a thin smile. "And that's meant to cheer me up how?"

"Hilarious," Chris leaned forward, removed his boots and flopped back, "I wish Granddad was here to see what happened."

***

Lizzy was sitting on her bed, drying her hair, when someone banged on her door.

"Lizzy, Lizzy," it was Chris, he sounded desperate.

"Go away."

"Lizzy this is serious, let me in."

Lizzy removed the towel wrapped around her waist and threw on a dressing gown then went to the door. Chris rushed in past her and shut the door.

"Chris," Lizzy said in alarm, "what...?"

Chris stood there wearing just his boxer shorts, his entire body covered in tattoos. A narrow band of interstellar space laced with constellation patterns spread across his chest just below his neck. The black shifted through thin, hazy layers and became a sky that changed from blue to stormy black as it spread around his body. Below the firmament, mountains, forests, deserts, plains and oceans, all rich with fantastic creatures, spread across his arms and body so none of his olive skin was visible. An azure river flowed through lush terrain. Exotic birds, dragons and other strange creatures swooped over herds of grazing beasts; a river gushed down a shimmering waterfall into a lake. Desert, jungles, volcanoes, mountains, Arctic islands. Only his neck, head, hands and feet remain unmarked.

"It's the atlas," he whispered, "it's all over me." Chris fell in the armchair by the tall mirror. "I think it happened back in Salem, when Melanie touched me.."

Lizzy gaped at him, her eyes scanning the images covering his body, then she peered closer at the animals on his chest. "The detail is amazing."

"Melanie said something about me not being finished. She did this."

Lizzy sat on the end of the bed, unable to take her eyes off him, "You sure? How?"

"She said something about me breathing in the spells. It mist have happened when I opened the glass case with the Thoth book inside."

"Why, why would she do that?"

"I don't think she knew herself. Stop looking at me like that."

"They're so realistic, almost 3D, it's unbelievable. The birds have feathers; there's even a rainbow effect in the spray on the waterfall. It's incredible."

"No it's not. I'm a freakin…" Chris threw his hands up, speechless, "a freaking freak show."

Lizzy smiled and, adjusting her dressing gown, crossed over and touched his chest, "I like it."

"What?" Chris smiled and leaned forward to kiss her and she put a hand between their lips.

"The power inside you," Lizzy lowered her hand, "we could start a revolution," she said and leaned her head forward.

This time Chris stepped back. "Hang on, what are you talking about?"

"First things first," She replied and pulled him towards her.

Summary guide for parents of Magician Children

Girls

Girls, although born with the magic, do not have hyperthymesia from birth. Most girls begin to retain memories from between the age of one year and eighteen months old. Parents are encouraged to allow their daughter's curiosity, and forms and methods of engagement with the world, to develop at a pace chosen by the child. Each child is best equipped to decide for herself the pace and ways in which she will choose to engage with and make sense of the world around her and become the unique woman she will grow up to be.

Individual pacing of a girl's sight will adapt at a similar pace. Over time, she will begin to see the uncertainty and probabilities of the reality she occupies as an extremely fine foam on the periphery of her visual range. As she grows, the shared space-time she occupies with her parents will become more familiar and your daughter will naturally begin to explore her magical potential.

Evolution has given girl magicians a powerful natural ability to sense their environment, know when it is safe and not safe to cast spells. Similarly, their survival instinct will ensure that when in danger, magic will only be used to keep them safe when no other options for self-protection are available. Unlike boys, girls are able to interact and communicate with sentient creatures from other realms.

Boys

The following occur when a young man's magic begins to arise:

His sight will be altered and he will begin to see the uncertainty and probabilities of the reality he occupies as an extremely fine foam on the periphery of his visual range.

He will experience some nausea as his hyperthymesia becomes active. That is, he will remember everything in the formed reality – the reality that becomes certain and fixed within the immediate space-time continuum – and never forget it. The nausea associated with the hyperthymesia will vary from person to person as will its duration. In all cases the nausea does not last more than fifteen minutes. If necessary, there is an incantation to minimise the nausea.

His minor innate ability, the magical force not requiring an incantation, that is present from puberty, will become stronger.

His primary elemental power, drawn from at least one of eleven dimensional forces, will become active.

Surgery, Transplants and Transfusions.

Removed from the body, filaments lose their magical properties; it is not possible for a straight person to have a transplant or transfusion to acquire magical powers. The original Lycus tests identified residual nanoscale variations in the masses of the neutrons. However, since the discovery and spread of Al-Hassani's spell of Limination, the test became redundant.

Limination affected the measuring instrument's ability to correctly output the actual measured mass of a neutron. The spell forced the instrument to output the generic or 'straight' mass measurement of any neutron, thus concealing the properties of those string filaments responsible for magic.

String Filaments and Magic

Magic is the result of 'Loop' strings. This is where closed strings vibrate in such a way that they curl to form a figure 8 and become fused in the centre. This fusion creates an anomaly that, in sufficient numbers, can fracture, cause a tear in, the brane that separates Universes.

Loop strings are unstable but they can cause other closed strings to Loop. In most cases, with most people, the number and propagation of Loop strings remains constant and the greater the number of Loop strings, the more powerful the magician.

The localised and unstable nature of common Loop strings results in the magic generated having a short life cycle. Spells fade away over a short period.

Sorcerers have a disproportionately high number of Loop strings which are very stable and, with the correct incantation, transferable, meaning that sorcery can generate spells that have a permanent presence.

Time

The 'Time' present in our universe permeates through from

neighbouring universes. It exists only as a constant where there is nothing that interferes with it. Time is subject to entropy through its interaction with the world of matter and anti-matter.

Where there is no matter attenuating, like a coffee filter, more time passes into our universe. This explains why, in the farthest reaches of the universe, galaxies are moving away from each other at a speed faster than light.

Multiple Universes

The omniverse exists as a multidimensional foaming mass, ever expanding, very much like an infinite cluster of bubbles – with one difference: the bubbles have complex affinities and relationships with one another. So even the bubble furthest away from the universe where our Earth is found in the cluster may be directly accessible by a magician because its origins may have a direct link to our universe. Time dilations in the omniverse are constantly moving the universes around.

Fae

Fae are creatures who can travel across realms unhindered. Originating in the realm of our Earth, they rapidly expanded and migrated to neighbouring realms. There are five main fae races that roughly correspond to our seasons. The fifth race, the Shadow Fae, is a destructive race. Thought to be the first fae to emerge on the Earth during the early days of its creation, they remained bound to the primal forces that shaped the early planet. While the evolving planet began to develop seasons, other forms of fae emerged from the energies generated by those seasons. The Shadow Fae fragmented into two clans. One migrated to the volcanic planets of other realms while others retreated to the dark, volcanic regions of the Earth, taking their feelings of bitter betrayal with them.